MOUNTAIN SOUTH

MOUNTAIN SOUTH

A Traveler's Guide to Kentucky,
Tennessee and Arkansas

by

Dana Facaros and Michael Pauls

HIPPOCRENE BOOKS
New York

 For information, address:
Hippocrene Books, Inc., 171 Madison Avenue,
New York, N.Y. 10016.

Published in the United States by Hippocrene Books, Inc.
in 1986.
ISBN 0-87052-238-8

Cover photo courtesy of Tennessee Tourist Development

Printed in the United States of America.

Contents

Foreword: The South

"Ah'm from the South, boy! In mah class ah graduated magnolia cum laude, and ah was voted the most likely to secede . . . When ah pass Grant's tomb ah shut both eyes. Ah never got to the Yankee Stadium! Ah won't even go to the Polo Grounds unless a southpaw's pitchin'!"

—Senator Beauregard Claghorn, the Dixie Foghorn

The honey warm names of the Southern states read like a list of belles at a ball at Mockingbird Plantation under a June moon—Virginia, Georgia, Florida, North and South Carolina, Louisiana. They encompass regions as diverse as the Okeefenokee Swamp, the Everglades, Louisiana's gator-filled bayous, sugar white beaches, cities like New Orleans and St. Augustine, which belong more to the Old World than the New, and others like Atlanta and Fort Lauderdale, toadstools of our own soggy age.

No region in the United States has attracted—or believed so fervently in—more of its own myths, nor has any region changed so drastically in the last thirty years. Yankees who formerly dismissed the South as the "Problem Child of the Nation," the home of poor sharecroppers, blustering pot-bellied sheriffs, fragrant demagogues, magnolia-scented women and country fried colonels, a land that its inhabitants willed them to forget, received a shock when Jimmy Carter, the technocratic symbol of the New South, was elected president. Overnight, on the cover of *Time Magazine,* the South had shed its hackneyed Dixie image to emerge as the "Sunbelt," and Northerners who had chortled at the jokes of Senator Claghorn, on Fred Allen's old radio show, found their employers moving the company plant to the South, where taxes and energy bills are lower and unionism stillborn.

It has been over a hundred years since the War and Reconstruction and now the South is getting its revenge. Not only are Southern industries, corporations and ports booming, often at the expense of their Northern counterparts, but regional exports like Bible beating T.V. evangelism, stock car racing and country music have infiltrated Yankeeland at an alarming rate, while 20th century Southern literati gleefully expose many of the Yankee's gods for the shams they really are.

The cultural exchange, however, has gone both ways, for better but usually for worse. Visiting the region isn't quite the journey to a foreign country that it used to be—desegregation is now a way of life, as are some of the North's biggest mistakes like suburban sprawl, shopping malls and urban renewal, all new and raw and perverting the landscape even more glaringly than in New Jersey. But it symbolizes one of the South's principal distinctions as a region, that it is unfinished, still waiting to fulfil its destiny.

Introduction

Getting Around

The South is not particularly blessed with public transportation; if you're not driving, a Greyhound or Trailways bus pass is the best bet for traveling around, particularly if you plan on visiting rural areas. If you are flying or taking a train, be sure to inquire about car rental packages (fly-drive) that are sometimes very economical.

By Air. The major international airports in the South are in Atlanta, Tampa, Miami, New Orleans, Washington D.C., Nashville, and Memphis. There are smaller airports in all the state capitals and resort centers, particularly in Florida. Don't neglect to check the ads in the travel section of your newspaper for discounts, charters, etc. Southern routes are very competitive; anyone who pays full fare hasn't done their homework.

By Train. Amtrak, the government subsidized passenger railway, has several daily trains to the South. From New York or Washington D.C. there is a coastal route that splits between Petersburg and Savannah, one line passing through Raleigh and Columbia, the other through Charleston and Fayetteville. From Savannah the route returns to the coast until Jacksonville, where it again splits, one fork running to Miami, and the other to Tampa. Another train from Washington goes to New Orleans, via High Point, Charlotte, Greenville, Atlanta, Birmingham, and Hattiesburg. You can also get to New Orleans from Houston, or from Chicago, via Memphis and Jackson. A line from Chicago to Texas crosses Arkansas. For detailed information on routes and stations, see the individual states. Families traveling Amtrak are eligible for discounts; see your travel agent, who can also make reservations—which are usually required.

By Bus. Greyhound and Trailways are the two major interstate carriers: each offers unlimited travel passes for a week, two weeks, or a month. Discounts are available to travelers over 65, between 6 and 11, while children under five ride free. On city buses and subways we have left out the fares, as these are always subject to increases. Note, however, that you'll always need exact change when boarding a city bus.

By Car. To rent a car in the USA you must have a major credit card for the deposit and be 21 years old. Foreign visitors, however, may pay the deposit in cash, and can rent a car if they're 18 as long as they have an International Driving Permit, and a return ticket home. Many companies let you rent the car in one place and return it to another. Most also offer unlimited mileage, and have lower prices the longer you rent the car. If there are more than two of you traveling, renting a car and splitting the cost may be less expensive than public transportation.

If you are cutting costs, consider the new breed of auto renting agencies that specialize in second hand cars. Two of these agencies have gone national and have toll free numbers to call for information: Rent-A-Wreck (800-228-5958) and Ugly Duckling (800-854-3380). In most cities there are independent companies that rent mechanically sound older cars—even Cadillacs, campers, and mini buses—for a small percentage of the fees charged by Hertz or Avis. Check the yellow pages in the telephone book when you arrive. Another good bet, if you plan to travel fairly long distances, are the Drive Aways, where you make arrangements through a company to drive someone's car in a certain amount of time from point A to point B. There are many of these to Florida in particular. Look in the yellow pages of the phone book under "Automobile Transporters and Drive Away Companies" and often times in the personal ads of newspapers for drive away opportunities.

Another possible option is to buy a used car and sell it when you're ready to fly home. The best place to look for one is the classified section of a small town newspaper. A decent used car may cost between $300 and $500; later models will be more, but probably not worth it. Shiny bargains often turn out to be lemons. After purchasing a car, you'll have to get a license for it (temporary ones are available) and in many states buy insurance. When it's time to leave, sell it through the newspaper or a used car dealer.

If you do drive, the first thing to do is buy a good road map, or pick up one at the state's tourist office. The Rand-McNally Road Atlas, covering the fifty states, is good and sufficiently detailed. It is also a good idea to join an auto club, like the American Automobile Association (AAA) which has offices in practically every town in the country. They offer not only advice, maps, and travel booklets, but also a discount on traveler's cheques, lists of campgrounds, a degree of insurance, bail bond, and cover the cost of a tow in an emergency. They can also help you get a license if you buy a car, and if you're from abroad, write to them for a copy of their *USA Travel Information* (AAA National Headquarters, 8111 Gatehouse Road, Falls Church, VA 22042), a free guide to all aspects of driving in the United States. If you want to join, a year's membership costs $28.

Driving regulations are standardized throughout the country: 55 mph speed limit on highways, and right turns on red are legal after giving pedestrians the right of way. In the South, small towns sometimes earn their main revenues by creating speed traps, so beware, and obey all posted signs. Gasoline is priced by the American gallon (a fifth less than an Imperial gallon, about 4½ litres) and is generally cheaper at self-service stations. Try to avoid buying gas along turnpikes or in the center of cities, where it's bound to be much more expensive.

Hitchhiking. The South is probably the worst region in the country to thumb a ride; the police are generally less tolerant, and motorists more suspicious and less likely to pick you up. Although it is technically not illegal in any state, each town may have its own ordinance on the subject. Stay off the Interstates (stand on the ramp in front of the "No Hitchhiking" sign) or the roadway, which in Arkansas is defined as the side of the highway as well as the paved section. Some general suggestions: always go to the edge of a town before you start, travel lightly (if you're from another country, sew your flag in a prominent place on your rucksack—Americans love foreigners), hold a sign stating your destination, avoid hitching at night, and smile. A good way to find rides is to ask around at gas stations, truck stops, or diners on the way.

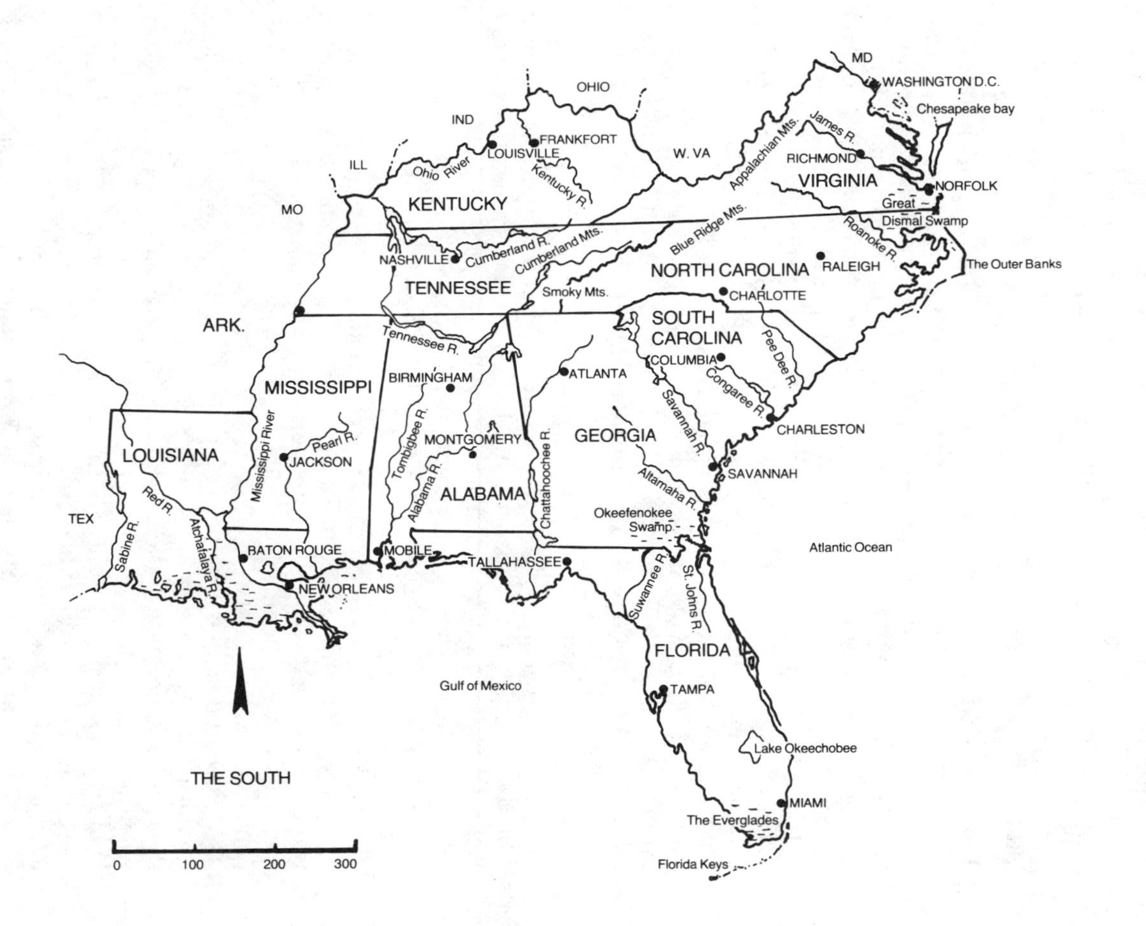
MD
WASHINGTON D.C.
Chesapeake bay
OHIO
IND
FRANKFORT
LOUISVILLE
ILL
Ohio River
Kentucky R.
W. VA
James R.
Appalachian Mts.
RICHMOND
VIRGINIA
NORFOLK
Great
Dismal Swamp
MO
KENTUCKY
Blue Ridge Mts.
Roanoke R.
Cumberland R.
Cumberland Mts.
NASHVILLE
RALEIGH
The Outer Banks
TENNESSEE
NORTH CAROLINA
Smoky Mts.
CHARLOTTE
ARK.
SOUTH
CAROLINA
Tennessee R.
COLUMBIA
Pee Dee R.
BIRMINGHAM
ATLANTA
MISSISSIPPI
Congaree R.
Savannah R.
CHARLESTON
Tombigbee R.
MONTGOMERY
GEORGIA
Pearl R.
Mississippi River
LOUISIANA
JACKSON
Chattahoochee R.
SAVANNAH
Alabama R.
ALABAMA
Altamaha R.
Red R.
Okeefenokee
Swamp
TEX
Sabine R.
Atchafalaya R.
Atlantic Ocean
BATON ROUGE
MOBILE
TALLAHASSEE
Suwannee R.
St. Johns R.
NEW ORLEANS
FLORIDA
Gulf of Mexico
TAMPA
Lake Okeechobee
THE SOUTH
MIAMI
The Everglades
0
100
200
300
Florida Keys

A woman thumbing alone is courting disaster, sad to say. On the positive side, there are many people who hitchhike even when they own cars, just for the interesting class of people who offer rides.

By Foot. The major trail of the east coast, the Appalachian Trail, passes through Virginia, Tennessee, North Carolina, and Georgia. For information and a list of hiking clubs in the region, write to the Appalachian Trail Conference, Box 236, Harpers Ferry, W.V. 25425.

Accommodation

Hotels and Motels. Outside the downtown areas of large cities and resort areas like Miami Beach, hotels are scarce; motels are common, but not always less expensive. We have listed after each state a small selection of the available commercial lodgings that do not belong to chains. We are not being elitist, merely saving space. If you prefer the security and reservation networks of a Hilton, a Holiday Inn, or an inexpensive Motel 6, look for their toll-free 800 numbers in the yellow pages of any city, and their operators will be happy to tell you where to find one of their establishments and make reservations for you. The South is well endowed with brand new chain lodgings; some good budget chains are Days Inn, L-K Penny Pincher Inns (tel. 800-848-5767), Scottish Inns (800-251-1962), Econo-Hotels (800-446-6900), Family Inns (800-447-4470), Motel 6, Knights Inn and Red Carpet Inns (800-582-6103). Inquire at the motel desks for free catalogs listing all the motels.

Prices vary widely. What is moderate in Miami in the winter season would be outrageously expensive in Mississippi. The easiest room to find is the double with a double bed; a single will be only a few dollars less, and an extra bed or cot a few dollars more in most cases. Almost all hotels and motels have at least a private shower and toilet, and it really is difficult to find one without a television. If you do not make reservations, the best place to look for reasonably priced accommodation is on the periphery of town, and along highways and access routes. This is unfortunate for the traveler relying on public transportation. We have tried to list all inexpensive and moderately priced downtown lodgings, but often the only choice is the local YMCA.

A place in this book listed as inexpensive will be up to $25 a night for a double room. Moderate ranges from $25 to $40, expensive from $40. Rates fluctuate, depending on the season and major events, like Mardi Gras, when a modest motel in New Orleans may charge over $100 a night. While prices in most of the South go up in the summer, they hit rock bottom in southern Florida. "American Plan" means three meals a day are included in the price; "Modified American Plan" means two meals. Hotels with arrangements like these are generally expensive resorts. Leave a tip if you spend more than one night in a place (at least a dollar per night).

Inns and Guesthouses. An "inn" usually means old and expensive, and there are several guidebooks that tell you where to find them in the South. In some places in the South, you can spend the night in ante-bellum plantation houses for $50 or $60 a night. Guesthouses (similar to Bed and

Breakfasts in Great Britain) are rooms in private homes, and are fairly inexpensive. For a list, write to the Tourist House Associates, Inc., P.O. Box 355a, Greentown, PA 18426 for their *Guide to Guest Houses and Tourist Homes USA* ($4).

Youth Hostels. The name is deceptive; these are for everyone, regardless of age. Although designed for travelers who arrive on foot or bicycle, there are now several hostels in cities as well. Almost all require a youth hostel card, issued either abroad, or, if you're an American, from the American Youth Hostel Federation (National Headquarters, Delaplane, Virginia 22025). A year's membership costs $14, or $7 if you're under 14 or over 59 years of age. When you join, you receive the *AYH Guide and Handbook;* the far more detailed *Hosteling USA,* which describes activities near each hostel, is also available from AYH headquarters for $5.95. Staying in an American Youth Hostel is not the rigid experience it often is in Europe, although there are certain rules, like no drinking or drugs, and you are sometimes expected to help out with the general chores. Check-out time each morning is 9.30. Reservations are recommended, and required at some of the more popular hostels. Prices average $5 a night and sometimes include meals. In summer, colleges and universities often have dormitory rooms for rent at modest prices.

Farm Vacations. These have a strong appeal to city families in particular, and range from old-fashioned farmhouse accommodation on working farms, to resort-style farms with many recreational opportunities. The best guide for these is *Country Vacations USA,* available from Adventure Guides, 36 East 57th Street, New York, N.Y. 10022.

Camping. Camping means different things to different people. There are commercial campgrounds throughout the South for the trailer and camper sets and state park campgrounds on a first come, first served basis. Backpackers and canoeists will find camping spots along major trails in the wilderness; a good book to read on the subject is *Wild Places of the South* by Steve Price, published at $7.95 by The East Woods Press, Fast & McMillan, 820 East Boulevard, Charlotte, NC 28203. Each state can provide information on campsites within its borders; another good source is Rand McNally's widely available *Southeastern Campground and Trailer Parks Guide.*

Handicapped Travelers. As time passes, airlines, airports, hotels, restaurants, museums, etc., are taking care to make themselves more accessible to the handicapped. For sound, specific information on facilities, *The Wheelchair Traveller* by Douglas R. Annand (write to Ball Hill Road, Milford, NH 03055) and *Where Turning Wheels Stop* (put out by the Paralyzed Veterans of America, 3636 16th St. N.W., Washington D.C. 20010) are good sources.

Senior Citizens. There are many discounts available to travelers over 65 years old. A good way to get in on them is to join the American Association of Retired Persons/National Retired Teachers Association, 1909 K Street NW., Washington, D.C. 20006.

Children. An alarming trend among newer establishments, particularly those with pretensions, is the banning of children. On the other hand, many chain motels take children for free or offer discounts. If you have very small children, bring a sleeping bag. Cribs are available in many places. Motels often provide lists of babysitters and many resorts have their own babysitters and special programs to accommodate the children of guests.

If you need help finding a place, or have any other questions, call or visit *Travellers Aid,* which has offices in most cities and is listed in the phone book. Foreign visitors can also call a toll-free number, 1-800-255-3050, for information; this is USADesk, and operators who speak a variety of languages are on duty from 9 am-10 pm Monday-Friday, and noon to 6 pm on Saturdays and Sundays.

Dining

Restaurants in this book (again we spurn the chains; they're harder to avoid than find, especially in the South) are rated by asterisks that reflect only the price, not the quality. One asterisk is inexpensive, around $5-$8 for dinner; two asterisks run from $8-$15, three will cost on the average $15 or more per person, for the average entree. In the world's largest democracy, people who work in restaurants receive sub-minimum wages, and are expected to make it up in tips; 15% of the final tab before tax is a rule of thumb. (Occasionally in Florida, however, you'll find the service included in the tab.) Only in fast-food restaurants and cafeterias are you not expected to tip.

Foreign visitors are often impressed by the large portions most American restaurants dish out, usually more than the average person can eat, a child certainly. Many offer children's portions at a low price, or have "kiddies' menus" with hamburgers, hot dogs, spaghetti and other foods the native children are addicted to. A popular restaurant feature these days is the salad bar, where you serve yourself as often and as much as you wish. Be wary of theme restaurants, another new trend, where you may dine in a castle or a cave, where the waiters on rollerskates dress up in gorilla costumes and bring you an indecipherable cutesy menu and bizarre food.

The coastal regions of the South and New Orleans are a gourmet's paradise, but the hinterland is another story altogether. Traditional, ballyhooed Southern cooking may be an acquired taste, particularly when you're confronted with the likes of collard and turnip greens, grits (white corn mush), chitterlings (pork intestines) and red eye gravy. Southerners eat more corn than anyone in more forms. Almost all main dishes are fried and accompanied by hush puppies—corn meal balls of deep fried batter that supposedly got their name in plantation kitchens, where the massa's hounds would pester mammy until she hushed them with these delicacies, hot from the pan. Judging by the number of restaurants that proudly advertize them, homemade baking powder biscuits are a Southern obsession for breakfast, so much so that you can even buy them at McDonald's. For lunch or dinner, try the fried catfish, fried chicken, Southern ham, or bar-b-qued meats, with a side order of black-eyed peas, sweet potatoes, or greens. Many restaurants feature gumbo, a Creole specialty that usually includes seafood or chicken, okra, corn, tomatoes, etc. "Tea" in the South means heavily sugared iced tea. Specify if you want it hot. Besides Southern-style restaurants, many towns in the South have Mexican, Louisiana-style, pizza, and Chinese restaurants, the latter, on the average, better than the Chinese restaurants in the north.

If you're on a budget, be sure to check out the menu by the cash register before you sit down. Prices are often lower at lunch time, so you may want to eat your main meal then. Buy your liquor in a state or retail package store, instead of ordering it in a restaurant where you'll pay twice as much. Even the lowliest motels have free ice.

American bars and taverns can be dark, gloomy places where no one talks to anyone, the television providing the only entertainment, or they can be lively and fun places to meet the natives. Ask around before you go. The drinking age varies throughout the country, from 18 to 21, and if you look a little young, you may be asked to show identification. Most bars close at one or two in the morning and on Sundays. Be sure to try the South's famous Mint Juleps, at least once. There are several good regional varieties of Tennessee whiskey and bourbon unknown in the rest of the country; ask the bartender.

Kentucky

The moonlight falls the softest
In Kentucky;
The summer days come oftest
In Kentucky
Friendship is the strongest,
Love's light glows the longest,
Yet, wrong is always wrongest,
In Kentucky.
James H. Mulligan (editor of the *Lexington Transcript,* c. 1920)

Any state whose major contribution to the nation consists of whiskey, tobacco and thoroughbreds can't be all bad. Obviously Kentucky, the essential Border State, is different. A long and colorful history, starting with old Dan'l Boone and culminating in the horsey Bluegrass aristocracy, has made it an almost mythical land that conjures up profound associations in the sentimental lobe of the American cerebrum. Tin Pan Alley for years made its living off the state; it was Kentucky this and Kentucky that, "She was bred in old Kentucky" and "Farewell to thee, old Kentucky shore," all following in the wake of the arch-sentimentalist Foster and "My Old Kentucky Home, good night."

The accidents of history that converted a state created by backwoods individualists into a bastion of aristocracy unusual even by Southern standards are of course reponsible for much of this aura. Kentucky is the state where, not too long ago, legislators had to swear that they wouldn't participate in duels, the state that creates honorary "Colonels" as the most luminous badge of honor and respect. In the old days when the Colonels had real commissions, they were usually running for office in order to take part in the great Kentucky folk ritual of the campaign stump, where the purest brand of Bluegreass braggadacio, blended into a legendary passion for political oratory, would be mixed with more than enough bourbon and burgoo—the stew of a hundred different recipes, some involving raccoon or possum, that is the State Dish—to create a communion so perfect that the Kentuckians would cheerfully forget how the politicians were running their state to hell with the brakes off.

Aristocracy has its pluses and minus. On one side there is the exquisite Bluegrass landscape and charming towns that make Kentucky one of the most beautiful of states. On the other, there's the social irresponsibility and intellectual torpor that, over a century, turned one of the greatest and most influential of states into a backwater. Still, the redemptive power seems to work better here than elsewhere in the Southland; if Kentucky remains relatively poor, according to the statistics, it doesn't show it (except in some corners of the mountains) and the backwardness that her accusers never lacked evidence for seems gone forever.

The Bluegrass isn't all there is to Kentucky; as in Tennessee, regional particularism is strong. The mountains offer spectacular unspoiled scenery, mountain folkways and the grimness of coal-mining areas, also the only place in the Western Hemisphere where you can see a moon rainbow. There's the estimable city of Louisville, and the other towns in the special world of the Ohio Valley, the western tobacco lands, the Pennyrile and one region known simply as the Knobs. Once you've seen the hills there, you'll know why. No, you won't listen; if you go at all you'll probably just visit Louisville for the Derby and drink mint juleps—but Kentucky, from the Cumberland Gap to the Mississippi, is a state worth exploring.

Getting to and Around Kentucky

By Air. Three interstate airports serve Kentucky, in Louisville, Lexington and Covington. The latter, Greater Cincinnati International Airport, is worth visiting for itself alone: inside are 14 giant mosaics salvaged from Cincinnati's Union Terminal when it closed. Smaller airports in the state with scheduled services are in Owensboro, Bowling Green and Paducah.

By Train. The only Amtrak stop in all of Kentucky is in Fulton, in the extreme southwest corner of the state.

By Ferry. A few ferries still operate on the Ohio River: at Constance (near Covington), Augusta, Etheridge and at Rt. 91 north of Marion in Crittenden County.

By Car. Kentucky has more toll freeways, confusing highway numbers and highway historical markers (1100 in all) than almost any state. Almost all of the freeways parallel lovely older highways that offer views of the countryside. State-sponsored visitors information centers are on I-65 at Franklin, I-75 at Williamsburg, I-64 at Grayson and at I-75/71 at Florence.

History

Kentucky got to be the first territory west of the mountains by a rather unusual circumstance: a lack of Indians. No one knows exactly why these rich lands, equally promising for hunting or agriculture, should possess no permanent inhabitants. It has been conjectured that the Shawnee, Cherokee and the other tribes that lived on its periphery used it as a kind of neutral hunting ground, to avoid the inevitable endless wars over ownership. Another intriguing possibility comes from recent archaeological research; apparently the lack of certain minerals in the soil caused chronic, crippling bone diseases among all the area's early inhabitants, the mound building Adena culture and the later, less advanced Fort Ancient people. Whatever, the land whose Cherokee name has been alternately translated "land where we live tomorrow" or "the dark and bloody ground" carried with it in its primeval state a small worrying mystery, a perfect frame for an unfolding history that was to be not without its romance, and not always happy.

Even without an Indian population, however, there were enough red men in the area to make life difficult for the first explorers. Kentucky lay along the route of the north-south "Warrior Trail," and all the neighboring tribes, whatever their differences with each other, found common ground in keeping the restless and land hungry Europeans on the other side of the Appalachians. Gabriel Arthur, perhaps the first Englishman to visit Kentucky in 1673, was captured, and many of those who followed were either warned away or killed. The colony that claimed this land, Virginia, typically had most of it given away before anyone had ever seen it, and other early explorers like Christopher Gist, a famous frontiersman who once saved George Washington's life, made their journeys as agents of various cabals of land speculators. Another of these, Thomas Walker, discovered and named Cumberland Gap in 1750. After the successful completion of the French and Indian War and Lord Dunmore's War, the westward movement began in earnest.

Most famous of all the explorers then as now, was a short pudgy fellow—not at all like the folklore and television representations—named Daniel Boone, born of Quaker parents in eastern Pennsylvania. The part of this legendary frontiersman's character that makes him such a fitting symbol of his type was his inability to ever sit still. Commencing his career with a trip to Florida at the age of 32, Boone caught the frontier fever and soon found it necessary to move whenever he could "look out the window and see the smoke from a neighbour's chimney." His knowledge of the territory, gained from numerous trips over the Appalachians, and his talent for being entirely at home in the wilderness, made him a valuable man for any would-be group of settlers; in his old age someone asked him if he ever got lost, and he replied "no, not exactly lost . . . but sometimes bewildered." In 1778 he was captured by the Shawnee, and so delighted were they to have a man of such reputation that they made him an honorary Indian, an adopted son of Chief Blackfish, and they took him up to Detroit to show him off.

Two factions, from Virginia and North Carolina, contended for leadership in the early days of settlement. Boone himself was often in the employ of the Transylvania Land Company, a famous scam operated by a Carolina judge named Richard Henderson who got all of Kentucky and part of Tennessee from the Cherokee for a few wagonloads of necessaries (the other tribes, and even most of the Cherokee, weren't consulted, and they resisted for years afterwards). At the same time, in the spring of 1775, that the company's grantees were founding Boonesboro, the Virginia group was installing itself at Harrodsburg, almost in the center of the state. Without too many Indians in the way, emigration to Kentucky was now reaching flood tide. Using the Ohio River or the Cumberland Gap as their routes, new arrivals dared to push as far west as Louisville (1778) and beyond. By 1792, Virginia had set aside her claims and there were enough Kentuckians to create the fifteenth state, the first beyond the Appalachians and the first to touch the Mississippi River.

In many ways Kentucky, as the first new state, served as the laboratory of the West. The process of settlement and the governmental machinery to facilitate it, proceeded by trial and error; there were errors enough to retard Kentucky's progress right from the start and trials enough to ruin nearly everyone but the lawyers. Legal vultures thrived on conflicting land claims, the result of speculative adventures and amateur surveying that made the state a crazy-quilt of misshapen parcels, usually with overlapping boundaries. The transplanting, almost intact, of the Virginia aristocratic social system brought all manner of evils. Deference to the gentry stunted Kentucky democracy as it gradually evolved into Southern-style government by courthouse clique. Their influence and the work of the lawyers, combined to spoil the dreams of thousands of would-be independent farmers and settlers or their children found themselves reduced to tenantage or pushed into marginal lands. Amazingly, the first Kentucky constitution made no provision for public education, setting the pattern for the scandalously low school budgets (except in Louiville) that have done so much to hold back the state until the reforms of recent decades.

From all this, it isn't surprising that Kentucky grew into a stratified society of limited opportunity in such a remarkably short time. The first great conflict came in the depression of the 1820's, when a movement for debt relief, stymied in the courts, led to a strange civil war within the legal system, where a "New Court" created by the legislature jousted with the "Old Court" that declared its successor unconstitional. As Kentuckians took their cases to whichever seemed most favorable, state government dissolved into anarchy until the conservative triumph in the elections of 1826.

In spite of the troubles and the poverty of most Kentuckians, the state had become a force to be reckoned with on the national scene. Already, the need to ship Kentucky's exports down the Mississippi River had occasioned the Louisiana Purchase, and Kentucky representatives had been among the loudest voices in the agitation that preceeded the War of 1812. "Kaintock" riflemen in that war helped Andrew Jackson to win the Battle of New Orleans. The state contributed a great political leader, House Speaker Henry Clay, who while a perennially unsuccessful presidential candidate was for years the very soul of the Whig Party and the engineer of all the difficult compromises between North and South that kept the Union together from 1820 to the Civil War.

By 1830 Kentucky was the sixth most populous state. Its fortune was made on its own unique agricultural products; unlike the South, cotton growing was never very important. The first of these was hemp, none other than our familiar *cannabis sativa,* not for smoking but for rope, used on Great Lakes ships and riverboats and for packing the Deep South's cotton bales. Tobacco, then as now, was a mainstay of the economy and Kentucky horses, for riding and for farm work, were in demand everywhere and made a good business for the aristocrats of the Bluegrass. Eventually a profitable export trade was established in one other commodity—slaves. Not as economical in Kentucky agriculture as elsewhere, slaves were sold by the thousands downriver into the cotton kingdom. As in Tennessee, sections of the state were always opposed to slavery and in a more tolertant atmosphere than exisited in the rest of the Solid South a considerable amount of abolitionist campaigning went on as late as the 1840's, led by a vigorous homegrown orator named Cassius Clay.

As a border state, Kentucky was well aware that one day it would be compelled to choose sides, but the arrival of the war nonetheless found the state unprepared. In the 1860 election her votes went hopefully to compromise candidate John Bell, and when that failed her Senator Crittenden worked feverishly to arrange an eleventh-hour deal that would keep the Union intact. After the formation of the Confederacy, Kentucky tried the clever but useless expedient of declaring its neutrality. Unionist sentiment had prevailed, but the state clearly wanted no part of war, particularly with equally large numbers of her sons marching north and south to enlist in the growing armies. Neutrality proved impossible, however, with Confederate troops occupying the southern portions of the state. Another native son, Abraham Lincoln (Jefferson Davis was a Kentuckian, too, ironically) for his part said, "I hope to have God on my side, but I must have Kentucky," and the state became one of the war's first battlegrounds, in a western front that saw Union generals like Grant and Sherman get their first taste of action.

With the Confederate defeat at Perrysville—not a defeat at all, but one of the many draws where outmanned and poorly supplied rebel armies were forced to retreat—Kentucky was safely in Union hands for the remainder of the war. Safe, but not secure, that is, for the following year another Kentuckian, John Hunt Morgan, with his small band of guerilla cavalry roamed across the state at will, capturing Yankee soldiers and supplies, tricking the enemy with false telegraph messages and thrilling the state's Confederate sympathizers with promises of liberation. Morgan drove the Yankees crazy until his capture—in northern Ohio—in 1863. By the end of the war other armed bands, serving neither side, and made up of criminals and deserters from both, were reducing parts of Kentucky to chaos in spite of the Union occupation forces. Violence continued even afterwards, with Ku Klux Klan atrocities in answer to the aspirations of the newly freed blacks.

In this atmosphere of reaction and social turmoil, the old Kentucky simply went to pieces. Political backwardness and brazen corruption reached new heights, as elsewhere, and if the iron grip of the old ruling class was somewhat lessened, a new and worse oppressor arrived on the scene, in the railroads and absentee capitalists. Of the former, the exemplar would be the Louisville and Nashville, one of the most predatory railroads ever, which kept its monopoly of trade for decades by wholesale purchasing of legislators. Outstanding among the other corporations were the coal companies; in the decades after the war they turned much of the eastern mountains into their own feudal satrapy while despoiling the land and destroying the fragile society of its people. (In places like Harlan County, they're still at it today.) A vicious circle was thus begun, as Kentuckians got poorer and fell further behind the rest of the nation, hopes of governmental reforms diminished and education and public welfare declined even further. In the mountains a society grown accustomed to violence reinvented the ritual vendetta, or clan feud, exactly as in Sicily or Corsica, only without the ritual musical accompaniment. More furtunate states, kept warm by underpriced non-union Kentucky coal, looked on with contempt. At the other end of the state, conflict between tobacco farmers and the monopoly American Tobacco Company turned into its own little war, with considerable burning of warehouses and even attacks on market towns by hooded "night riders."

When reform finally seemed to arrive, it was only more trouble. Out of the good German city of Covington, in the 1890's, a brilliant lawyer named William Goebel arose to do battle with the railroads, employing an innovative combination of populist rhetoric and big-city machine organization. Nothing is more illustrative of the times than this man of good intentions, who never won a political battle without deceit and strong-arm tactics, and who never failed to alienate even his political allies. In such a way, after a memorably bitter party convention that attracted nationwide attention, did Goebel achieve the Democratic nomination for governor in 1899. What followed was an even nastier reprise of the court conflicts of the 1820's, after an unusually close election confused by an election law written by Goebel himself and contested in the Courts. Goebel the apparent loser, was assassinated in front of the state capital in January, 1900, and sworn into office by the Democrats before he died. For a while it was old anarchy again, with the governors, two rump legislatures and hundreds of thugs supplied by the railroad interests crowding the capital. When the Democrats finally won control in the courts, it was found that a conspiracy had existed to kill Goebel; the Republican gubernatorial candidate, William Taylor fled to Indiana to avoid prosecution and his Secretary of State, Caleb Powers, was caught and convicted. Whether they were guilty, and who actually did the shooting, are still unknown.

Hardly an auspicious start for the new century; even with the generally unlikeable Goebel now become a holy martyr and symbol of all the poison that afflicted Kentucky, progress would continue to be glacially slow. Several later reform governors proved flops, most notably the celebrated Happy Chandler in the 1930's, who distinguished himself by cutting back even further on education and went on to higher office—as Commissioner of Baseball. A better progressive, Alben Barkley, was a renowned storyteller and whiskey-and-branch water man who became Harry Truman's Vice President. Things got better in the quiet upheaval after World War II, but Kentucky's Constitution still, uniquetly, allows the Legislature to meet only once every two years, to keep damage to a minimum.

Just the same Kentucky looks none the worse for all the tribulations of its past. The state is improving its condition economically, reclaiming much of the ground lost after the Civil War. Education and social services are no longer such a scandal. Thousands of miles of new roads have finally brought many of the mountainous areas into the modern world, although other parts are among the most depressed in the nation. Rural Kentucky still seems to be one well-tended garden; its towns and cities are on the whole finer and prettier than those of any state in the South. The old perversions seem to have passed and a quieter, saner Kentucky now has some breathing space to recover its old distinctions.

Bluegrass and Central Kentucky

Few regions in America are as prettily civilized as Kentucky's Bluegrass, a rolling region of park-like tidiness, of lush green pastures and lawns ("bluegrass" is only bluish in May when it produces tiny blue flowerets), of miles and miles of white and black plank fences and hundred-year-old fieldstone walls, behind which some of the world's finest horses graze contentedly under stately descendants of Kentucky's primordial hardwood forests. On the hilltops, overlooking all, are the old Kentucky homes of generations of horse breeders and horse-loving tycoons, and the equally palatial barns, solariums and whirlpools of their blue-blooded quadrupeds. This pastoral aristocracy reaches its highest plane of perfection in the six counties known as the "inner bluegrass" surrounding **Lexington,** the "Horse Capital of the World."

Kentucky's second city and the fourth fastest-growing metropolis in the U.S., Lexington, was named in 1775 when news of that first Revolutionary battle reached a group of frontiersmen camped at the spot. A town grew up to fit the name, and it became the seat of Fayette County, one of the original three that encompassed the entire state. The main ingredients of the city's present prosperity—education, tobacco and horses—can be traced back to its earliest days. In 1787, Transylvania, the first university west of the Appalachians, was moved to Lexington from Danville, where it had been floundering; in Lexington it thrived to such an extent that in the 1820's it was considered the most enlightened college in the US. The city became known as the "Athens of the West," a reputation somewhat revived when the University of Kentucky was founded in 1862. Lexington also served as a major hemp and tobacco market, particularly after a local farmer around the time of the Civil War developed a strain of tobacco known as white burley. Air-cured in ventilated barns, white burley became an essential ingredient in another novelty of the era, cigarettes. Today Lexington is the world's largest burley tobacco market, its 24 warehouses the scene of colorful winter auctions that enrich Kentucky's farmers and perplex the uninitiated visitor with their rapid-fire dealing.

Lexington's phosperous-rich bluegrass was producing noted horses and mules by the end of the 18th century. Early settlers from the Carolinas and Virginia (like Henry Clay) brought their favorite "light" horses with them to Kentucky and finding the Lexington area so favorable to their development, imported thoroughbred English stallions to improve the breed, producing an exceptional racing stock, both thoroughbreds and standard-breds (used in harness racing) as well as developing a new breed, the American Saddle Horse. The country's first celebrity thoroughbred, aptly named Lexington, was born on an area farm in 1850; his phenomenal success at the track and his 16 years as the country's leading thoroughbred sire are still unmatched, and did much to create the local equine empire (stuffed, Lexington now stands in the Smithsonian Institution). One of his greatest progeny was another local celebrity, Man O' War.

The importance of the horse to Lexington's society and economy is symbolized by the golden stallion weathervane on the **Fayette County Courthouse,** a Romanesque pile in the center of downtown. From here there are a number of activities to enthrall the horse lover. The **Kentucky Horse Park,** on Iron Works Pike, is a large-scale introduction to the horse world, featuring the International Museum of the Horse, the tomb and statue of Man O'War, a daily parade of breeds, cinemas, race tracks, polo grounds, farm tours and carriage and horseback riding (open daily 9-5, adm.). The **Kentucky Horse Center,** 3380 Paris Pike, offers tours of its facilities, designed for the training and breeding of thoroughbreds; special features include a unique 5/8 mile covered race track for year-round training and a multimedia presentation (tours Mon-Sat at 10 am, adm.). The **Lexington Convention and Tourist Bureau,** 421 N. Broadway, has a list of horse farms open to visitors; area tracks include the **Keeneland Race Course,** a non-profit model track on Versailles Road, where thoroughbreds race in April and October meets on land deeded by Patrick Henry to his cousins, the Keenes, and the **Red Mile Harness Track,** 847 S. Broadway, built in 1875. Considered the world's fastest harness track, Red Mile is the scene of the last leg of trotting's triple crown (races April-October).

The Old Frankfort Pike northwest of Lexington is the loveliest road for driving tours of the bluegrass, lined with a canopy of trees and picture-postcard farms, and at no. 4435, the astonishing **Headley-Whitney Museum,** located on the family farm of George Headley, who is responsible for most of the exhibits. These are arranged in three small but curious structures. The first houses a collection of Chinese porcelain, furniture and robes; the second an extravaganza of mullusk art called the "Sea Shell Grotto"; in the third, the Jewel Room, is Mr. Headley's collection of *bibelots,* gem encrusted bric-a-brac rendered by a small army of jewellers according to Headley's designs. Some of these costly oddities rotate, like the *bibelot* portraying man's flight to the moon; others, like the green obelisk with hands holding a collection of baby obelisks, are merely stupifying. Don't miss it (Wed-Sun 10-5, adm.).

Downtown Lexington has made a brave but not entirely successful attempt to stem the blight caused by outlying shopping malls. What it has preserved well, however, are several fine neighborhoods, most notably around **Transylvania University** and Third Street, the latter lined with Victorian homes, residential courts and alleys of modest frame houses—the latter a rare relic of old Southern cities. Transylvania's landmark, **Morrison Chapel,** was designed in 1833 by Lexington architect Gideon Shryock; its oldest structure, nicknamed the "Kitchen," stands in the middle of lovely **Gratz Park,** the old college lawn, named for a wealthy hemp manufacturer named Benjamin Gratz who lived on the park at 231 N. Mill Street. His sister, Rebecca, a gracious lady who devoted her life to charity, was a friend of Washington Irving, who described her to Sir Walter Scott when the latter mentioned his plan to write a novel with several Jewish characters. This turned out to be **Ivanhoe,** with Rebecca of York modeled after Rebecca Gratz.

Magnificent Federal and Victorian style town houses enclose the park. One of these, the **Hunt-Morgan House,** 201 N. Mill, was the home of Kentucky's first millionaire, John Wesley Hunt, and his descendants, General John Hunt Morgan, the "Thunderbolt of the Confederacy," the leader of Morgan's Raiders, and Thomas Hunt Morgan, the pioneer geneticist who won the 1933 Nobel Prize for medicine. Tours of the house are offered Tues-Sat 10-4, Sun 2-5, adm. Henry Clay's tiny law office is also on the park and nearby, at 578 W. Main, the **Mary Todd Lincoln House,** an 1803 Georgian home where Lincoln's wife spent her childhood. Orphaned at six, Mary Todd was raised by her grandmother, who lived at Parker Place at 511 W. Short Street, ticket office and orientation center for the Lincoln House (April-December, Tues-Sat 10-4, adm.), The most famous home in Lexington, Henry Clay's **Ashland** is off E. Main Street. Clay lived here from 1811 until his death in 1852, and although his private race course no longer exists, the smoke, carriage and ice houses remain on the grounds of the elegant estate (open daily 9:30-

4:30, adm.). Clay is buried under a towering monument in **Lexington Cemetery** at 833 W. Main; other local notables interred in the landscaped grounds include John Hunt Morgan and Buchanan's Vice President, John Breckinridge, later Presidential candidate of the violently pro-slavery Southern Democrats in the fateful election of 1860. A memorial to Breckinridge stands by the courthouse in Cheapside Park, where slaves were auctioned on the block.

Clockwise, north of Lexington: The South's smallest state capital, **Frankfort,** is a pleasant community tucked in a mountain valley on an S-shaped bend in the Kentucky River. The only state capital with three distilleries and one of the few where legislators meet only once every other year (from January to April), Frankfort was founded in 1786 and named, not for the German city (although the ensemble of the city hall, library and Church of the Good Shepherd spires give it a decidedly Old World air), but for a man named Frank shot by the Indians. Frankfort became the state capital in 1796, as a compromise between Lexington and Louisville, the two major contenders for the plum.

Like many state capitals, Frankfort has two capitol buildings. In South Frankfort, the new **Capitol Building** (funded by the 1904 million dollar settlement of a suit Kentucky brought against the federal government, for damages that occurred in the Civil War!) features a dome copied from the Invalides, and a sweeping interior of stairways and frosty Ionic columns of Vermont granite. In the rotunda stands a tall bronze statue of Lincoln-Jefferson Davis, on a lower pedestal, gazes at him gloomily, while two other Kentuckians—Henry Clay and Dr. Ephraim McDowell, the father of abdominal surgery—stand in attendance. The State Reception Room was modeled after Marie Antoinette's drawing room. Behind the main entrance to the capitol, the **Floral Clock** moves its hands over 20,000 flowers and plants (capitol open Mon-Fri 8-4:30, Sat 9-4:30, Sun 1-5).

The Greek Revival **Old Capitol** in North Frankfort was designed by Gideon Shryock in 1827 and built of stone from the bluffs of the Kentucky River. A plaque marks the site where William Goebell fell to an assassin's bullet in 1900; his statue, with sonorous inscriptions, stands in front of the building. Inside, Kentuckians are proudest of Shryock's beautiful self-supporting double stairway of "Kentucky River marble," of which the upper landing acts as a keystone. In the Old Capitol annex the **Kentucky Memorial Museum** presents chronological exhibits on the commonwealth's history, two slide shows and the coat Goebel wore when he was shot (Mon-Sat 9-4, Sun 1-5).

Frankfort has two historic houses: haunted **Liberty Hall,** built by Senator John Brown in 1796, and the **Orlando Brown House,** designed by Shryock for the senator's son in 1835. Located at 208 and 202 Wilkinson Street, the homes are open Tues-Sat 10-5, Sun 2-5; combined or separate adm. Also open are Frankfort's three distilleries, where you can learn how bourbon (whiskey with a content of at least 51% corn and aged in a charred white oak barrel) is made. At **Old Taylor Distillery** on Glenns Creek Road, it's distilled in an 1887 castle and honored in a Hall of Fame (Mon-Fri 8:30-3:30); **Ancient Age Distillery** on US 421, with its one barrel warehouse, is located on the site of a 1773 village founded by George Rogers Clark (Mon-Fri 9-2); **Old Grand Dad Distillery,** on US 460 is open Mon-Fri 8:30-3:30. All tours are free.

Overlooking the town, at 215 E. Main Street, is **Frankfort Cemetery,** where Daniel and Rebecca Boone are buried under a marker carved with scenes from his almost legendary life.

North of Frankfort, near the Ohio River, **Big Bone Lick State Park** (Rt. 338) was a popular Ice Age rendezvous for mastodons, mammoths, bison and giant ground sloths, who fled the advancing sheets of ice into the Ohio Valley. Many who came for the salt sank in the encompassing gelatinous mud and perished, leaving a massive quantity of giant bones that amazed the Indians and early settlers alike—some of them used the exposed mastodon ribs as tent poles. Although most of the bones have been scattered in museums around the world several remain in a small park museum; lifesized models of the beasts dot the park.

The "South side of Cincinnati," **Covington** and **Newport,** are picturesque river towns in their own right that have long served as rollicking outlets for Cincinnati fun seekers, with bars on every block and nightclubs the size of supermarkets. Covington, the larger of the two towns, wears its German heritage on its sleeve with its narrow brick homes, lovely churches and the new **Main Strasse Village,** a redecorated business and residential area with a Goose Girl Fountain and the **Carroll Chimes Bell Tower** (6th and Philadelphia, in Goebel Park) where from spring to Christmas a 43-bell carillon rings out the hours between 10 am and 6 pm, while mechanical figures act out the legend of the Pied Piper of Hamelin.

Covington boasts four exceptional churches. The **Cathedral Basilica of the Assumption,** a copy of Notre Dame, towers over retail district at Madison and 12th, its 24 by 67 foot stained glass window believed to be the largest in the world. Inside are four murals by Covington's own Frank Duveneck (1848-1919; other Duveneck works hang in the **Duveneck Gallery** at Robbins and Scott Sts.). **Mother of God Church,** 119 Sixth Street, built in 1871 in the Italian Renaissance basilica style, contains works by Johann Schmitt, whose work may also be seen in the Vatican. **Saint Aloysius,** at Seventh and Bakewell, is in the seldom seen Roman Etruscan style, and contains an underground grotto with a German diorama of the miracle at Lourdes. The fourth church, **Monte Casino,** at Thomas More College in Fort Mitchell, was built by economy-minded Benedictine monks in 1897. Measuring all of 9 by 6 feet, it is one of—if not the—smallest church in the world. While in Fort Mitchell (a southwestern suburb of Covington) don't miss the **Vent Haven Museum** on 33 W. Maple Avenue, the world's largest collection of retired dummies and other ventriloquist paraphenalia; American ventriloquists hold their convention here in July (open May-September by appointment, call (606) 341-0461).

Covington's oldest residential district, **Riverside** (four square blocks off Riverside Drive) has been elegantly restored. One of the homes, 322 E. 3rd Street, belonged to Daniel Carter Beard, founder of the Sons of Daniel Boone—later renamed the Boy Scouts of America. The **Carneal House,** 405 E. Second, has a rear tunnel believed to have been a station of the Underground Railroad. Riverside's homes overlook the Cincinnati skyline, the ungainly Riverfront Stadium and the bright blue **Suspension Bridge** (1866), the oldest to span the Ohio. Designed by John Roebling as a prototype of the Brooklyn Bridge, it was at one time the longest suspension bridge in the world (1057 feet). Having proved the engineering feasibility of such a bridge here in Covington, Roebling immediately went to work in Brooklyn. If you cross it, notice that you are not welcomed to Ohio until you've completely crossed the river. When Kentucky joined the Union, it claimed as its northern border the north bank of the Ohio. When Ohio became a state in 1803 it took Kentucky to court over the issue, claiming the boundery should be, as customary midpoint in the river. Still in the courts today, the Ohio River dispute may well be the longest running and most tedious suit in US history. Docked near the bridge are the B.B. Riverboats, offering sightseeing and dinner cruises on the Ohio (tel. 261-8500).

Newport, just upriver from Covington, is a pretty town with a German touch and one of Kentucky's loveliest courthouses, built in 1884. Further up the Ohio, **Augusta,** located at one of the Ohio's last ferry crossings, is an old-fashioned 18th century river town of brick row houses, located on a low bluff over the river; **Maysville,** at a bridge crossing, is located on a steep slope by Limestone Creek—hence its original name, Limestone (and Limestone Street in Lexington). Daniel and Rebecca Boone operated a tavern in Maysville from 1786-89; the town has since grown into the second largest burley tobacco market. Near the central business area a fine collection of French style homes has lent Maysville the nickname "Little New Orleans," a name the town tries to live up to with its pretty wrought-iron bus shelters. An informative introduction to Maysville is available in the **Mason County Museum,** 215 Sutton St., Tues-Sat 10-4, summer Sundays 2-4, adm. Just south of town, **Washington** was founded in 1786 and has changed little since that time, its 18th century flagstone streets lined with 18th century log structures. The first incorporated town west of the Alleghenies, it was the hometown of Confederate General Albert S. Johnston, who died in the Battle of Shiloh. (Tours from the Paxton Inn, May-mid August, Mon-Sat 12-4, Sun 1-4).

Southwest of Washington, at **Blue Licks Battlefield State Park,** US 68, the "last battle of the Revolution" took place a year after Yorktown, when 50 British and 500 Indians ambushed and defeated a small band of Kentuckians, killing 60, including Daniel Boone's son Israel. When a great army of Kentuckians rose up to retaliate, the British fled across the Ohio. A museum in the park tells the story of the battle and of the Buffalo Trace, the oldest road in the state, blazed by buffalo seeking the salt at Blue Lick (daily 9-5). **Paris,** the seat of Bourbon County (where Kentucky's corn "likker" was first distilled and received its name) is a major thoroughbred center; Claiborne Farm on Winchester Road produced Kelso, and Secretariat, two of the great all time money winners. Near the Bourbon County Courthouse is the stone **Duncan Tavern,** built in 1788 and frequented by Simon Kenton, Daniel Boone and other pioneers. The library and manuscripts of Kentucky novelist John Fox Jr. (1863-1919) are in the tavern; one of his books, *Little Shepherd of Kingdom Come,* portraying life in the Kentucky Mountains, was the first novel to sell a million copies in the US. (open Tues-Sat 10-12 & 1-5, Sun 1:30-5, adm.)

South of Lexington: The 1775 Transylvania Company-sponsored settlement of Boonesboro, built by Daniel Boone on the banks of the

Kentucky River, has long disappeared, but survives in a facsimile erected in **Fort Boonesborough State Park** (Rt. 627), where Kentuckians perform pioneer crafts and music in the manner of their ancestors. Films are shown in the blockhouse, and the **Dixie Belle Riverboat** offers tours into the Kentucky River palisades (April-Labor Day, 10-6:30, adm.). Boone's Wilderness Road from the Cumberland Gap to the Kentucky River passed through **Richmond** where Kentucky's great abolitionist Cassius Marcellus Clay lived, his home now **White Hall State Shrine** on US 421 North. Built in the Italianate style, the mansion contains most of its original furnishings (open April-Labor Day, 9-5, adm.) The college Clay helped establish with fellow abolitionist John Fee, **Berea,** lies twelve miles south. Founded in 1855 it was one of the first colleges in the country to offer non-sectarian, racially intergrated classes for the youth of the Southern Appalachians. After John Brown's raid at Harper's Ferry the college was forced to temporarily relocat in Ohio; at the end of the war the teachers returned and for forty years Berea was harmoniously intergrated. The infamous Day Law of 1904, however, mandated segregation and Berea divided its endowment to create Lincoln Institution, a black college in Shelbyville. Only in 1950 was the college able to readmit black students.

Berea is an unusual, tuition-free institution that sponsors the Student Craft Industries and the Boone Tavern Hotel, to give its students jobs to finance their other school expenses. Their efforts have attracted other craftsmen, most famously the **Churchill Weavers** (founded 1922), on the north edge of town, making Berea a leading center of traditional Appalachian handicrafts. The college's **Appalachian Museum,** in College Square, features photographs of the Southern Appalachian people taken in the 20's and 30's by Doris Ullman; audio-visual demonstrations of traditional folk arts by modern craftsmen; and exhibits of Appalachian tools and utensils (daily 9-6, till 8 pm in the summer, Sun 1-6, adm.). Lovely hiking trails are open to the public in the college forest; outside of Berea **Indian Fort Mountain** is a 1,442-foot high Hopewell Indian mound, possibly used for defense.

Danville to the west was the first capital of Kentucky, when in 1785 the Supreme Court of Virginia declared it the seat of government west of the Alleghenies. Nine conventions were held in Danville preceding Kentucky's admittance as a state; the commonwealth's first constitution was drawn up in Danville's town square, now **Constitution Square State Shrine,** containing the first office in the West, along with replicas of the state's first courthouse and jail. Danville is also the site of **Centre College** (1819), home of the "Praying Colonels," and the **Kentucky State School for the Deaf** (1823), the first tax supported school for the deaf in the U.S. In the **McDowell House and Apothecary Shop** on S. 2nd Street, Dr. Ephraim McDowell became the father of abdominal surgery when he removed, without anesthetics, a 22-pound ovarian tumor from a patient in 1809—after which she lived to the ripe old age of 78 (open Mon-Sat 10-12 & 1-4, Sun 2-4, adm.)

Harrodsburg, founded in 1774, is the oldest town in Kentucky and the first American town beyond the mountains. A reproduction of the original settlement has been constructed. in **Old Fort Harrod State Park,** on US

68/127 in the city; inside are the George Rogers Clark Memorial, honoring the early leader of Harrodsburg and explorer of the Northwest Territory, dedicated in 1934 by President Roosevelt; the Pioneer Cemetery; the Lincoln Marriage Temple, where Abe's parents were wed; the Mansion Museum, housing artifacts from all periods of Kentucky's history; several log cabins and the state's first school—where the children filled their pens with the juice of ox galls; and the Old Fort Amphitheater, where outdoor drama, *The Legend of Daniel Boone* is presented mid-June to late August, Mon-Sat 8:30 pm. The park is open March-November daily 9-5, and has information on self-guided walking and driving tours of town. In **Morgan Row** (220 S. Chiles St.) Kentucky's oldest row houses, built in 1809, the Harrodsburg Historical Society has a small museum open in the summer.

Shakertown at Pleasant Hill, just north of Harrodsburg on US 68, was founded by the Shakers (the United Believers in Christ's Second Appearing) in 1805. A sect founded by Mother Ann Lee, who established the first Shaker town in New Lebanon, New York, the Shakers lived a communal and celibate life as brothers and sisters supporting themselves by making furniture, raising livestock and selling seed and tools. Noted for their ingenuity, the Shakers at Pleasant Hill (who reached their peak of 500 members in the 1820's and dissolved in 1910) made use of original inventions like the clothes pin and washing machine. A National Historic Landmark, the original Georgian-Shaker buildings have been restored by a non-profit organization. Craftsmen in Shaker costumes demonstrate the chores and handicrafts of the Shakers in the village, sing Shaker hymns in the Meeting House and offer wagon or sled rides on the weekends. Lodging for guests is available in the old Shaker dormitories; the Trustee's Land Office, with its lofty spiral stair, is now a dining room serving meals cooked from Shaker recipes (craft buildings open daily 9-5, adm. tel. (606) 734- 5411 for lodging or dining reservations and more information).

The crucial battle for Kentucky in the Civil War took place at **Perryville Battlefield** south of Harrodsburg, on October 8, 1862, when 22,000 Federal soldiers under General Don Carlos Buell clashed with 17,000 troops under Confederate General Braxton Bragg. Although Bragg had the upper hand at the end of the day, he was forced to withdraw to Tennessee when he realized that he had engaged only a portion of the Union force. Battle relics and diorama are in a museum at the battlefield (April-October, 9-5, adm.).

Loretto, to the west in Kentucky's scenic Knobs region, has been the home of **Maker's Mark Distillery** since 1840. One of the last family distilleries in the U.S., five generations have produced old-style sour mash whiskey at Star Hill Farm, a picturesque historic landmark (tours on the half hour, Mon-Fri 10:30-3:30). To the north in Nelson County Trappist monks founded the **Abbey of Our Lady of Gethsemane** in 1848, the first Trappist monastery in North America, a white Gothic complex where the monks live under vows of poverty and silence, communicating with each other by sign language. Gethsemane is locally famous for its Trappist cheeses, which women may purchase in the monastery gift shop while men tour the grounds.

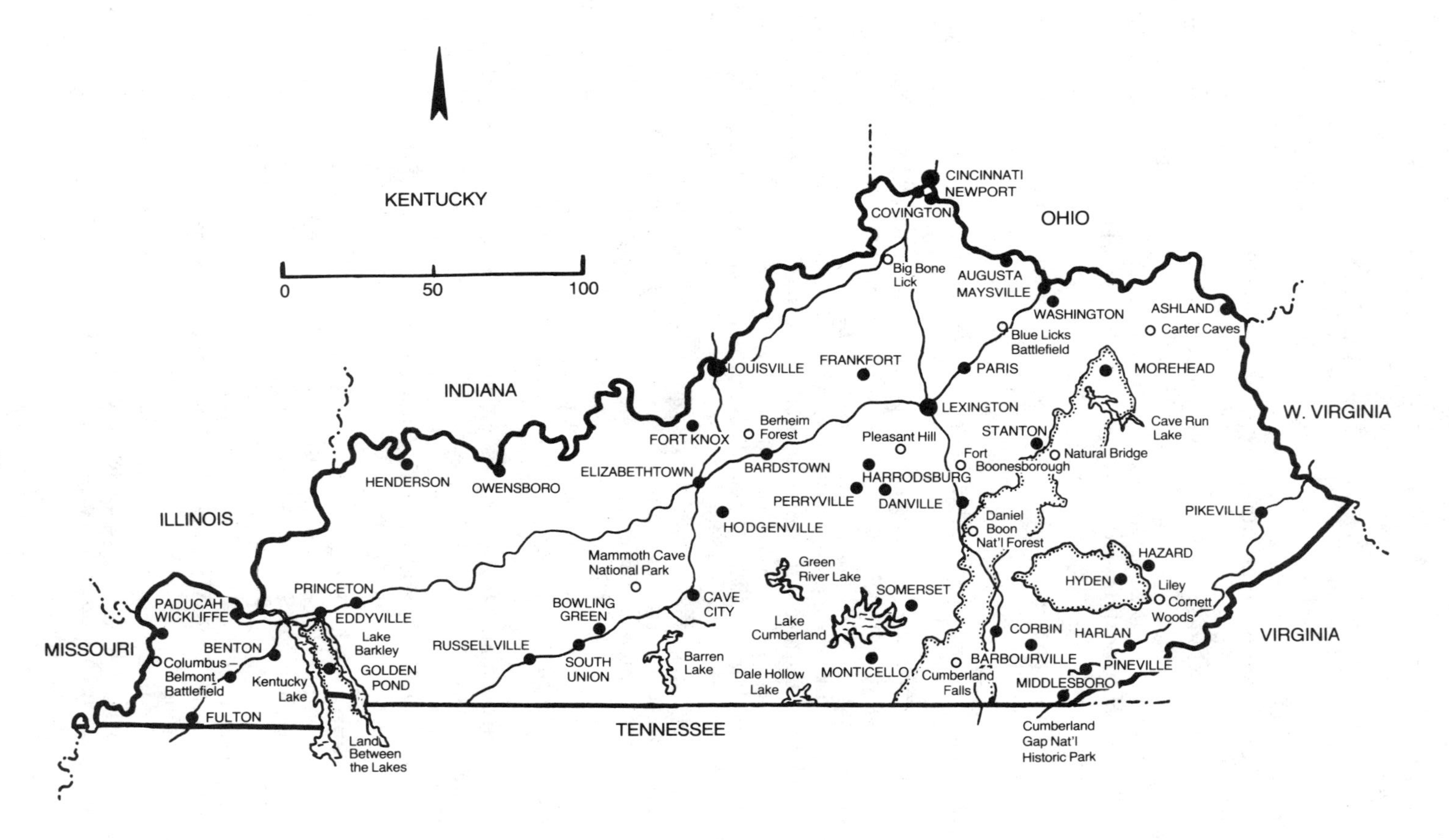
KENTUCKY
0
50
100
OHIO
INDIANA
ILLINOIS
MISSOURI
W. VIRGINIA
VIRGINIA
TENNESSEE
CINCINNATI
NEWPORT
COVINGTON
Big Bone Lick
AUGUSTA
MAYSVILLE
WASHINGTON
Blue Licks Battlefield
ASHLAND
Carter Caves
MOREHEAD
Cave Run Lake
PARIS
LEXINGTON
FRANKFORT
LOUISVILLE
FORT KNOX
Berheim Forest
Pleasant Hill
STANTON
Natural Bridge
Fort Boonesborough
BARDSTOWN
HARRODSBURG
PERRYVILLE
DANVILLE
ELIZABETHTOWN
HENDERSON
OWENSBORO
HODGENVILLE
Daniel Boon Nat'l Forest
PIKEVILLE
HAZARD
HYDEN
Liley Cornett Woods
Mammoth Cave National Park
Green River Lake
SOMERSET
PRINCETON
PADUCAH
WICKLIFFE
EDDYVILLE
BOWLING GREEN
CAVE CITY
Lake Cumberland
Lake Barkley
BENTON
RUSSELLVILLE
SOUTH UNION
Barren Lake
CORBIN
HARLAN
Columbus – Belmont Battlefield
Kentucky Lake
GOLDEN POND
Dale Hollow Lake
MONTICELLO
Cumberland Falls
BARBOURVILLE
PINEVILLE
MIDDLESBORO
FULTON
Land Between the Lakes
Cumberland Gap Nat'l Historic Park

Bardstown to the north has more than once been tickled by the fickle fingers of fame. By its wonderful old courthouse is a monument to the 18th century inventor of the steamboat, John Fitch, who retired to the wilderness of Bardstown when the public failed to acknowledge and support his invention; he committed suicide in Bardstown in 1798. The Duke of Orleans, Louis Philippe, is said to have taught French and dancing to Bardstown children in 1797. The first Roman Catholic cathedral west of the Alleghenies, **St. Joseph's Proto-Cathedral** at 310 W. Stephen Foster Street, was built here in 1819—several paintings inside are said to have been donated by Louis Philippe, others were given by Pope Leo XII (open Mon-Sat 9-5:30, Sun 12-5:30). In 1852 Stephen Collins Foster paid a visit to his cousin John Rowan's home, "Federal Hill" just east of Bardstown and was so charmed by the Southern hospitality and mint juleps he encountered that he was inspired to compose his classic ballad, "My Kentucky Home," now the state song, and further exalted in **My Old Kentucky Home State Park,** encompassing Federal Hill, shown by ladies in flouncy hoop skirts. From mid-June to Labor Day, an outdoor musical drama by Paul Green, **The Stephen Foster Story,** is presented Tues-Sun at 8:30 pm, with Saturday matinees at 3; tel. (502) 348-5971 for reservations. Federal Hill is open 9-5, closed Mon in the winter, adm.). Bardstown also has two museums: the **Spalding Hall Museum** at 5th and Flaget Sts., displaying—somewhat incongruously—the coronation stole worn by Pope John XXIII and Jesse James' hat. (Memorial Day-Labor Day, Mon-Fri 10:30-5:30, Sun 1:30-5:30), and the **Barton Museum of Whiskey History,** at the Barton Distillery on Barton Road, with a collection of whiskey memorabilia, from moonshine stills, antique booze bottles and Prohibition artefacts to Abe Lincoln's whiskey selling license (daily 8-12 and 1-5, free). Bardstown, with its fourteen area distilleries, has crowned itself the Bourbon Capital of the World.

West of Bardstown in Clermont, the popular **Bernheim Forest Arboretum and Nature Center** (Rt. 245) features a landscape arboretum, wildlife refuge and beautiful gardens (March 15-November 15, 9-dusk, free); in nearby **Fort Knox,** home of the U.S. Army Armor School, Uncle Sam hoards $40 billion of gold in the **U.S. Gold Depository.** Built in 1936, the two-storey, bombproof treasury is visible from Gold Vault Road, and very much closed—behind a 30-ton vault door—to the public. Open, however, is the **Patton Mueum of Cavalry and Armor,** 4554 Edmunson Avenue in Fort Knox, containing General George Patton's staff car and his Colt .45, a garden of tanks, exhibits on the evolution of the helicopter and German and Japanese weapons captured in World War II (open Mon-Fri 9-4:30, Sat & Sun 10-4:30, free).

Elizabethtown, and much of the area to the south, is in the **Pennyrile** region, the local pronunciation of Pennyroyal, an annual mint that grows abundantly in the sometimes sharply rolling land. Elizabethtown's most poular attraction is devoted to the eau de South—**Schmidt's Marvelous Museum of Coca Cola,** at the bottling plant on US 31 W., displays the world's largest collection of Cocacoliana, with items dating back to 1886 (Mon-Fri 9-4, free). A building in Elizabethtown's Public Square still bears a cannonball hurled into it bv Morgn's Raiders.

Abraham Lincoln was born in **Hodgenville** to the south in a humble log cabin now enshrined in a granite case, at the **Abraham Lincoln Birthplace National Shrine** on US 31 E. Fifty-six steps, one for each year of his life, lead up to the shrine. The grounds include much of Thomas Lincoln's original farm, including the ancient boundary oak; the visitor's center presents a film on Lincoln's Kentucky boyhood (open June-August 8-6:45, September-May 8-4:45, free). In Hodgenville's public square there is a seated statue of Lincoln by Saint-Gaudens' pupil, A. A. Weinmann.

Mammoth Cave National Park to the south comprises the world's largest cave system, with over 200 miles of underground passages—and sections still wait to be explored. Discovered at the end of the 18th century, the cave was used as a saltpeter mine during the War of 1812. Although parts of Mammoth Cave are stunning, like the "Frozen Niagara" section included in most of the Park Service's tours, the single most awesome thing is the cave's great size. If you have the energy the best way to get a feel for it is on the six hour, wild cave tour, where the only light comes from mining helmets and hand-held torches. Between the wild cave tour and the half mile, least strenuous (you'll notice how the rangers are always warning about the "strenuousness" opf the tours—thery tend to exaggerate) Frozen Niagara Tour, the Park Service offers six other tours, including an historic tour through the natural entrance of the cave, a handicapped tour and a detailed three-hour tour to the cave's Echo River. The longer tours stop for lunch in the underground Snowball Dining Room. Prices and times for all tours are posted in the Visitors Center, which also has an orientation film (open 7:30-7 in summer, 8-5 winter). Note that Mammoth Cave maintains a year-round temperature of 54 deg.; sturdy footwear is advised.

The National Park also has a hotel, motor lodge, campsites (for back country camping get a free permit at the visitors center) and miles of scenic trails along the bluffs of the Green River. From April to October, one-hour cruises of the river depart from the visitors center. Outside the borders of the park are the usual hubbub of commercial attractions—wax museums, water slides and roadside shops peddling chunks of colorful glass slag. There are, however, two other caves of note: **Crystal Onyx Cave,** on Rt. 90 in Cave City, with unusual onyx formations, an ancient Indian burial ground and a lake (Memorial Day-Labor Day 8-8, rest of the year 8-5, adm.) and **Mammoth Onyx Cave** on Rt. 335 in the town of Horse Cave, with bountiful stalactites, stalagmites and overhanging bridges; on the surface roams a herd of bison (open summer 8-6, winter 8-5, adm.).

When the first white men visited the Pennyrile, they were surprised to find much of the region void of trees. They named it the Barrens and its major waterway the Barren River, not learning until later that the Indians had burned all the trees on the plains to support a grazing herd of buffalo. The chief city on the Barren River, **Bowling Green,** was founded in 1780 by two Virginians, Robert and George Moore, who carved wooden balls to play their favorite game in the fields. Bowling Green, as the town became known, served as the Confederate capital of Kentucky until Grant captured nearby Forts Henry and Donelson in Tennessee. A market for burley and smoke-cured dark tobacco (used for chewing) Bowling Green is also the home of **Western Kentucky University,** where a collection of Kentucky folklore and crafts, photos and literature is displayed in museum in **The Kentucky Building** (Tues-Sat 9:30-4, Sun 1-4, free). In the center of Bowling Green 19th century **Fountain Square Park** is a little oasis of unusual charm, with statuary representing the four seasons.

South Union, southwest of Bowling Green on US 68, was like Pleasant Hill a Shaker Community, from 1807-1922, the last Shaker town in the west. The four-storey **Centre House,** residence of the South Union Shakers, has been restored as a museum, featuring Shaker furniture and hundreds of other items from their lives (open mid-May-Labor Day, Mon-Sat 9-5, Sun 1-5, weekends only September & October, adm.).

East of Bowling Green there are a number of recreational lakes; Barren River Lake, Green River Lake, Dale Hollow Lake and Lake Cumberland are the largest. On farms in the area you may see yet a third type of Kentucky tobacco—Green River tobacco—used in snuff.

Restaurants. *In Lexington*: Le Cafe Chantant***, 137 Vine St.; Stanley Demos Coach House***, 885 S. Broadway; Gennero's Lexitalia***, 1765 Alexandria Dr.; Levas**, 141 W. Vine; The Little Inn**, 1144 Winchester Rd.; Thoroughbred*, 1483 Leestown Rd. *In Frankfort*: Jim's Seafood**, 950 Wilkerson Blvd.; Scotty's Pink Pig Bar-B-Q*, 581 E. Main. *In Covington*: Covington Haus**, 100 W. 6th St.; Szechuan Garden**, 1504 Dixie Hwy.; El Greco**, 2440 Alexandria Pike. *In Maysville*: Carponi's**, Rosemary Clooney St. *In Berea*: Boone Tavern**. *In Harrodsburg*: Beaumont Inn***, US 68. *In Pleasant Hill*: Trustee's House**, Shakertown. *In Bardstown*: Old Talbott Tavern***, 107 W. Stephen Foster Ave.; Old Stable**, 116 W. Stephen Foster Ave. *In Bowling Green*: House of Wan**, 401 E. Main St. *In Perryville*: Elmwood Inn**, 205 4th St.

Louisville

Kentucky's metropolis, the center of a metropolitan area in two states that is home to almost 900,000 people, has just recently celebrated its own bicentennial. Two hundred years is a long time, by American standards, and this is one city that has made good use of each of them. Louisvillians smiled when a visiting journalist pronounced their home "all attic, no first floor" but on the whole they enjoy living in a place with a patina of age and quality on it that is unusual in this part of the world. This isn't to say that Louisville is an antique; on the contrary, it comes across as unexpectedly slick, polished and well-kept and it offers a sophisticated big-city air without the concomitent traffic and confusion, a perfect counterpoint to the immaculately bucolic Kentucky countryside.

Not many people are on to Louisville. After reaching its greatest commercial importance over a century ago, the city gradually faded into the background as the newer industrial giants crowded the stage, and today most Americans give Louisville a thought once each May for the running of the Kentucky Derby. That's a pity, for few cities are as capable as Louisville of showing its guests a good time. Its civic virtues are many;

progressive and able government, steadfast support of the arts, general tidiness and not too many acres of parking lots. It has traditions, political, social, even culinary; you may encounter such favorites as the "Hot Brown," Derby Pie or Benedictine sandwiches and, of course, there's bourbon, one of the city's economic mainstays.

Getting Around

Louisville is well served by a bus line called **TARC,** Transit Authority of River City. Fares are quite cheap outside of the morning and evening rush hours and there are two convenient downtown loop routes. Information, good maps and schedules may be obtained at their headquarters at 1000 West Broadway in the Old Union Station (585-1234) or at the **Visitor's Information Center** in Founder's Square, operated by the Louisville Convention and Visitor's Bureau.

History

Louisville has a famous founding father, George Rogers Clark, who played an important role in the obscure western front of the Revolutionary War. Clark, with both soldiers and settlers, arrived in May, 1778, for the purpose of creating a military base to aid in the reduction of British forts at Kaskaskia and Vincennes. The spot he chose was the only falls on the length of the Ohio River, not only strategic militarily but a logical point for the development of a town, where a portage would have to be established to circumvent the hazard to navigation. The settlement began at Corn Island and a fort was completed on the Kentucky side of the river in 1782. Clark's victories in the west encouraged more settlers and Louisville, named for the King of France who helped so much with the war effort, began an immediate and rapid growth after Kentucky gained statehood and river traffic increased.

In 1828 Louisville became a city and two years later the first canal around the falls was completed. Even at this early stage, visitors like Charles Dickens (who never fails to inform his readers which American hotels had clean sheets) were noting their surprise at how such a comfortable and civilized town had miraculously appeared in the West. Impressive new public buildings were going up, such as Gideon Shryock's courthouse that remains today, and railroads and civic improvements were changing the face of the city. Prosperity brought with it new citizens: Irish laborers, German political refugees from the revolutions of 1848 and Southerners seeking their fortunes from out of Virginia and the Carolinas. This mixture began the diversity and border-town outlook that characterizes Louisville today, a city at the crossroads of South and Mid-west that understands a little of both. The Germans, in particular, a cultured, asute and politically active lot, contributed as much solidness to Louisville's nature as they did to its fierce commercial rival upstream, Cincinnati. They were not always well received, however. In the 1850's, the anti-foreign Know-Nothing movement briefly seized control of the city and their depredations against both Germans and Irish reached a climax in bloody election day riots in 1855, when dozens of foreign citizens were murdered and their neighborhoods burned and looted.

The outbreak of the Civil War found Louisville, then the tenth largest city in the nation, fervently wishing it had never happened. Although the city had sentimental attachments (and trade relations) with both sides, opinion favored the North. After a half-hearted attack by Confederate General Simon Bolivar Buckner, however, the war troubled Louisville no more; business even got better, first in the city's role as the major Union supply center in the West and afterwards from finding opportunities provided by the collapsed Southern economy. Louisville went all out for Progress in the postwar years, managing a moderate boom in industry and railroads just to stay even with Cincinnati. In this era, the city's leading figure was a journalist, Henry Watterson, whose *Courir-Journal* is today one of America's most respected newspapers. A fitting symbol of his class and age, Waterson started his career as a toady for the industrilists and ended it baiting German-Americans during World War I, but Louisville still reveres his memory enough to have named its big circumferential freeway after him.

One event still remembered by older Louisvillians is the great flood of 1937, which left almost all of the central city under water for a month. The city did, however, dry out in time to make an important contribution to victory in World War II; one area along the river is still called "Rubbertown" from the huge government synthetic rubber plants established during the conflict. In recent years, Louisville has attracted attention over its struggle with school desegregation; the nation's first country-wide busing program, begun in 1975, continues today with relative success. Another issue, strangely enough, is historic preservation. Louisville has always built well, and it has become over the years a fascinating museum of American architecture, from ornate Victorian homes to the austere downtown office building on Main Street by Mies van der Rohe. Few cities anywhere have done as much as Louisville to preserve its urban fabric—both downtown and in the neighborhoods—but the very success of the effort has sparked a lively debate over goals and values, especially while the city is undergoing a building boom. The restored buildings and revitalized neighborhoods, meanwhile, are Louisville's epitome and pride.

Downtown. The old prints, understandably enough, show Louisville's riverfront as the busiest part of town, docks lined with elegant sidewheeler river packets, long warehouses and merchants' offices, the market and haymarket. All this is long gone, its decline starting as far back as the 1840's with the coming of the railroads. Today's Louisville is trying to reclaim its riverfront, and there is plenty of new development going up all around; to partially compensate for the mistake of the inevitable riverfront freeway, the city has built a park over a part of it, the **Riverfront Plaza and Belvedere.** Here, next to the new skyscrapers, you may look out over the broad Ohio and its once more important traffic, but you won't see the falls that made the city. Despite the railroads, the Ohio carries more freight than any American river, and the little falls (a trivial affair, really a rapids and only visible at low water) were removed long ago. Corn Island, site of Clark's settlement, is gone, too. The commercial docks have all migrated up or downstream, but one remains for the *Belle of Louisville,* not the usual replica but a genuine old paddlewheeler, c. 1914, one of the last to be built. Every year at Derby time this spry old Belle races Cincinnati's *Delta Queen* for the river championship (the prize for which is the traditional pair of antlers, installed on the winning boat), and she spends the rest of her time carting Louisvillians and tourists up the river on daytime excursions and dance cruises at night (Memorial Day-Labor Day, daily except Mon, 2 pm for the two-hour trip, fare $5, tel. 582-2547 in summer, 778-6651 in winter, for information).

Behind the Belvedere on Main Street, the **Kentucky Center for the Arts** (under construction) is a project Louisvillians are very excited about. When completed, the center will be home for the Louisville Orchestra, the Louisville Ballet and the Kentucky Opera Association. Few cities of Louisville's size pursue the arts so fervently. Another institution, perhaps the best known outside the city, is just a block away on Main, in the innovatively recycled 1836 Bank of Louisville building; if Louisville is a city that sends plays to Broadway instead of getting them second-hand as road shows, it is entirely because of **Actor's Theatre,** one of the nation's outstanding repertory companies, also one of the best-subscribed. The building itself is interesting. Architect James Dakin (who also did the old Louisiana State Capitol) apparently couldn't decide whether he wanted Greek Revival or Egyptian Revival and so used a little of both.

West Main Street, in the last century, was Main enough, but around the turn of the century fashion and commerce moved south towards Broadway, leaving this wonderful time-capsule of Victorian commercial buildings to be rediscovered by preservationists of the 1970's, a rare, intact downtown streetscape, mixing the elegant and the quirky, that hasn't changed much since the 1890's, containing the largest collection of decorative cast-iron fronts outside of lower Manhattan. Restoration for new shops, restaurants and offices is going on at an intense pace, spearheaded by the **Preservation Alliance** at no. 712, which offers a bookstore of Louisvilliana and information on city affairs old and new. On the same block, an 1878 cast-iron building has become the new **Louisville Museum of History and Science,** with a little bit of everything, from an Apollo space capsule to an Egyptian mummy, with a hand-carved model circus as the star attraction (open Mon-Sat 9-4:30, Sun 1-4, adm.) **The American Saddle Horse Museum** is just across the street, with all the history and lore of this galloping Kentucky invention, paintings, carriages and a horsey hall of fame (Mon-Sat 10-4, Sun 1-5, adm.). At the corner of Seventh, the **Fort Nelson Monument** commemorates the 1781 settlement on this site.

After the Civil War, Louisville tested the winds and found it expedient to become, at least temporarily, a thoroughly Northern city; in so doing it embraced the cult of industry with the kind of piety only a convert can muster. The magnificently overstuffed 1871 **City Hall,** at Sixth and Jefferson, makes a fitting memorial to this period. Its sculptural programme includes a chugging locomotive bearing the motto PROGRESS on the pediment, and protruding heads of mules, pigs, horses and cows, perhaps to remind us of the city's role as a junior Porkopolis. Across the street, looking somewhat ashamed, the chaste Greek Revival **Jefferson County Courthouse** was designed in 1835 by

Gideon Shryock. There's a statue of Louis XVI out front and a map showing Civil War action around Louisville set in the pavement. The courthouse was originally intended as the state capitol, an honor Louisville at the time was trying to snatch. This area is Louisville's Civic Center and the other offices of city and state cluster around. One block south, what once was Walnut Street now goes as Muhammad Ali Boulevard, in honor of Louisville's most famous son. The city's **Vistor Information Center** is here, at Fifth Street on **Founders Square,** facing the 1849 Gothic **Cathedral of the Assumption.**

When downtown shifted south, it moved along **Fourth Avenue,** still the major shopping and business street of town. To keep it that way, the city has made five blocks of it, from Market to Broadway, into the River City Mall for pedestrians only. For decoration, they have added a bit of whimsey called the **Louisville Clock,** which besides telling the hours provides a daily horse race at exactly noon. Daniel Boone, Thomas Jefferson, George Rogers Clark, Louis XVI and Belle of Louisville, as sculpted by a local artist named Barney Bright who created this contraption, are the competitors; a computer secretly decides the winner, and wagers in the crowd are not unknown. Behind this, they're putting part of the street under glass, the **Louisville Galleria.** This project, full of shops and flanked by new office towers, is designed to breathe new life into the retail district, and it faces two of the older downtown landmarks, Stewart's Department Store and the grand, recently reopened Seelbach Hotel, which has a famous Rathskeller done in tile from the Rookwood studios in Cincinnati in 1907.

Further south, Fourth becomes Louisville's renascent theater district, with its leading lady the recently restored **Louisville Palace;** once a first-run movie house from the 20's, called Loew's Grand, it now serves to astound us moderns with the opulence of that era. The theme is Spanish-Moorish, with an illuminated firmament and clouds overhead, and Louisville stages its bigger concerts and stage shows here. The southern end of the Mall is at **Broadway,** the city's grand thoroughfare, impressively broad and lined with some fine buildings. At Tenth Street, one of the city's landmarks, the 1891 **Union Station,** showpiece of the Louisville and Nashville Railroad, was saved from demolition to become the offices of the municipal bus line. Traveling the other way, east, on Broadway, you'll encounter the equally lovely Gothic **Jefferson Community College,** at First, built in 1903 as a Presbyterian seminary, before passing into the new extension of downtown known as the **Medical Complex,** where the hospitals of the University of Louisville dominate a number of other institutions in a still-growing renewal area north of Broadway.

Downtown continues (and "downtown" in Louisville is an area much larger than that of other cities Louisville's size) south of Broadway, though at a decreasing intensity. One attraction, at 118 W. Breckinridge, is the **Filson Club,** a graceful, lonely old townhouse on an otherwise vacant street. Any city worth visiting will have one dusty museum of historical bric-a-brac whose contents are occasionally downright peculiar (Philadelphia, the champion in this department, has at least a dozen). In Louisville, this is the place. Downstairs, the club (named for Kentucky's first historian, also Daniel Boone's mythographer and dedicated to the state's antiquities) maintains a large library, always full of genealogical researchers; upstairs, the museum has its documents, swords, Shaker furniture, grim-faced portraits and the like, and also some genuine Civil War chewing gum, a plaster cast of the hand of the seven foot eight "Kentucky giant" with an account of his career and, most famously, the slice of tree trunk where Daniel Boone inscribed his legendary communiqué "D. BOON KILLED A BAR 1803", reputed to be the real McCoy (Mon-Fri 9-5, also Sat 9-12, from October-July, free). Further south, downtown gradually merges into the city's finest residential district, **Old Louisville.**

Just as in their flamboyant City Hall and commericial buildings, the leaders of booming, confident, post-Civil War Louisville wanted their homes to be monuments, the domestic side of progress in a city that has always taken homes and home life very seriously. They built so prodigiously and so well that Old Loiusville, roughly the area between Second and Sixth north of Hill Street, is left to us as one of the outstanding Victorian neighborhoods in all the U.S. After a long and gradual decline, the city rediscovered the district, and it became the first Louisville neighborhood to be restored, a process that continues today. Every style in the trick-bag of the eclectic era can be found here, Renaissance, Romanesque, Queen Anne, Second Empire, and the rest (sometimes all in the same house!). The architectural detail, in stone or terra cotta, is rich and fascinating and almost every house in this museum of a neighborhood is built in brick, here as in all the Ohio River towns the preferred material.

A walk through this area is a delight and a good place to start would be the information center of the Old Louisville Preservation Association in **Central Park,** Fourth and Magnolia, where there's also an outdoor theater where Louisvillians enjoy Shakespeare in the summer months. Central Park had its beginnings as part of the grounds for the 1883-7 Louisville Southern Exhibition, a successful trade fair of the early New South that lent this new part of town much prestige and made it the prime location for Louisville's burgeoning industrial elite. Fourth and Third are the best streets to see, along with **St. James Court** and **Belgravia Court,** directly south of the park. These courts (the main building of the expostion was on this block), under spreading lindens and horse-chestnuts, and decorated with a lovely cast-iron fountain, are probably the zenith of residential elegance between the East Coast and New Orleans.

Continuing south from Old Louisville along Third Street, you eventually meet the tall column of the **Confederate Monument,** topped by a rebel soldier defiantly facing north. Support for the seceded states was limited in Louisville, but somehow the political disapointment that followed the war made the Lost Cause fashionable. There is no Union memorial here. All around is the campus of the **University of Louisville,** the oldest, and one of the largest of America's municipal universities. One of its landmarks is just across the street, the **Belknap Playhouse,** a theater remodeled from the 1874 Gothic chapel of the reform school that once occupied this site. Adjacent to the campus on Third, the **J. B. Speed Art Museum** was built in 1927 by a branch of one of the city's famous families; its comprehensive collection is strong in European painting and contemporary sculpture, and there is also a film center named for another of the city' sons—D. W. Griffith (Tues-Sat 10-4, Sun 2-6, free).

Not far away, on Fourth Street at Central Avenue, the holiest shrine of the horse world stands in a quiet and unpretentious neighborhood, **Churchill Downs,** its twin Victorian spires a landmark familiar to touts from coast to coast. When founded in 1874, by Colonel M. Lewis Clark—he had to be a Colonel, of course—this was known as the Louisville Jockey Club. Colonel Clark brought over new betting and stakes systems from England, and his creation played a major role in racing's transition from an informal, county-fairish attraction to major urban spectator sport. The Jockey Club itself was a subtle though important power in state politics for many years, quite understandably in an age when the blackguards of Prohibition were looking around for other diversions to stamp out. Since a horse called Aristides won the first Kentucky Derby in 1875, the race and the track have acquired a lore and accumulated pageantry unique in America. Each year, before the traditional playing of "My Old Kentucky Home" makes everyone misty-eyed and serious, the devotees are as likely to be recalling past champions like Whirlaway, Carry Back and Citation as discussing the prospects of the day. Derby Week is Louisville's festival, where not only horses are raced, but bicycles, marathon runners, and even hot air balloons, while the bartenders put everything else away and concentrate on making mint juleps. Churchill Downs may be the prettiest racetrack in the nation, an ornate affair built in 1895 and famous for its flower gardens. The Derby isn't its only function; there are spring and fall racing seasons, and whether you play the ponies or not you might wish to stop in at the **Kentucky Derby Museum,** a place, for sure, where old times are not forgotton (daily 9:30-4:30, free). Another sport that has been making Louisvillians' blood run warmer of late is played nearby at the **Kentucky Fair and Exposition Center** the modern home of the State Fair on Crittenden Drive. Louisville has a minor league baseball team called the Redbirds that is the best-run such outfit in the nation; not only are they successful, but they have been drawing more fans than some of the major league teams. There's more racing—harness racing—two miles to the east at **Lousville Downs,** at 4520 Poplar Level Road, with seasons February-April and June-September.

More Neighborhoods. Even though Old Louisville gets most of the attention, it is not the only interesting corner of this cozy and beautiful city. Two riverfront communities even older are **Portland,** just west of downtown, and **Butchertown,** to the east. The former, around Northwestern Parkway and 34th Street, was founded in 1814 as a competitor to Louisville on the downstream side of the falls. The first canal around the falls began Portland's decline, but it also brought the Irish laborers who made the community their own. Even after annexation, this tight-knit area continued to elect its own, Honorary "mayor." Many of the fancy shipowners' homes and workmen's cottages remain, and also a landmark in the 1847 **U.S. Marine Hospital,** on the Parkway, designed by Robert Mills. Today navigation around Portland is facilitated by the **McAlpine Dam and Locks,** with an observation deck accessible from Marine Street on the riverfront.

Butchertown, along Washington Street, a block north of East Main, grew up in the 1830's around the Bourbon Stock Yard (still in operation on Main Street, and you may arrange for a tour by calling 584-7211). Here the Germans made up most of the population; they built the neighborhood centerpiece, **St. Joseph's Church** on Washington and Webster, in 1883. Across the street, a complex of shops and restaurants in a restored old German bakery called **Bakery Square** is the symbol of the new Butchertown, an almost entirely restored neighborhood that maintains its charm and vitality even though it's quite small, and surrounded by industry. At 729 Washington, the **Thomas Edison House** was the home of the young inventor for a time while he worked for Western Union as a telegraph operator. Tom got himself fired when one of his early experiments wrecked a train car (open Mon-Fri 9-5, weekends 2-4, free; tours on weekends only). Both Portland and Butchertown have plenty of examples of a Louisville specialty called the "shotgun house," a narrow, deep frame cottage perfectly suited to thwart early tax laws, where rates were based on frontage and height. Some architectural historians trace both the name and design to Africa, from which it reached Louisville by way of the West Indies and New Orleans, courtesy of the slaves, who built their own cottages in imitation of the council houses they had back home. The very tidiest of all shotgun houses can be found in **Germantown,** between Shelby Street and Eastern Parkway, one of those rare ethnic communities that has always politely declined to be in any sort of transition whatsoever. There are some popular restaurants here, and the local political organization is called the "All Wool and a Yard Wide Democratic Club."

A lovely, tree-shaded neighborhood called the **Cherokee Triangle** was the East End's garden suburb counterpart to Old Louisville, developed beginning in the 1870's. Fine houses can be seen here along Cherokee Road, Willow, Everett and Longest Avenues, and also monuments to Daniel Boone and John B. Castleman, a parks commissioner who planted many of Louisville's trees. One side of the Triange is bordered by **Cave Hill Cemetery,** which has a beautiful gatehouse on Baxter Avenue surmounted by a beckoning angel. George Rogers Clark and most famous Louisvillians since are buried here, as well as the brother of the poet Keats, who lived here as a prominent businessman. The eastern leg of the triangle is **Cherokee Park,** showpiece of the city park system, designed in the 1880's by the firm of the two Frederick Law Olmsteds, father and son; as with their plans for Boston, Baltimore and Kansas City, the Olmsteds connected large, fine parklands with a network of tree-lined boulevards, an embellishments that also serves to subtly unify the city. From this park, Eastern and Southern Parkways join **Iroquois Park** on the southern edge of town, with riding stables and an amphitheater used for various entertainments in the summer, and the Algonquin Parkway continues westwards to **Shawnee Park** on the banks of the Ohio in the West End.

But back east, however, there's more to see among the growing suburbs of this posh area of town. If you take the River Road east from downtown along the Ohio, at Zorn Road, you may visit one of the most decorative pieces of engineering anywhere, the 1860 **Louisville Water Works,** a Greek temple and a tall shaft adorned with mythological statuary (and one Indian chief, added after a tornado knocked down an original) that seems to be a monument, but is really the water tower. No longer in use, this elegant fantasia undoubtedly feels more at home now as the headquarters of the Art Center Association, for classes and local exhibitions. At 2825 Lexington Road, the campus of the Southern Baptist Seminary holds two small museums, the **Eisenberg Museum of Egyptian and Near Eastern Antiquities,** and the **Nicol Museum of Archaeology** with more from the Middle East (both open Mon-Fri 8-10, Sat 9-4, free). The **Louisville Zoological Garden,** at 1100 Trevilian Way, has 600 animals but is proudest of its Siberian tigers (summer, Mon-Sat 10-6, Sun 10-7; winter Tues-Sun 10-5, adm. $2.50).

Two early 19th century homes are administered by the Historic Homes Foundation; **Farmington,** built in 1810, was the home of the Speed family, and was constructed after a design by Thomas Jefferson. Abe Lincoln spent a few weeks here (at 3033 Bardstown Road; Mon-Sat 10-4:30, Sun 1-4:30, adm.) **Locust Grove,** the oldest house in Louisville, was the last home of George Rogers Clark (same hours as above; at 561 Blankenbaker Lane, off I-71). Near the latter, one thoroughly forgettable president rests at the **Zachary Taylor Monument and National Cemetery,** at 4701 Brownsboro Road.

One could spend a very unusual vacation in Louisville just taking factory tours. The city has its share of the more prosaic sorts of industry—two of the biggest employers are Ford Motor and General Electric, which makes all its household gadgets at a giant installation called "Appliance Park" south of town—but there are also some local specialties whose makers are always glad to show off to visitors. Two distillers, of course, offer tours: **Joseph E. Seagram & Sons,** on Central Avenue and Seventh (Mon-Fri 10-2, no kids), and the **Old Fritzgerald Distillery** southwest of Louisville on Fritzgerald Road (weekdays, call 448-2860 for information). Tobacco is represented by **Philip Morris,** who is the Marlboro Man's boss, at Broadway and the Dixie Highway (Mon-Fri 8-2 & 3-4). For almost a century, big and little leaguers have rubbed pine tar on "Louisville Sluggerts," and it is disconcerting that today the **Hillerich and Bradsby Co.** has moved itself across the river to Indiana, where besides the tour (and a souvenir) there's a museum of bats (1525 Charleston-New Albany Road, Jeffersonville, Ind., just across from downtown Louisville; Mon-Fri 10:30 and 2:30 for the baseball bat tour, 9:55 & 1:55 for the golf club tour). Handcrafted pottery is another old local industry, and you can see it at **Hadley Pottery,** 1570 Story Avenue, near Butchertown (Mon-Fri, 2 pm. no kids).

Restaurants: 610 Magnolia***, 610 W. Magnolia; Casa Grisanti***, 1000 E. Liberty; New Orleans House***, 412 W. Chestnut; Hasenour's***, 1028 Barrett Ave.; The Atrium***, 1028 Barrett Ave.; Cafe Metro**, 1700 Bardstown Rd.; Fifth Quarter**, 1241 Durrett Lane; House of Hunan**, 916 Depont; Myra's**, 2420 Grinstead Dr.; Monarch Club**, 16600 Dixie Beach Rd.; Hickory House*, 2225 Taylorsville Rd.; (for Kentucky burgoo); J. P. Kayrouz Delicatessen*, 130 St. Matthews Ave.; La Normandie*, 2616 Bardstown Rd.

Eastern Kentucky

Eastern Kentucky is the state's mountain region, rich in coal, dotted with bleak, seemingly always depressed towns, once shattered by generations of feuding, today the victims of the big business which, as Harry Caudill so graphically depicted in his classic *Night Comes to the Cumberlands* has destroyed not only the mountains, but their inhabitants as well. Yet at the same time old Appalachian crafts are flourishing with an hitherto unheard-of prosperity; traditional folk songs and clog dancing are enjoying a popularity far beyond the mountains as towns, abandoned by the coal companies, now make rugs and quilts sold in Manhattan boutiques.

Running diagonally across the west edge of Eastern Kentucky, the **Daniel Boone National Forest** is a scenic wonderland noted for its high cliffs, waterfalls and recreation areas. A hiking trail, the **Sheltowee Trace,** stretches the length of the forest from the Tennessee border to Morehead. The most striking part of the forest, the **Red River Gorge Natural Area** lies off the Mountain Parkway southeast of Lexington; here 12 natural stone arches, (most notably the 300 foot Sky Bridge), sheer precipices, three waterfalls, and an unusual diversity of plant and animal life may be explored via miles of hiking trails, or the Red River Gorge Loop Drive (Rts. 715 & 77). In Stanton, outfitters rent canoes for paddling down the Red River. In **Slade,** just south of the Mountains Parkway, **Natural Bridge State Resort** encompasses the scenic area around the 65 foot Kentucky Natural Bridge, carved by the wind out of sandstone. To the north near **Morehead,** (the seat of Rowan County, once so corrupt that the state considered abolishing it all together), is **Cave Run Lake,** one of the most scenic in Kentucky, surrounded by lofty mountains and famous among anglers for its muskie.

East of the National Forest in Olive Hill, **Carter Caves State Resort Park** (Rt. 182) is another beautiful area, with cliffs, streams, a mountain lake and abundant wildflowers. There are 29 caves in the park, one the home of the rare Social Bat; tours are offered five times daily from the trading post, adm. **Ashland,** on the Ohio River, is the major industrial center of Eastern Kentucky, where "coal meets iron." Today oil refining and steel are the most prominent concerns. Much of Ashland was built on top of Hopewell Indian mounds, several of which remain in the city's **Central Park.**

The tier of counties south of Ashland along the West Virginia border were the scene of some of mountains' worst feuds, most famously the Hatfield and McCoy feud of Pike County. Kentucky touchily likes to emphasize that such bloody rows are now a thing of the past, and that as a state its crime rate is one of the lowest. To get a first-hand look at the ruggedness and remoteness of Pike County's terraine, visit **Breaks Interstate Park** near Elkhorn City overlooking the great "break" in the eastern edge of the Cumberland plateau, the Grand Canyon of the South (see Virginia).

In isolated **Pippa Passes** (named for Browning's poem), **Alice Lloyd College** was founded in 1919 by Alice Lloyd of Boston to educate East Kentuckians; today its Appalachian semester is an important introduction to the region for outside scholars. From Pippa Passes a series of twisting mountain roads leads to the equally remote **Lilley Cornett Woods** (Rt. 1103), 554 acres of primeval forest a remnant of the ancient Mesophytic forest that once covered the Cumberland Plateau. Guided tours of the woods are offered from April to October.

To the west in **Hyden,** the **Frontier Nursing Service** was founded in 1925 by Mary Breckinridge, to serve the medical needs of a 700 square mile area that had no resident doctors. Because women in the Appalachins had traditionally attended births, Breckinridge staffed the nursing service with midwives, many of whom had to be trained in Europe because of American reluctance to accept midwifery. Now the FNS is itself one of America's leading trainers of midwives, at the Frontier School of Midwifery & Family Nursing; FNS's Chapel contains 15th century stained glass. South of Hyden, **Harlan,** a major coal mining center, is nationally known as "Bloody Harlan" for the numerous homocidal labor disputes; when the miners are on strike no place in the world is more suspicious or mean as convoys of scabs and company guards riding shotgun roll into town. Harlan itself is a dismal place, drab as if the houses and trees themselves were coated with a fine layer of coal dust, a fitting monument to the free enterprise system. Between Harlan and Whitesburg, near Lilley Cornett Woods, extends the 38 mile gravel **Little Shepherd Trail,** named for John Fox Jr.'s novel, which is set in Harlan County.

The tri-state **Cumberland Gap National Historic Park** holds great significance for Kentucky. Until Dr. Thomas Walker became the first white man to see it in 1750, and Daniel Boone the first to make extensive use of it, the land beyond the mountains was subject to the wildest imaginings. When Boone passed through the natural 800 foot cleft in the mountains, he discovered the ancient Athiamiowee Trail used by countless Indian hunters; this became the basis for the Wilderness Road, the main route from Virginia to the west, making Kentucky indeed the "land of tomorrow." As Frederick Jackson Turner commented in 1893: "Stand at Cumberland Gap and watch the procession of civilization marching single file—the buffalo following the trail to the salt springs, the Indian, the fur-trader and hunter, the cattleraiser, the pioneer farmer—and the frontier has passed by." The National Visitors Center is near **Middleboro,** a town founded as a kind of model British community in 1886; streets were given names of English shires and one of America's first golf courses was laid out. The venture collapsed with the failure of the London bank of Naring Brothers and Company, and only revived slowly through coal mining, a story symbolized by the **Coal House** at N. 20th Street, built in 1926 of 40 tons of coal. In **Pineville's** Pine Mountain State Park Amphitheatre (US 25E), an outdoor musical, *Song of the Cumberland Gap* tells the story of Daniel Boone, from late June-August, tel. (606) 337-3800.

In **Barbourville** to the northwest, the **Dr. Thomas Walker State Shrine** (Rt. 459) commemorates the discoverer of Cumberland Gap (see Charlottesville, Virginia). A replica of his log cabin, the first built west of the Alleghenies, stands on the grounds (open March-October, daily 9-9, free). Corbin nearby is the main point of departure for Kentucky's greatest natural wonder, **Cumberland Falls,** 120 feet long and 70 feet high, famous for its rare moon-bow, a phenonemon it shares only with Africa's Victoria Falls. The force of the falls is so great that a mist always hovers over the water, which in the light of a full moon is reflected to form a night-time rainbow, especially colorful in cool, clear evenings. White water rafting trips, easy enough for the greenest novice, are available below the falls down the Cumberland River, May-October; tel. (606) 523-0629. Cumberland Falls State Resort Area also encompasses the high tumbling **Little Eagle Falls,** sacred to the Indians.

West of Cumberland Falls, Wayne County's Sunnybrook Cemetery has a number of unique East Kentucky grave houses—wooden shelters built over the graves, sheltering collections of memorabilia of the deceased. Near **London,** north of the Falls in Daniel Boone National Forest, **Levi Jackson Wilderness Road State Park** marks the site of one the most vicious Indian massacres that occured in Kentucky, when in 1786, 24 newly arrived settlers on the Wilderness Road were surprised and killed. Sections of the original Wilderness Road and Boone's Trace remain in the park, which also features the **Mountain Life Museum,** a collection of log cabins housing pioneer relics, a vast collection of millstones, a prarie schooner, a mill, and a backwoods Methodist church (open May 15-October 15, 9-5).

Restaurants. *In Morehead*: Windmill*, I-64. *In Ashland*: Chimney Corner*, 1624 Carter Ave. *In Hyden*: Appalachian Motel*, Rt. 80. *In Middlesboro*: Front Porch Steak House**, US 25 E.; Clancy's*, 1521 E. Cumberland. *In Corbin*: Yeary's*, 107 18th St.; Dixie Cafe*, 208 S. Main St.; *In London*: Chadwell's London Inn**, N. Main St.

Western Kentucky

Western Kentucky encompasses several regions—the Pennyrile, the Western Coal Fields, and the Jackson Purchase, the westernmost corner of the state, between the Ohio, Tennessee and Mississippi Rivers, purchased from the Chickasaw Indians by President Jackson. Kentucky's rolling hills smooth out in the west—some patches resemble the prarie—yet the presence of TVA's vast Land Between the Lakes makes the region an increasingly popular recreational area.

Owensboro on a high bluff over the Ohio, is the largest city in the region and the third largest in Kentucky. The state's largest dark tobacco market, Owensboro, like Louisville, goes out of its way to patronize the arts (its motto is "Bourbon, Barbeque and Beethovan)—with a fine symphony orchestra, the **Owensboro Museum of Fine Arts,** 901 Frederica Street, with 18th and 19th century American and English paintings (Mon-Fri 10-4, Sat & Sun 1-4, free), and the **Owensboro Area Museum,** 2829 S. Griffith Avenue, featuring local history, reptiles, planetarium shows, and exhibits on the various -ologies Mon-Fri 8-4, Sat & Sun 1-4, free). Some of Owensboro's finest homes are along Griffith Avenue, lined with dogwoods and azaleas. The botanical specimen Owensboro is proudest of, however, is the world's largest **Sassafrass Tree** at 2100 Frederica Street, estimated to be between 250 and 300 years old. Owensboro's barbeque comes in the form of the International Barbeque Festival in May; its bourbon, Glenmore, is distilled at Hardinsburg Road and US 60 E. (tours weekdays at 2). **Glenmore's Little Museum** at the distillery has an assorted collection of whiskey memorabilia (always open).

Henderson, down river, was the home of John James Audubon from 1810-1820. Here he first began studying and painting the many migratorv birds he encountered in nearby forests, while failing at several business enterprises; eventually he had to declare bankruptcy. **John James Audubon State Park,** on US 41 & 641, is quite appropriately a bird sanctuary as well as a park noted for its many varieties of wildflowers. On the grounds the Audubon Memorial Museum contains 126 first edition prints of *Birds of America,* as well as Audubon family items (April-October, 9.5, adm.).

The western coal fields extend to the south into the Pennyrile. In Muhlenberg County, one of Kentucky's leading coal producing areas, strip mines have scarred the landscape in gaping, awesome pits. Amidst this environmental rape, **Lake Malone State Park** is a picture postcard. The lake is surrounded by tall cliffs in many places and a dense forest of hardwoods. **Fairview,** south of the park, was the birthplace of Confederate President Jefferson Davis (1808-1889); the **Jefferson Davis Monument State Shrine** on US 68 is marked by an audacious obelisk 351 feet high—the fourth largest dedicated in 1924. An elevator takes visitors to the top for a panoramic view.

The TVA's **Land Between the Lakes** (see Tennessee) was formed by impounding the Cumberland and Tennessee rivers; between the dams in **Lake City** the Army Corps of Engineers operates a Visitor Center (US 62) with information on the dams and the area.

Paducah, at the confluence of the Ohio and Tennessee Rivers, may well have more historical markers per block than any city. Founded by explorer William Clark, who inherited the land from his brother, George Rogers Clark, the city was named for the Chickasaw Indian chief, Paduke, Clark's friend, whose statue by Lorado Taft stands at 19th and Jefferson. During the Civil War Paducah was a prize coveted by both sides for the long stretches of river it controlled. Grant captured the town in 1861, and for a while it's federal garrison was commanded by General Lew Wallace, the author of *Ben Hur.* Another writer more closely associated with Paducah was journalist and humorist Irving S. Cobb (1876-1944), creator of the famous Jedge Priest stories; he is buried in the city's Oak Grove Cemetery. Truman's popular Vice President, Alben W. Barkley, affectionately known as the Veep, also hailed from Paducah. The **Barkley Monument** stands at 28th and Jefferson, and the **Barkley Museum** at Madison and 6th (open Sat & Sun 1-4).

Yet more Paducalia is on display in the **Market House** complex at Broadway and S. 2nd Street, near the Ohio River. Also in the collection are American decorative arts, an early drug store, sea shells, Indian relics and an art gallery (Tues-Sat 2-4, Sun 1-5, adm). **Paducah City Hall,** at 300 S. 5th Street, is by Edward Durell Stone, featuring his typical inner court; indeed, the building is a copy of his U.S. Embassy in New Delhi.

South of Paducah, **Benton** hosts the only festival commemorating the sweet potatoe, east of the Mississippi on Tater Day, a popular event since 1843. Big Singing Day in May, celebrated since 1884, demonstrates the almost forgotton art of shape note singing, using the 1833 Southern Harmony book. **Mayfield,** in a county aptly named Graves, was the home of a mildly obsessed horse trader named Henry C. Woodridge, who prior to his death had 16 life-sized stone stautues carved of his favorite people and animals to keep his cemetery monument company; over his mortal remains stands a procession of hunting dogs, a deer, a fox, Woodridge's sisters, girl friends, mother, brother, and himself riding his favorite horse Pop. Known as the **Woodridge Monuments** they may be seen during daylight hours in Maplewood Cemetery on US 45.

More funerary relics, these of the Temple Mound Builders, are in **Wickliffe,** at the confluence of the Ohio and Mississippi Rivers (nearby Mound City, Illinois, was a major Mississippian center). The **Ancient Buried City,** on US 51, 60 and 62 contains mound burials, some as deep as five layers, as they were discovered by archaeologists. A museum on the site houses ornaments, tools and furnishings found in the "city" (open Mon-Sat 9-5, Sun 12-5, adm.). On the bluffs over the Mississippi, **Columbus-Belmont Battlefield State Park** is where the Confederates labored to build an impregnable fortress to protect Southern shipping. Besides fortifying both sides of the river with 140 guns, they built a floating battery and stretched an enormous chain across the river, all to little avail. In November, 1861, General U.S. Grant, in the Union's first major western campaign, captured Belmont on the Missouri side of the river, but was unable to subdue the heavy artillery at Columbus. He retreated and pursued a new strategy, outflanking the Southerners by capturing Forts Henry and Donelson in north Tennessee. In February, 1862, the Confederates at Columbus were forced to withdraw, and Federal troops occupied their positions, taking the first step in the drive to capture the Mississippi and split the Confederacy. In the park, a museum presents an audio-visiual account of the battle. A trail leads through the Confederate-dug trenches; part of the great chain and its six ton anchor may still be seen along with Civil War artillery (museum open June-August 9-5, weekends only in May & September).

The extreme southwest corner of Kentucky, the **Kentucky Bend** (accessible only from Tennessee) is tucked in a horseshoe bend of the Mississippi. This geographical oddity was caused by the 1811-12 New Madrid earthquake, one of the strongest in history, which changed the course of river, separating this little island of Kentucky from the rest of the Commonwealth.

Restaurants. *In Owensboro*: Gabe's**, 1816 Triplett; House of Canton**, 1019 Old Hartford Rd.; Royce*, 704 W. 2nd St. *In Henderson*: Wolf's Tavern**, 31 N. Green St. *In Paducah*: Ninth Street House**, 323 Ninth St.; Stacey's**, 1300 Broadway; Pasta Vino*, 2711 Jackson St. *In Benton*: Marquita's Place*, US 68. *In Mayfield*: Devanti's Steak House**, Mayfield Shopping Plaza.

Annual Events in Kentucky

Late March-early April: Sue Bennett Folk Festival, *London.*
April: Tater Day, *Benton.*
Late April-early May: Derby Week Festival, in *Louisville,* a week of events that culminates in the Kentucky Derby, including the Great Steamboat Race, the Pegasus Parade, and the Running of the Rats, a parody of the Kentucky Derby.
May: Big Singing Day, *Benton*; May Festival and Chili Cook-off Fest, *Covington*; Kentucky Guild of Artists and Craftsmen's Fair, *Berea*; Kentucky Mountain Laurel Festival, *Pineville*; Kentucky Fiddlers

Contest, *Elizabethton*; Kentucky Horse Trials, *Lexington.*
June: National Mountain Style Square Dance, *Slade*; Festival of the Bluegrass, *Lexington*; Capital Expo, *Frankfort*; Appalachian Celebration, *Morehead*; Bluegrass National Open Sheep Dog Trials, *Lexington.*
July: Shaker Festival, *South Union*; Kentucky Lake Indian Pow-wow, *Gilbertsville*; Renfro Valley Bluegrass Festival, *Renfro Valley*; Fourth of July Jamboree, *Cumberland*; Founders Day Weekend, *Hodgenville.*
August: International Banana Festival, *Fulton*; Kentucky State Fair, *Louisville*; Great Ohio Flatboat Race, *Owensboro.*
September: Admirals Day, *Boonesboro*; Septemberfest Square Dance Fest, *Gilbertsville*; Kentucky Highlands Folk Festival, *Prestonsburg*; Cow Days, *Greensburg*; Black Patch Tobacco Festival, *Princeton*; Great Dulcimer Convention, *Pineville*; Apple Festival and Fair, *Liberty.*
October: Logan County Tobacco Festival, *Russelville*; Sorghum Festival and Flea Market, *Springfield*; October Court Days, *Mount Sterling*; Butcherton Oktoberfest, *Louisville*; Daniel Boone Festival, *Barbourville.*

Accommmodation in Kentucky

Bluegrass and Central Kentucky

Campbell House Inn, 1375 Harrodsburg Rd., Tel. (606) 255-4281, *Lexington.* Expensive.
Spring Motel, 2020 Harrodsburg Rd., tel. (606) 277-5751, *Lexington.* Fine moderate rooms, some with kitchens.
New Circle Inn, 588 New Circle Rd., Tel. (606) 255-3337, *Lexington.* Moderate.
Kimball House, 267 S. Limestone, tel. (606) 252-9565, *Lexington.* Inexpensive.
Bryan Station Inn, 273 New Circle Rd., tel. (606) 299-4162, *Lexington.* Inexpensive.
Gateway Motel, 225 Scott St., tel. (606) 291-7100, *Covingtn.* Moderate.
Lookout Motel, 1700 Dixie Hwy., tel. (606) 431-5141, *Covington.* Inexpensive.
Alexandria Motel, 7725 US 27, tel. (606) 635-2124, *Newport.* Moderate.
Brown's Motel, US 52 W. Aberdeen, *Maysville.* Inexpensive.
Colonial Motel, 1493 S. Main, tel. (606) 987-3250, *Paris.* Inexpensive.
Boone Tavern Hotel, Main Street, tel. (606) 986-9358, *Berea.* College run, with student made furnishings; moderate.
Mountain View Motel, Rt. 21, tel. (606) 986-9316, *Berea.* Inexpensive.
Prince Royal Motel, I-75 exit, tel. (606) 986,8426, *Berea.* Inexpensive.
Beaumont Inn, 638 Beaumont Dr., tel. (606) 734-3381, *Harrodsburg.* Built in 1845, furnished with antiques; moderately expensive.
Stone Manor Motel, US 127, tel. (606) 734-4371, *Harrodsburg.* Inexpensive.
Shaker Village at Pleasant Hill, US 68, tel. (606) 734-5411, *Pleasant Hill.* Moderate.
Talbott Tavern, 107 W. Stephen Foster Ave., tel. (502) 348-3494, *Bardstown.* Five antique furnished rooms over tavern, one featuring murals painted by Louis Philippe; expensive.
Bardstown-Parkview Motel, 418 E. Stephen Foster Ave., tel. (502) 348-5983, *Bardstown.* Moderate.

Old Kentucky Home Motel, 414 W. Stephen Foster Ave., tel. (502) 348-5979, *Bardstown*. Inexpensive.
Lincoln Trail Motel, 905 N. Mulberry St., tel. (502) 769-1301, *Elizabethtown*. Very inexpensive.
Lincoln Memorial Motel, US 31 E. & Rt. 61, tel. (502) 358-3197, *Hodgenville*. Inexpensive, with restaurant.
Mammoth Cave Hotel, tel. (502) 758-2225, *Mammoth Cave National Park*. Moderate; restaurant adjacent.
Oasis Motor Inn, Rts. 70 & 90, tel. (502) 773-2151, *Cave City*. Inexpensive, near Mammoth Cave.
Park Mammoth Resort, US 31 W., tel. (502) 749-4101, *Park City*. Resort with many activities, adjacent to Mammoth Cave National Park; moderate.
Cardinal Motel, 1310 US 31 W. Bypass, tel. (502) 842-0328, *Bowling Green*. Inexpensive.
Crossland Motel, 421 US W. Bypass, tel. (502) 842-0351, *Bowling Green*. Inexpensive.

Louisville (Area Code 502)
The Seelbach Hotel, 500 Fourth Ave., tel. 585-3200. Recently renovated; four-posted beds. Deluxe.
Galt House, Fourth & River, tel. 589-5200. A new hotel with the old name; expensive.
Breckinridge Inn, 2800 Breckinridge Lane, tel. 456-5050. East of downtown; moderate-expensive.
Louisville Inn, 120 W. Broadway, tel. 582-2241. Moderate-expensive; downtown.
Executive Inn, 978 Phillips Lane, tel. 367-6161. Near fairgrounds; moderate-expensive.
Milner Hotel, 231 W. Jefferson St., tel. 452-6361. Moderate.
All of Louisville's inexpensive motels are along the Dixie Highway between the city and Shively.

Eastern Kentucky (Area Code 606)
Natural Bridge State Resort Park, Rt. 11, tel. 663-2214, *Slade*. Moderate; many activities in scenic setting.
Mountain Lodge Motel, 205 Fraley Dr., tel. 783-1555, *Morehead*. Inexpensive.
Carter Caves State Resort Park, US 60 & 182, *Olive Hill*. Moderate, many activities.
Western Hills Motor Lodge, 3466 13th St., tel. 325-8461, *Ashland*. Inexpensive.
Appalachia Motel, US 421, tel. 672-2327, *Hyden*. Inexpensive.
Pine Mountain State Resort Park, Rt. 190, tel. 337-3066, *Pineville*., Moderate, with golf course.
Cumberland Falls State Resort Park, Rt. 90, tel. 528-4121, *Corbin*. Moderate, pretty mountain setting.
Holiday Motor Lodge, Rt. 90, tel. 376-2732, *Corbin*. Inexpensive.
Yeary's Motel, 107 18th St., tel. 528-2311, *Corbin*. Inexpensive.
Westgate Inn Motel, Rt. 80, tel. 878-7330, *London*. Inexpensive.

Western Kentucky (Area Code 502)
Executive Inn Rivermont. One Executive Blvd., tel. 926-8000, *Owensboro*. Moderate.
Tower Motor Inn, US 231 & 20th, tel. 684-8835, *Owensboro*. Inexpensive.
Henderson Downtown Motel, 425 N. Green St., tel. 827-2577, *Henderson*. Inexpensive.
Kentucky Dam Village State Park, US 62 & 641, tel. 362-4271, *Gilbertsville*. Overlooking Kentucky Lake; moderate.
Kenlake State Resort Park, US 68 & Rt. 80, tel. 474-2211, *Aurora*. Resort overlooking Kentucky Lake.
Lakeland Motel, Aurora Rd., tel. 474-2292, *Aurora*. Inexpensive; near Kentucky Lake.
Shawnee Bay Resort, Rt. 962, tel. 354-8360, *Benton*. Expensive; on Kentucky Lake.
Lake Barkley State Park Resort, US 68 & Rt. 80, tel. 924-1171, *Cadiz*. On Lake Barkley, many activities; moderate.
Eddy Creek Resort & Marina, Rt. 93, tel. 388-7743, *Eddyville*. Resort cottages on lake inlet, moderate.
Drury Inn, US 60 & I-24, tel. 443-3313, *Paducah*. Moderate.
Diplomat Inn, 2701 H.C. Mathis Dr., tel. 443-6573, *Paducah*. Moderate.
Diamond Inn Motel, 2301 S. Beltline Hwy., tel. 443-5323, *Paducah*. Inexpensive.
Mid-towner Motel, 513 E. Broadway, *Mayfield*. Inexpensive.

For more information on Kentucky, write the Kentucky Department of Tourism, Fort Boone Plaza, Frankfort 40601. Camping and other recreational information is available from the Department of Parks, Capital Plaza Tower, Frankfort 40601; for hunting and fishing regulations, write the Department of Fish and Wildlife Resources, 592 E. Main St., Frankfort 40601. The state's tourist office has a toll free number 1-800-626-8000 to answer your queries; within Kentucky dial 1-800-372-2961.

Channing, Steven A., *Kentucky, A History,* W. W. Norton, 1977
Federal Writers Project, *Kentucky: A Guide to the Bluegrass State,* Hastings House, 1954.
Federal Writers Project, *Lexington and the Bluegrass Country,* E. M. Glass, 1938.
Klotter, James C., *William Goebel; The Politics of Wrath,* University of Kentucky Press, 1977.
Yater, George H., *Two Hundred Years at the Falls of the Ohio: A History of Louisville and Jefferson County,* The Heritage Corporation, 1979.

Tennessee

> "It is certain that every man who arrives here and determines to become a Citizen appears to feel and I believe does feel an Independence and Consequence to which he was a Stranger in the Atlantic States . . ."
>
> —William Blount, former territorial Governor, in 1797

So much of the American character had its birth in the frontier experience, and so much of that experience began in this quietly remarkable state of Tennessee. Settlement began here even before the Revolution, a purely private matter that no colonial government promoted or desired, and only fifteen years after Yorktown the land became, after its sister state Kentucky, the second new state to form itself out of the West. And no sooner was that done than those independent-minded men, who had thought nothing of climbing up and down mountains into unknown territory to make their homes, and who had already nonchalantly created democratic commonsense governments for themselves, set to work making their new state an important member of the Union both economically and politically; when they first elected one of their own as president they rewrote the ground rules of American democracy.

Of course there isn't much frontier left in the state that once sent Davy Crockett to Congress, but there is a good deal that survives from the early days: a talent and a love for music and politics, a tacit but well understood devotion to individualism that goes beyond the usual American cliches, and especially in the mountains of the East, a surviving folk culture that has landed on its feet in spite of being jerked into the twentieth century with a startling abruptness in the 30's and 40's. Another strong old trait is friendliness; Tennesseans may well be the most cussedly friendly people in the nation, and they are the people with whom out-of-state license plates are most likely to elicit an open conversation and a wonderfully unaffected "Y'all come back now, hear?"

It is a state of curious proportions, about 450 miles by 110; Bristol, at its northeastern corner, is closer to Philadelphia than to Memphis on the Mississippi. In longitude it reaches from the level of the Florida coast to that of Davenport, Iowa. The historical carelessness that gave it such boundaries also destined Tennessee to have as sharply defined regions as any state. There are three, all different but none any more or less Tennessee than the rest (a trinitarian mystery!) and the virtues, faculties, favorites and faults of each are as well-known to the others as if they were all children who have grown up in the same apartment-house. East Tennessee is Appalachian ridges and the Cumberland Plateau, dulcimer players and physicists; it sells nuclear fuel to the Europeans and ginseng root to the Chinese, and it always votes Republican. Middle Tennessee, as solid a heartland as any state could hope for, has more bluegrass than Kentucky, miles of white board-fenced horse farms, famous distilleries in dry counties and the admirable but often confusing city of Nashville. Across the Tennessee River and the smooth stairway of TVA dams that the New Deal built, West Tennessee dreams the dreams of old cotton-planting, steamboating Deep South. It too has an interesting city, Memphis—but already the voice of the East pipes up, claiming neglect of the others: Knoxville and Chattanooga.

That's a paradox, and one of many; this Tennessee that most of us think of as a woodsy pastorale has four big cities, more than any other Southern state. Tennessee is in many senses a border state—it touches eight neighbors, more than any other except Missouri—and it often finds itself caught in the middle between North and South, industry and agrarianism, forward-looking and backward-looking politics, custom and modernity. Such a situation doesn't make life simple for the Volunteer State, but it's the best way to gain experience.

Getting To and Around Tennessee

By Air. The major airports in Tennessee are in Memphis and Nashville, with regularly scheduled flights from as far away as Canada; other interstate airports are in Knoxville, Chattanooga, Jackson, Clarksville, and the tri-city area of Johnson City, Bristol, and Kinsport in the extreme east of the state.

By Train. The only Amtrak train that passes through Tennessee is the Chicago-New Orleans train, which stops at Memphis and Dyersburg. For information call toll free 800-874-2800.

By Bus. To make up for its lack of public rail transportation, Tennessee is served by a wealth of bus companies besides Greyhound and Trailways.

By Car. The Natchez Trace (see Mississippi) begins in Nashville.

By Boat. An increasingly popular way to spend a vacation in Tennessee is renting a house boat on the TVA-created "Great Lakes of the South". Addresses of houseboat rentals may be found in the "Outdoors in Tennessee" booklet (see below).

By Foot. The Appalachian Trail follows the Tennessee-North Carolina border through Cherokee National Forest and Great Smoky Mountains National Park; write the Appalachian Trail Conference, P.O. Box 236, Harpers Ferry WV 25425 for more details. Another good source is the "Outdoors in Tennessee" booklet published by Tennessee Tourist Development, P.O Box 23170, Nashville 37202.

History

There was no easy way into the country across the Appalachian mountains, only the circuitous route through the Cumberland Gap, at the point where the present states of Tennessee, Virginia and Kentucky meet. Of necessity, military affairs preceded settlement; in the 1700's both France and Britain had traders and agents among the Cherokee and Chickasaw of Tennessee, and both nations intrigued to bring this barely explored land into their sphere of influence. In 1756, with the advent of the French and Indian War, Fort Loudoun was established on the Tellico River, the westernmost British outpost in the New World. The Cherokee themselves had asked for the fort, as protection from the neighbors and the

French, but they and the British soon fell out over settlement rights. In spite of the fact that their leading chief, Attakullakulla, was a firm friend of the colonists—he had paid an official visit to London and had his portrait done by Hogarth—the war party prevailed, and Fort Loudoun was taken in 1760. In response, Colonel James Grant, who figured prominently in the capture of Fort Duquesne (the main business street of Pittsburgh is named for him), came over the mountains to destroy the Cherokee's villages and burn their crops. By the end of the war, in 1763, control of the mountains was secure enough for the first settlers to begin trickling in from North Carolina, Pennsylvania and Virginia.

In a sense, all the early history of Tennessee is the story of land deals, and competition between rival groups of speculators created the territory's first political factions. In 1775, a group of North Carolinians cashed in on the greatest speculation of all when their Transylvania Land Company purchased land from the Cherokee amounting to almost all of Kentucky and a third of Tennessee. The settlers themselves, frontier farmers to whom land deals were only insurance for future prosperity, were a hardy and clever mix of Scotch-Irish Presbyterians, English, and French Huguenots, and they proved perfectly suited to the task before them. One thing they had to do was form a frame of government. Neither the British nor the North Carolina authorities were much interested in them, preferring instead to keep a hard-won peace with the Cherokee, and consequently the first Tennesseans were compelled to look after their own interests. In 1772, they met to form the Watauga Compact and the Watauga Association, an important early experiment in self-government paralleling those of the New World's first colonists a century and a half before. Five years later, the Wataugans found their dearest wish granted—to go out of business. North Carolina agreed to claim the territory just as the American Revolution was getting under way.

That revolution did not leave Tennessee untouched, or rather, the Tennessee frontiersmen did not fail to leave their mark on it. When the British imperiously sent a demand over the mountains that the settlers submit to the King's arms in 1780, they responded by raising an army overnight (a habit that came with living next to the Cherokee) and marching into South Carolina to rout the force of Tories on King's Mountain and preclude any further threat to their lands. Their achievement should not be underestimated; the victory at King's Mountain came at a time when the patriot cause in the South looked bleak, and it was the first in a string of successes that ended only at Yorktown. At the same time that the frontier army was getting itself ready, another group of pioneers was embarking on one of the most dramatic westward migrations ever. To reach their promised land in the Cumberland Valley, and to join the small band that had preceeded them a year before over the difficult Cumberland Plateau, two hundred men, women and children under John Donelson sailed the length of the Tennessee River through a gauntlet of hostile Indians, up the Ohio and back down the Cumberland to establish the first settlement in Middle Tennessee, at what is today the city of Nashville. One of the company, Donelson's little daughter Rachel, would eventually be the celebrated wife of Andrew Jackson.

After the war, North Carolina once more put in a claim to the transmontane territories, and this caused the settlers to begin their first movement for separation and statehood. The heart of the issue again was land, and whether the anticipated killings from the sale of it would end up in the pockets of the Carolina legislature and its friends, or of the settlers themselves. Once more John Sevier, the man who had led the attack on King's Mountain, came forth to assume command. This frontier gentleman, a worthy contemporary of Daniel Boone (himself no stranger to these parts) was a descendant of French Huguenots and one of the first men to make his home in the old Cherokee lands. His friends, meaning almost everyone in Tennessee, called him "Chucky Jack" from his home on the Nolichucky River, and he proved as adept at statemanship as he did at soldiering, pioneering and land speculating. In 1784, he presided over the birth of what the settlers called the State of Franklin; originally Frankland, the "land of the free," Sevier had it changed to flatter old Ben into using his influence with Congress to have the state admitted into the union. It didn't work; Sevier's backwoods revolution not only failed to enlist any sympathy from Congress, but North Carolina sent an expedition over the mountains to arrest him. Even though a group of Chucky Jack's friends had little trouble springing him from the jail in Morganton, North Carolina, the experiment was over and the "Lost State of Franklin," whose Constitution and Bill of Rights can still be seen at the Tennessee Historical Society in Nashville, slipped to the bottom of the page as a curious footnote in the nation's history.

Eventually, the U.S. forced North Carolina and all of the original states to renounce claims on any western lands and another speculator, William Blount of North Carolina, managed to secure appointment as territorial governor, the perfect post from which to watch over his western lands. The first territorial census revealed that a population surpassing the 60,000 necessary for statehood had already grown up along the Tennessee River and its tributaries. The first settlers had set themselves down along little streams with names like Watauga, Holston, French Broad and Clinch, all deep in the mountains. Despite the rapids at Chattanooga and the rocks at Muscle Shoals, however, the broad Tennessee was beginning to serve as the highway to the west the promoters always hoped it would be and the settlements at Nashville and the rest of Middle Tennessee were already competing with the east for prominence. On June 1, 1796, the territory became the fifteenth state of the union; in the deliberations of the convention that preceded this event, the name of Tennessee was first suggested—some say by Andrew Jackson, an up and coming young lawyer who had moved to Nashville from North Carolina, and who already was a force in local politics and an enemy of Tennessee's first governor, none other than John Sevier. Knoxville, at the time the only sizable town, became the first capital.

It was not, however, to remain so for long. Within a decade, the rich lands of Middle Tennessee attracted enough settlers for it to surpass the east, and later, in the 1820's the boom reached to West Tennessee, good land for cotton and slavery. A clause in the constitution allowed the growing state to move its capital to Nashville, and East Tennessee, particularly the city of Knoxville, began a long slide into political and economic impotence. In the War of 1812, Tennessee picked up its "Volunteer State" nickname for the numbers of recruits it contributed to the cause. Already a leader among the expansionist western states and eager for a war with Britain, Tennessee was just beginning the most glorious period of its history, when the state would exert a greater influence over national politics than it ever would again. Of course, the state's own Andrew Jackson would parlay his victory at New Orleans into national prominence and eventually the presidency, but in a sense the "Age of Jackson" was also the Age of Tennessee.

Ever since the days of the Watauga Association—and the Cumberland Association drafted by the settlers at Nashville—Tennesseans showed a genuine zest for politics, Court sessions and political campaigns were among the biggest social events, and every candidate's oratory was expected to be at least as strong as the whiskey he was generously pouring out. Parade wagons and banners were everywhere and discussions of the issues were not an unknown occurrence. Jackson's platform, designed for the land-speculating classes and prospective westward migrants, swept them off their feet. By no means, however, was Old Hickory the only noteworthy character on Tennessee's stage. One of his strongest supporters was popular governor Sam Houston, who disappeared in 1829—in the middle of his term and a few weeks after his marriage—and turned up a year later in the Texas Revolution. An opponent was Congressman Davy Crockett, the legendary pioneer who made himself overnight the most popular man in the state when he courageously fought Jackson's and the State of Georgia's genocide against the Cherokee. Davy was last seen in Tennessee emerging stark naked from the Mississippi at Memphis, after a steamboat wreck on his way west, leaving the message for his constituents that "You can go to Hell; I'm going to Texas." These two heroes of the Alamo and San Jacinto and the thousands of other Tennesseans who followed them, made the new Republic of Texas almost a Tennessee colony.

That Jackson could control national politics for a decade did not mean he could always do it in his home state; Tennesseans were so comfortable with their political dominance by 1836 that after Jackson's two terms they wanted another Tennessee man, Hugh White, to succeed him. When Jackson selected New Yorker Martin Van Buren instead, the state rebelled and voted Whig in the next five presidential elections (along with only Kentucky, Vermont and Massachusetts—a strange coalition!). The state even voted against another of its sons, James K. Polk, in his successful bid for the presidency in 1844, although they were quite pleased with Polk's successful aggression against Mexico. The 1840's were the high-water mark of the importance of Tennessee, fifth among the states in population and a leader in cotton, tobacco and most other agricultural products as well as politicians.

As far as anyone knows, the first and only abolitionist newspapers to be published in the South appeared in East Tennessee, in Jonesboro and Greenville, around 1820. Although the movement in Tennessee didn't last, its presence alone presaged the state's future as the reluctant rebel, the last state to join the Confederacy and the first to be parted from it. The first referendum to decide whether there should be a state secession convention failed and it took all the bullying that the rabid pro-secessionist governor, Isham Harris, was capable of to turn that vote around. After Harris signed a military pact with the Confederacy, a

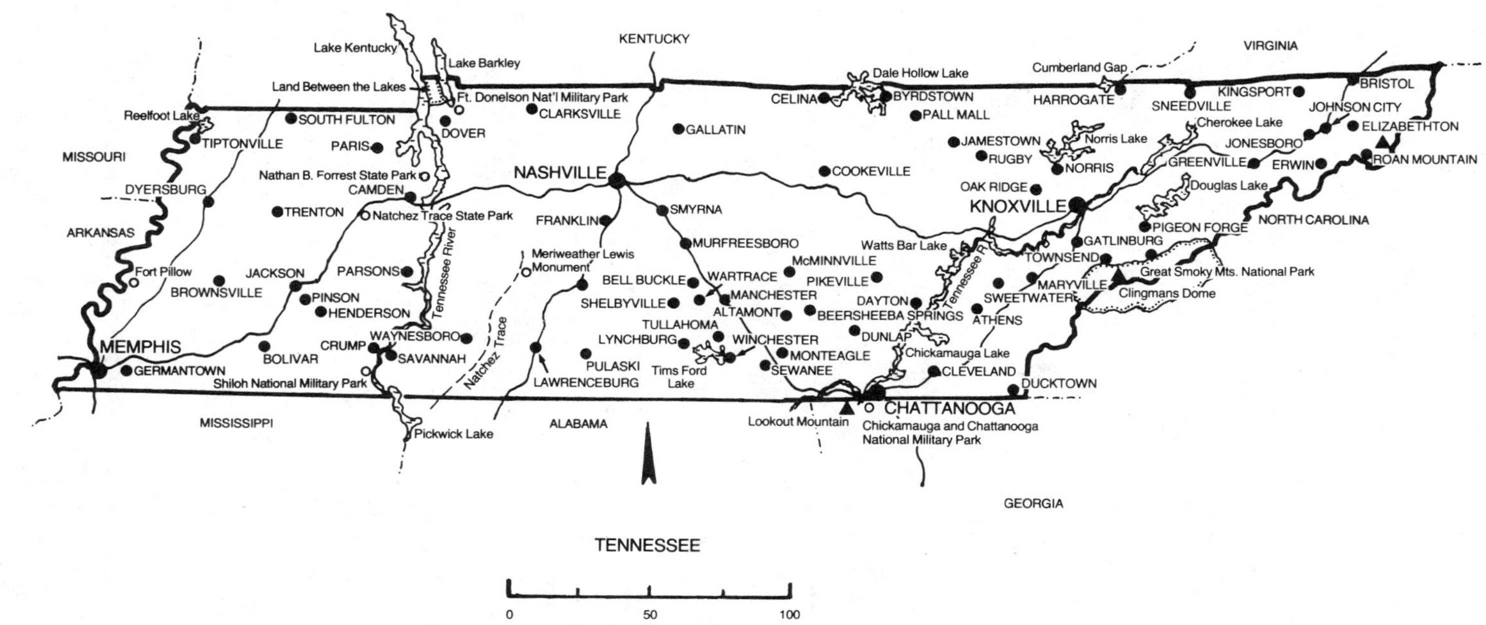
KENTUCKY
VIRGINIA
Lake Kentucky
Lake Barkley
Land Between the Lakes
Ft. Donelson Nat'l Military Park
CLARKSVILLE
Dale Hollow Lake
Cumberland Gap
CELINA
BYRDSTOWN
HARROGATE
SNEEDVILLE
KINGSPORT
BRISTOL
JOHNSON CITY
ELIZABETHTON
Reelfoot Lake
SOUTH FULTON
PALL MALL
Cherokee Lake
JONESBORO
TIPTONVILLE
PARIS
DOVER
GALLATIN
JAMESTOWN
Norris Lake
RUGBY
GREENVILLE
ERWIN
ROAN MOUNTAIN
MISSOURI
Nathan B. Forrest State Park
NASHVILLE
COOKEVILLE
NORRIS
OAK RIDGE
Douglas Lake
DYERSBURG
CAMDEN
KNOXVILLE
NORTH CAROLINA
TRENTON
Natchez Trace State Park
SMYRNA
FRANKLIN
PIGEON FORGE
ARKANSAS
MURFREESBORO
Watts Bar Lake
GATLINBURG
Tennessee River
Meriweather Lewis Monument
McMINNVILLE
TOWNSEND
Great Smoky Mts. National Park
Fort Pillow
JACKSON
PARSONS
BELL BUCKLE
WARTRACE
PIKEVILLE
Tennessee R.
MARYVILLE
BROWNSVILLE
PINSON
MANCHESTER
SHELBYVILLE
DAYTON
SWEETWATER
Clingmans Dome
HENDERSON
ALTAMONT
BEERSHEEBA SPRINGS
ATHENS
TULLAHOMA
WAYNESBORO
Natchez Trace
DUNLAP
MEMPHIS
CRUMP
LYNCHBURG
WINCHESTER
BOLIVAR
SAVANNAH
MONTEAGLE
Chickamauga Lake
PULASKI
GERMANTOWN
Tims Ford Lake
SEWANEE
CLEVELAND
Shiloh National Military Park
LAWRENCEBURG
DUCKTOWN
CHATTANOOGA
MISSISSIPPI
ALABAMA
Lookout Mountain
Chickamauga and Chattanooga National Military Park
Pickwick Lake
GEORGIA
TENNESSEE
0
50
100

second referendum passed. Tennessee joined the rebels in June, and only eight months later found itself the victim of the first successful Union offensive, led by an obscure recently re-commissioned general named Grant. Governor Harris and his speedily-assembled state army made the wrong guess at every turn and Grant's forces occupied both Nashville and Memphis by June, 1862. Still, the war wasn't over for the Volunteer State (which sent thousands of volunteers to both sides; pro-Union East Tennessee very nearly seceded itself, as did West Virginia). In all, Tennessee saw more fighting than any state except Virginia, from the first battle at Fort Henry to the last desperate Confederate attempt to retake Nashville in 1864.

Tennesse's Reconstruction experience was different from the other states'. A sympathetic military governor, future president Andrew Johnson, attempted to get the state peaceably back into the Union in 1863, but Congress refused it. A new constitutional convention was begun in 1865, abolishing slavery and disenfranchising the rebels. In the elections that followed, the irascible Unionist writer William G. Brownlow became governor, and under him the state was readmitted and made its difficult passage through radical rule. An embarassing sidelight was the founding of the Ku Klux Klan in Pulaski, by former slave trader and Confederate general Nathan Forrest. This warped genius, a revolutionary strategist and originator of the old saw about "getting there the firstest with the mostest," was Tennessee's greatest contribution to the Confederacy; his campaigns were studied by the Nazi high command and contributed much to the Blitzkrieg. Despite its founding, the Klan was never as active in Tennessee as other states and Forrest himself disavowed it when the game started getting out of hand.

In the decades that followed, Tennessee led the South in its economic recovery; Tennesseans discovered that they had a great talent for business and they created important mining and iron industries without much Northern capital or help. One consequence of this was the growth of Chattanooga into an important city, and another was the "convict wars" of the 1890's, waged by miners in East Tennessee against the use of convict labor for strikebreaking; in 1892 miners were storming the prisons and sending the cons to Nashville to get rid of them. Politics after Reconstruction followed the usual Southern pattern, only with the Republicans actually electing a governor now and then. One campaign still remembered in Tennessee was that of 1886, where the two Taylor brothers, Democrat Bob and Republican Alf, came out as opposing candidates and followed the old Tennessee custom of stumping the state together to publicly argue, sing, play fiddle duets, steal each other's speeches and laugh at each other's jokes. Voter turnout was the largest ever and Bob, the winner, showed what a swell guy he really was the following year by introducing a poll tax and other measures to disenfranchise blacks and poor whites.

Twentieth-century Tennessee saw a curious blend of the old and new, North and South; while Boss Crump's political machine ran Memphis and the state with modern efficiency, the grim-faced maidens of Prohibition stalked the counties and precincts to keep alcohol the longest-running hot issue. Thriving industrial cities existed side by side with mountain hollows which even the 19th century hadn't quite reached

Parts of Tennessee—especially East Tennessee, were poor and backward and used-up. The New Deal, which probably did more for Tennessee than any other state, changed everything. Not only TVA (see below), but agricultural price supports and rural electrification wrought a quiet revolution in the state. Political modernization wasn't far behind; after the big war that Tennessee industry, TVA and, of course, Oak Ridge contributed so much towards winning, the lessons of democracy were brought home by GI's in the "veterans' revolts" against courthouse rings in Athens and elsewhere. Tennessee began to depart from usual Southern behavior by sending Republicans and even progressive Democrats to state and national office, useful citizens like Estes Kefauver—Adlai Stevenson's running mate, famous for his Senate organized crime investigations.

In a way Tennessee has much in common with Florida; for perhaps entirely different reasons, they are the two Southern states that have most clearly escaped from Southernism. Tennessee is growing economically, but it is a calm and orderly growth, nothing like Atlanta, Tampa or the Gulf Coast. With its two-party politics, businesslike, inclined to compromise and relatively free of Southern obsessions, Tennessee is getting a chance to play the Border State role it passed up in 1861. Today, there's a little of the best of both North and South in her.

TVA: In the 1930's and 40's, a tune called the *TVA Song* was popular among the folk singers of Kentucky and Tennessee, to honor the piece of New Deal alphabet soup that John Gunther called "the greatest single American invention in this century":

. . . All up and down the valley
They heard the glad alarm
"The Government means business!
It's working like a charm . . ."

Remarkably, the man most responsible for the Tennessee Valley Authority had no connection at all with the region; he was a determined, unassuming Progressive Senator from Nebraska named George Norris. Back during World War I the U.S. had begun a dam and nitrate plant at Muscle Shoals, Alabama, on the Tennessee, and in the course of using his committee chairmanship to keep three Republican presidents from giving the unfinished project away to private industry, Norris became interested in the flood control problems of "America's worst river" and in the tremendous waste of natural and human resources in the area, including parts of seven states that are drained by the Tennessee and its tributaries. Those same presidents vetoed two Norris bills for the improvement of the river, but with the election of Franklin Roosevelt Norris got a blank check; apparently it was Roosevelt himself who had the idea of placing all the possible goals for the Tennessee Valley under a single non-political planning authority.

As one of the first acts of the Hundred Days, TVA came into being in May, 1933, and work on the first dam—Norris Dam—began within months. The extent of the job was staggering; TVA was mandated to stop floods, make the Tennessee navigable, generate electric power to sell to publicly-owned utilities, introduce new farming techniques, reclaim marginal lands, and provide recreational opportunities. In all of these, it succeeded brilliantly. Fifteen years and 26 dams later (all built for a total of less than $1 billion) the economy of the area had been transfigured. Tennessee became the first public power state, with new industries flocking to the region for the advantage of cheap electricity; TVA power contributed immeasurably to the war effort, not least of all for the Manhattan Project at Oak Ridge. Valley farmers were becoming as modern and prosperous as any in the nation, and TVA reservoirs, the "Great Lakes of the South," developed into the region's playground. The whole story of this great experiment in democracy, of its myriad innovations and improvisations, is perhaps better known in some places overseas than in the U.S. Students and officials from all over the world came to see it, and still do, not just because it represents the biggest attempt at regional planning outside of the socialist bloc, but for the ideal it embodies. Of all the attempts made by the U.S. Government to improve the conditions of its people, TVA was the most successful.

Of course there was always opposition; the big utility corporations (behind Wendell Wilkie's Commonwealth & Southern holding company) kept TVA in the courts for eight years. When the Republicans gained power in 1953, they prepared to sell off the whole thing—only the near-unanimous protest of Tennessee prevented them. They did succeed, however, in drawing out much of the initial idealism. Lately the authority seems to have grown distant both from its original purpose and the people it serves. A nasty dispute over its land acquisition tactics at the Land Between the Lake project caused much unfavorable publicity, and TVA's wholesale plunge into nuclear power has made it quite unpopular with many Tennesseans. Recently it has suffered the embarrasment of announcing the scrapping of four half-completd reactors, begun after the planners had wildly exaggerated the region's future power needs.

In spite of this, there's still much to be learned from TVA. All of the dams and power plants may be visited (Norris, Fontana and Hiwassee are perhaps the best). They have few frills—nothing like Hoover Dam—but their builders gave them a strikingly modern and consistent sense of design that makes them almost beautiful. They are monuments and they were built to last.

East Tennessee

In East Tennessee, the Appalachian and Cumberland Mountains meet in the Tennessee Valley, their combined pressure forming the land into a series of ridges and valleys. This rugged, sometimes fertile terrain, has traditionally appealed to the individualistic, rugged temperament of the Scotch-Irish, people willing to tame the land with "guts, grit and gizzard." Their roots in the mountains run deep; in Eastern Tennessee's "hollers" singers still read shape notes and sing ballads their ancestors brought over with them in the 18th century.

The largest city in southeastern Tennessee, **Chattanooga,** is located at the Tennessee River's hairpin Mocassin Bend near the Georgia border. Its poetic name, from the Cherokee *Tsantanugi,* means "rock coming to a point," referring to famous Lookout Mountain, the dominant feature of Chattanooga's geography, of its past, and of its present tourist industry.

Because of Lookout Mountain (which extends almost a hundred miles into Georgia and Alabama) and the surrounding ridges, Chattanooga's location in the geographic center of the Tennessee Valley as a gateway between the south and midwest has long been important. Several major Indian trails converged here, the impetus for a Scotch-Cherokee trader to set up the area's first trading post in 1817, called Ross's Landing. In 1837 Ross's Landing was the central staging area of the Cherokee removal, and the beginning of the Trail of Tears. A year later, freed from Indian claims on the land, it incorporated under the name Chattanooga.

During the Civil War Chattanooga was an important prize. Its railroad links to Atlanta, Memphis, Nashville and Knoxville formed the South's major east-west transportation hub; once the Union captured Chattanooga, Sherman's March to the Sea was unstoppable. After the Confederate victory at the Battle of Chickamauga on September 20, 1863 (see North Georgia), General Braxton Bragg made a major error in waiting a day to press home his advantage over General William S. Rosecrans' Federal Army of the Cumberland. Rosecrans used the day to entrench his army in Chattanooga, and Bragg, realizing the folly of an open attack on the Federals, trapped them in the city, setting up positions on Lookout Mountain and Missionary Ridge.

Bragg cut off Rosecrans' communications with the outside world and prevented fresh supplies from entering the city. Meanwhile Lincoln, realizing how close he was to losing an entire army in Chattanooga, sent General Hooker and 20,000 men from the Army of the Potomac by train, and General Sherman and two corps of his Army of the Tennessee by boat to relieve the besieged Army of the Cumberland, now under Rosecrans' replacement General Thomas, "the Rock of Chickamauga." Grant, commander of the Military Division of the Mississippi, was in charge and he ordered Hooker to first reopen the line of communications to Chattanooga and send in suppplies and reinforcements (October 28).

Early in November, Bragg made a second major miscalculation when he sent off part of his besieging army to aid Longstreet's attack on Knoxville. In the fog of November 23-24, Hooker captured Lookout Mountain in the "Battle above the Clouds," while Sherman simultaneously attacked Confederate positions on Missionary Ridge. When his offensive bogged down on November 25, Grant sent General Thomas and the Army of the Cumberland to take some of the rifle pits on the western slope of Missionary Ridge. Recalling their defeat at Chickamauga, Thomas' troops quickly seized the rifle pits, and by sheer momentum and anger stormed up the steep ridge and captured it on their own initiative—much to the amazement of Generals Thomas and Grant. The Confederates retreated, and Chattanooga, in the hands of the Federals, opened up Atlanta and Georgia to Sherman's campaign of "total war."

After the war, Chattanooga's railroads were rebuilt, the most famous being the Cincinnati-Southern Line, completed in 1880, the first municipal railroad, and the first since the Civil War to connect North and South. A reporter covering the maiden run of the train nicknamed it the "Chattanooga Choo-Choo," a name that became world famous during World War II when Tex Beneke sang it with the Glenn Miller band. Although Chattanooga's hopes of becoming an iron or mining center in the late 19th century died when the ore proved too hard to abstract, the city earned a footnote in history with the *Chattanooga Times,* one of the best papers of the era, published by young Adolph Ochs, who in 1896 would purchase the bankrupt *New York Times* and turn it into one of the world's leading newspapers.

Today Chattanooga, the former "Dynamo of Dixie," emphasizes its outdoorsy aspects with a new nickname, the "Scenic Center of the South," a mountain playground that manufactured the golf balls the astronauts hit on the moon. The city itself, piled between the twisting Tennessee River and the slopes of Missionary Ridge has, like many Southern cities, a very broad Broad Street for its main thoroughfare, several fine old commercial buildings, a big urban renewal project (built by the TVA), and some pretty Victorian era homes on the hillsides. At 1400 Market Street, the city's best-known institution the **Chattanooga Choo Choo Hilton** is a sprawling complex of restaurants and shops in the great domed 1909 Terminal Station. Guests sleep in Victorian style sleeping cars connected to an 1880's woodburning engine, similar to the Choo-Choo that made the first run from Cincinnati. A trolley takes visitors around the terminal to an arcade housing an enormous model railroad and a scale model of Chattanooga in its railroading heyday. Near the Choo-Choo in the **National Cemetery** (1080 Bailey Ave.), Captain James J. Andrews and seven of his "raiders" are buried beneath a miniature replica of the *General,* the Confederate engine they hijacked in 1863 in an escapade known as "The Great Locomotive Chase." After kidnapping the *General* in Kennesaw, Georgia, Andrews and his men drove it north towards Chattanooga, destroying bridges and equipment on their way, with the Confederates in hot pursuit. When the locomotive ran out of fuel just over the Tennessee border, the daring raiders tried to escape into the woods, but were captured. Those who escaped execution in Chattanooga went on to become the first Americans to receive the Congressional Medal of Honor, the nation's highest award.

Chattanooga's two museums are near the Tennessee River: the **Houston Antique Museum,** at 210 High Street, specializes in antique glass pitchers, with over 15,000 in the collection: shaving mugs, music boxes, lamps and other antiques are also displayed (open Tues-Sat 10-4:30, Sun 2-4:30, adm.). The **Hunter Museum of Art,** at 10 Bluff View overlooking the river, contains 18th-20th century American paintings and sculpture including several paintings by Charles Burchfield (open Tues-Sat 10-4:30, Sun 1-4:30, free). From the central city, Dodson Avenue heads north to the **Tennessee Valley Railroad Museum,** at 2202 N. Chamberlain Avenue at the foot of Missionary Ridge, where a collection of antique steam and diesel locomotives take visitors on short excursions (open May-October, Sat 10-5, Sun 1-5, adm.).

Broad Street connects downtown to **Lookout Mountain** and its bevy of attractions; the first, **Confederama,** is just off Broad at 3742 Tennessee Avenue. Here some 5,000 miniature soldiers—made in South Africa—electronically reenact the major battles for Chattanooga on a miniature battlefield, accompanied by music, lights, smoke and a historical narrative (open Memorial Day-Labor Day, Mon-Sat 9-9, Sun 1-9, till 5 the rest of the year, adm.). Nearby, signs point out the **Lookout Mountain Inclined Railway,** a National Historic Site on St. Elmo

Avenue. This mile-long incline is considered the world's steepest, with a 72.7 grade, and it affords a magnificent view, with the Tennessee Valley slowly unfolding down below (June-August Mon-Sat 8:30 am-9:30 pm, Sun 10 am-9:30 pm; the rest of the year, Mon-Sat 9-5:30, Sun 10-6:30; trips every 15-20 minutes, round trip fare $3). In the summer, a bus at the incline's Cloud High Station offers scenic tours of Lookout Mountain; another bus provides the connection to **Rock City,** the world's most heavily advertised tourist attraction; "See Rock City," says every bird house, barn door, boulder and cow within a five hundred mile radius of Chattanooga, elevating Rock City into the ozone layer of folklore. The man who painted all of these signs made enough money to open his own attraction in Alabama. Well then, what is there to see at Rock City? Ten acres of unusual sandstone formations on the precipice of Lookout Mountain, encompassed by the Enchanted Trail. This leads through tunnels and narrow passageways with cute names like Fat Man's Squeeze and over a suspension bridge to Lover's Leap, where seven states are visible on a clear day. Fairyland Caverns and Mother Goose Village, at the end of the Enchanted Trail, are illiminated by black lights (open daily 8 am-sundown, adm.).

The other major commercial attraction atop Lookout Mountain, the **Ruby Falls-Lookout Mountain Caverns,** are on Lookout Mountain Scenic Highway, the main route up the mountain. Ruby Falls, a majestic 145-foot cascade 1,120 feet down in the caverns, is reached by elevator; views of the Tennessee River and Chattanooga may be had from the castellated lookout tower (open May-September, daily 7 am-9 pm, 8-8 the rest of the year, adm.). Surrounding this entire area is the Tennessee section of **Chickamauga and Chattanooga National Military Park** (headquarters in Chickamauga, Georgia). The "Battle above the Clouds" took place near the incline station at **Point Park,** overlooking the famous Mocassin Bend in the Tennessee River. In the park are the **Ochs Memorial Museum and Observatory,** honoring Chattanooga's most famous citizen, and depicting the siege and battle of Chattanooga. The **Cravens House,** nearby on Rt. 148, was used first as the Confederate, then as the Union headquarters in the Battle above the Clouds (all sites in the National Military Park are open daily 9-6, 9-5 in the winter, and are free). At the foot of Lookout Mountain, off Scenic Highway 41, **Reflection Riding** is a picturesque, drive-through garden, home of the Chattanooga Nature Center. Remains of one of the old trails that converged in the area, the Great Indian Warpath, may still be seen along with double profile "Father Stone" (Mon-Sat 9-dusk, Sun 1-dusk, fee per car). Several hang-gliding endurance records have been made off of Lookout Mountain; for instruction and outfitting information write Air Space Inc., P.O. Box 6009, Chattanooga TN 37401 (tel. (615) 867-4970).

From Chatanooga, Cherokee Boulevard crosses the river north of the city for **Signal Mountain,** the southernmost tip of Walden's Ridge. Both the Cherokee, and later the Confederates, used the mountain for signalling to their cohorts. From Signal Point and James Point on the mountain there are wonderful views of the **Grand Canyon of the Tennessee,** a magnificent gorge cut between Signal and Raccoon Mountains through Marion County. Prentice Cooper State Forest, on top of Signal Mountain, is a terminus of the **Cumberland State Scenic Trail** to the Sequatchie Valley. **Raccoon Mountain** (take US Scenic Highway 41 from Chattanooga) is another hang-gliding center; a sky ride eliminates the chore of walking back up the bluff after a ride. Raccoon Mountain is also well known in energy circles for the TVA's new Raccoon Mountain Pumped Storage Project, an innovative dam where the water passes through the turbines during periods of high power demand, and is pumped back up to the reservoir in the evening when demand is low.

Monteagle, a small resort town to the east, has been the seat of the Cumberland Mountains' Chautauqua Assembly for a century. Every July and August, lectures, concerts and classes in the arts are held in the tradition that once made the Chautauqua popular all over the country. In nearby **Sewannee,** the Episcopalians built their **University of the South** in 1857. Reorganized after the Civil War, the campus features the **Breslin Tower** (1888), a replica of Oxford's Magdalan Tower, and **All Saints' Chapel,** a neo-Gothic jewel. **University View** overlooks a valley a thousand feet below. Allen Tate, a member of the Fugitive group, founded the University of the South's *Sewanee Review,* still one of America's notable literary reviews.

North of Chattanooga, **Chickamauga Lake** is one of the TVA's Great Lakes, fringed with several swimming beaches. Noted for its breezes, the lake hosts several national sailing championships. Square dances take place every weekend at **Primitive Settlement** off US 64 in **Cleveland,** where a collection of log cabins brought in from the surrounding area are furnished with frontier antiques and handmade tools (daily 10-6, adm.). East of Cleveland are two of Tennessee's principle floatable rivers: the **Ocoee River** and the Hiwassee River, the latter Tennessee's first designated Scenic River; headquarters are in Delano (tel. 263-1341). Both of these rivers pass through **Cherokee National Forest,** running parallel with the North Carolina border and surrounding Smoky Mountains National Park.

Athens, the seat of McMinn County, made national news in 1946 when a group of young GIs, disgusted by the local machine's graft, election stealing and downright viciousness, stormed the local jail after an election with dynamite and rifles, wounding a number of people, where the sheriff and his hoodlums had retired to rig the votes. After their coup d'etat, the GIs restored order, and public opinion prevented the state from taking any action against them.

An even more famous incident took place in the **Rhea County Court House** in the town of **Dayton.** When Tennessee passed a law in 1925 prohibiting the teaching of evolution in the public schools, a group of citizens sitting around Robinson's Drug Store decided to test the new law in court and found a substitute biology teacher named John Scopes willing to lend his name to the cause. Although they lived in the heart of the "Bible Belt," their motives for bringing the issue to court stemmed not entirely from an interest in the conflict between the secular and the religious; Dayton, after all, could use a little publicity to boost business. Soon it had more than it ever dreamed possible, as the case captured the interest of the entire world.

The so-called "Monkey Trial" took place in the court house for eight sweltering days in July, the crowd of reporters hanging on every word of the debate between the silver-tongued fundamentalist and one-time presidential candidate, William Jennings Bryan, and Clarence Darrow, the most famous lawyer of his day. Even the papers in China followed the trial as eight overworked Western Union operators worked day and night to get the news out. The citizens of Dayton sold thousands of souvenirs and Robinson's Drug Store concocted a drink called the Monkey Fizz. Although Scopes was found guilty and fined, both sides proclaimed victory. Tennessee, however, has just recently shaken off its image as the Monkey State (dropping the anti-evolution law in 1967), while Dayton preserves the memories of its moment in the world spotlight in the basement museum of the courthouse, and in Robinson's Drug Store, where the walls are covered with photographs from the trial that inspired the play and movie "Inherit the Wind."

The Cumberland Plateau west of Dayton is endowed with several spots of exceptional natural beauty. On Rt. 30, near **Pikeville,** magnificent virgin forests, chasms and the sheer 256-foot Fall Creek Falls are contained in scenic **Fall Creek Falls State Resort Park.** To the south, near **Altamont,** the **Savage Gulf State National Area** and the adjacent **Great Stone Door State Environmental Educational Area** consist of three sheer rock gorges, created by the Collins River, Savage Creek and Big Creek, forming an enormous crow's foot on the edge of the Cumberland Plateau. An ancient earthquake formed the natural gateway into the gorge, a 150-foot high crevice known as the Great Stone Door, and released an underground spring that formed the focus of an antebellum spa called Beersheba Springs. There are several trails through the park for day hikers and over-night backpackers. To the north, on US 127 in Crossville, the **Cumberland Mountain State Rustic Park** (cabins, restaurant) encompasses another large stretch of virgin hardwoods on the lofty Cumberland Plateau.

Halfway between Chattanooga and Knoxville, the world's largest underground lake, the **Lost Sea,** covers 4½ acres. Stocked with enormous rainbow trout, visitors to the caverns are taken on a glass-bottomed boat excursion; cave flowers and other formations may be seen in caves surrounding the lake (daily 9-sundown, adm.). In **Vonore,** just east of Sweetwater, the Colony of South Carolina built Tennessee's first English structure, diamond shaped **Fort Loudoun** in 1756, on the banks of the Tellico River (made famous recently by the Army Corps of Engineers' Tellico Dam project, to be built at the expense of the rare snail darter). In recent years Fort Loudoun has been reconstructed to resemble its 1760 appearance (located off US 411; open daily 8-4, free).

When John Gunther visited **Knoxville** in 1946 he was appalled. "Knoxville is the ugliest city I ever saw in America, with the possible exception of some mill towns in New England," he wrote in the bestseller *Inside U.S.A.* Not only was it ugly, but it was extremely blue-nosed, disallowing Sunday movies and baseball and alcohol, which led Gunther to the conclusion that "it is one of the least orderly cities in the South—Knoxville leads every other town in Tennessee in homicides, automobile thefts, and larceny."

If his portrayal of Knoxville was true, then the city has gone through an amazing metamorphosis. It no longer even comes close to being the ugliest or most disorderly city, compared to boom towns like Houston or Atlanta, and it long ago repealed most of its blue laws. But for decades

Knoxvillians remembered and smarted from Gunther's comment (long after everyone else had forgotton about it), and they worked to redeem their city. By 1982 Knoxville was ready to show off to the entire universe with a World's Fair.

Knoxville began in 1786 when Revolutionary War Veteran James White built a collection of cabins in a stockade he called White's Fort on First Creek, one of two creeks that poured into the Tennessee on either side of a level bluff. The first governor of the territory, William Blount, changed the name of White's Fort to honor his immediate boss, Washington's Secretary of War, Henry Knox, and made it the first capital of the territory, and eventually the state. One of the settlers who had accompanied Blount to Knoxville was a soldier of fortune named George Farragut, who had fought for North Carolina in the Revolution. His son, David, born near Knoxville, would grow up to become a hero of the U.S. Navy in the Civil War. The Farragut Hotel was for many years a Knoxville institution.

Although Knoxville soon lost its status of state capital, it continued to grow as the major marketing town in the Great Valley of East Tennessee, and at one point, produced a candidate for the presidency, Hugh Lawson White, a son of Knoxville's founder. White had been a strong supporter of Andrew Jackson and hoped to succeed him in office in 1836. Jackson, however, had already given Martin Van Buren the nod, and this began a rift between East Tennessee and the Democratic Party that has never healed.

Salt was rubbed in the wound by a Methodist circuit rider named William G. "Parson" Brownlow, who arrived in Knoxville in 1849, where he published a paper called *Brownlow's Knoxville Whig*. Knoxville's most vituperative citizen of all time, Brownlow hated almost everything except slavery *and* the Union, and was quite as much hated in return; one Kentucky editor growled, "He is a loathsome fistula of the body politic . . . Heaven, earth, and even Hell abhor him—though the latter will somehow manage to gulp him down." When Knoxville was occupied by the Confederates, Brownlow fled, and went on the Northern lecture circuit, spewing such venom that the *New York Times* commented, "He is himself a legion and might safely be pitted against the whole Confederacy."

Brownlow was far from being the only Unionist in Knoxville, as Confederate General Felix K. Zollicoffer found out in November, 1861, when Union sympathizers burned a number of important railroad bridges. When Federal gains forced the Confederates to concentrate their forces in Chattanooga and north Georgia, General Ambrose Burnside moved a Union army into Knoxville (September 1, 1863) amid cheering throngs. Robert E. Lee sent Longstreet and part of the Army of Northern Virginia to retake the city. After failing in both a siege and a direct attack, he withdrew, leaving Knoxville in Union hands for the rest of the war.

Along with Burnside's occupation, Knoxville suffered the return of Brownlow, who began republishing his paper under a new title, the *Knoxville Whig and Rebel Ventilator*. After the war, he became Tennessee's Reconstruction governor, and made even more enemies, particularly with West Tennesseans and the Ku Klux Klan. Knoxville, meanwhile, grew quickly as a transportation, wholesale, milling, and mining center. With its booming industries, visitors described it as a very Northern city, although as a city of mountaineers it was always quick to erupt into wanton violence—shootouts on Gay Street, Knoxville's main business street, continued until the turn of the century.

Knoxville's boosters had visions of grandeur for their rapidly growing city; they held two Appalachian Expositions in 1910 and 1911, and a National Conservation Exposition in 1913 to introduce Knoxville to the world. By the Great Depression, however, it was becoming increasingly apparent that Knoxville was in a sad state of decline, with little hope of revival.

Help came from an unexpected corner: the federal government. Knoxville attributes its present prosperity to three major institutions, the TVA, Oak Ridge and the University of Tennessee, which expanded by leaps and bounds after World War II, thanks to government subsidies. The well-educated newcomers and technocrats employed by these institutions have changed the character of conservative Knoxville, although the city, which profitted more from the New Deal than any other, still votes Republican. In 1982, the general feelings of prosperity and success Knoxville has experienced in the last few decades culminated in the holding of the first sanctioned World's Fair in the South since Atlanta's 1895 Cotton States Internation Exposition, on a theme that Knoxville knows well—energy.

The 70-acre site of the fair, Knoxville's Lower Second Creek Valley was a dismal depression of abandoned railroad tracks, industrial buildings and crumbling housing, a barrier between downtown and the University. In 1976 it was chosen as the site for the fair, with the proviso that afterwards it would be redeveloped with a park and lake, new housing, shopping and entertainment complexes. The 266-foot **Sunsphere,** the symbol of the fair, will remain with its observation decks and restaurants, along with the multi-use **U.S. Pavilion,** the renovated **L & N Railroad Depot,** housing shops and restaurants, and the **Tennessee Amphitheater.** At writing, the verdict isn't in on the Knoxville World's Fair, but in one respect, at least, it was disappointing. World's Fair pavilions are nothing if not experimental proving grounds for new ideas in architecture whether successfully (most recently, the geodesic dome and Habitat apartments at the Montreal Expo in 1967) or unsuccessfully (the futuristic monstrosities at the 1964 New York World's Fair). The architecture at the Knoxville World's Fair, touted as futuristic, was glorified shopping mallish or variations on a circus tent. The Chinese dancing girls, fireworks and exhibits of Appalachian folk art were more interesting than the pavilions or their exhibits. The World's Fair, did, however, lead to a number of civic improvements in Knoxville. New hotels were built, streets improved and downtown was given a facelift. It also brought about some civic embarrassments, as local landlords booted out long-time tenants to soak World's Fair visitors and participants.

Gay Street has been Knoxville's main thoroughfare since the city's earliest days; near the foot of Gay Street, the **Governor Blount Home** (a National Landmark) was the first frame house built west of the Alleghenies, in 1792. The early log cabin dwellers admiringly called it a mansion, and here Territorial Governor William Blount signed the documents creating the state of Tennessee. The adjacent Craighead-

Jackson House, built in 1818, serves as a visitors center (open Tues-Sat 9:30-5, summer Sundays 2-5, adm.). The **Knox County Courthouse** and two theaters have been renovated along Gay Street. The **Bijou Theater,** in the Lamar House at 807 Gay Street, hosts performances of the local opera company in its classical auditorium, while the **Tennessee Theater,** at 508 Gay Street, presents classic old films and newsreels on the weekends in a 1928 Rococola movie palace, complete with a large illuminated Wurlitzer organ. The glass tower of the United American bank and the undistinguished modern headquarters of the TVA at the top of Gay Street dominate the Knoxville skyline. Near the TVA, Knoxville once had a prosperous, three-storey market house in the middle of what is now **Market Square,** but the city's fathers saw fit to tear it down in the 1960's, replacing it with a typical pedestrian mall (a restaurant on the square has pictures of the old market on its walls). Despite the destruction of a major focal point, Knoxville's downtown held its own until 1971, when the city became the last metropolis of its size in the U.S. to sell its soul to a suburban shopping mall. Although Gay Street now has covered walkways, potted trees and other beautifications, it still cannot compete with the alluring lights of the surrounding sprawl for the affection of Knoxville shoppers.

Below downtown, in a bleak valley of unsuccessful urban renewal, **James White's Fort** (205 E. Hill Ave.) is an incongruous vision. A replica of Knoxville's original 1786 settlement, the seven log houses and stockade contain pioneer furnishings; a museum displays artifacts relating to the settlement of the Great Valley of the Tennessee (open February-mid December, Mon-Sat 9:30-5, Sun 1-5, adm.). Near downtown and the World's Fair grounds at 422 W. Cumberland Avenue, the **Medical Museum,** at the Knoxville Academy of Medicine features doctors' instruments, medical books, furniture and other items from bygone days. It is open by appointment; call 573-3464.

The sprawling campus of the **University of Tennessee,** just west of downtown, was born of tiny Blount College founded in 1795. Since the war, enrollment at the university has increased over ten-fold to make U.T. the 16th largest university in the U.S. The spate of new building to accommodate all of the new students engulfed much of the pretty Victorian Fort Sanders neighbourhood, now confined to a few streets on the opposite side of Cumberland Avenue. The **Frank H. McClung Museum** on U.T.'s Circle Park contains the university's exhibits on Tennessee's Indians, the state's early settlement, fine arts, science and natural history (open Mon-Fri 9-5, free). The **Estes Kefauver Memorial Library** on campus honors Tennessee's colorful one-time presidential candidate.

Cumberland Avenue turns into Kingston Pike (US 11 & 70) further west, where there are two museums. At no. 3148, Bleak House (named for Dickens' novel) served as Longstreet's headquarters during the siege of Knoxville in 1863. When a Confederate sharpshooter, hidden in the tower of Bleak House, fatally wounded a Union General, it became a favorite target of the North's artillery men. The Daughters of the Confederacy have recently converted the house into **Confederate Memorial Hall** and filled it full of memorabilia of the Lost Cause (open April-October, Tues-Sun 2-5; rest of the year 1-4, adm.). John Russell Pope, architect of the

National Gallery in Washington, designed the mansion housing the **Dulin Gallery of Art** at 3100 Kingston. The gallery displays temporary and permanent exhibits, the most famous being nine Thorne Miniature Rooms, furnished with miniature antiques (open Tues-Sun 1-5, adm.). At the Crescent Bend in the Tennessee, the **Armstrong-Lockett House** (2728 Kingston Pike) contains 18th century American and English furniture and decorative arts, as well as a collection of 17th-19th century English silver (open Tues-Sat 10-4, Sun 1-4, adm.).

East of Knoxville, off I-40, the **Knoxville Zoo** is home to over a thousand animals from around the world. The first African elephants in the Western Hemisphere were born at the zoo; children may ride on some of the younger pachyderms (open summer 10-7:30, winter 10-4:30, adm.). South of Knoxville, a two-storey log cabin was the home of Indian fighter, congressman and first Governor of the State of Tennessee, John Sevier (at Neubert Springs Rd. and Sevier Memorial Hwy.; open Mon-Sat 10-12 & 2-5, Sun 2-5, adm.).

In 1900, "Old John" Hendrix, resident of a Cumberland Mountain hollow west of Knoxville, had a peculiar vision: "I tell you that Bear Creek Valley some day will be filled with great buildings and factories and they will help toward winning the greatest war that will ever be . . . there will be a great noise and confusion and the world will shake." Forty-two years later, President Franklin D. Roosevelt authorized the Manhattan Project to design and build the atomic device that Albert Einstein and Enrico Fermi feared the Nazis would build first. The government appropriated two billion dollars for the top secret project and the Bear Creek Valley-Black Oak Ridge region west of Knoxville was selected as the site of a secret city that would create the bomb's essential ingredients. **Oak Ridge,** as the city became known, was at once remote but near an abundant source of power (nearby are the TVA's Norris, Fort Loudoun and Watts Bar dams); at one point during the war, Oak Ridge used one tenth of all the electricity in the United States. What astounds us today, in the age of the mass media, is how well the secrecy of Oak Ridge was kept. Although thousands of local Tennesseeans worked on building Oak Ridge, although it had a population of 75,000 by the end of the war, although scientists and technicians labored long hours in the new plants and factories of what they knew as the Clinton Engineer Works, almost nobody knew what the end result of their labors would be: to produce enriched uranium 235 in the world's first nuclear reactor. As property of the Atomic Energy Commission, the city was off limits, caged in by wire fences and military guards until March, 1949. In 1959 Oak Ridgers voted to establish a municipal government, although the Department of Energy still maintains a major operation at the Oak Ridge National Laboratory.

When the late David Lilienthal lamented that the TVA lacked an urban plan, he was thinking of Oak Ridge. During the war, Oak Ridge, designed by Skidmore, Owings, and Merrill, was a raw, hastily built collection of prefabricated houses—"flattops," plywood "hutments," and cement and asbestos board "cemestos"-trailers, new factories and the **Chapel-on-the-Hill,** the interdominational church where workers could worship in shifts. When Oak Ridge's fences were taken down, many of these temporary structures were remodelled into army post-ranch style bungalows. Oak Ridge may boast of having more Ph.D.s than any other city in America, but they live in a vast faceless atomic suburb. People in Oak Ridge find their way around by the numbers given each traffic light in the business district—itself a sterile shopping mall.

At Traffic Light 10 a sign directs visitors to Oak Ridge's most popular attraction, the **American Museum of Science and Energy,** devoted to the peacetime glories of the atom. It contains gadgets, models, a Van de GraaF generator that makes your hair stand on end, computer games and numerous demonstrations throughout the day (open Mon-Sat 9-5, Sun 12:30-5, free). Nearby, the Oak Ridge National Laboratory features the **Graphite Reactor,** the world's first nuclear reactor (or second after Fermi's University of Chicago prototype) and a National Landmark. Retired in 1963, the Graphite Reactor, along with a similar reactor in Hanford, Washington, produced the enriched uranium for the bombs dropped on Hiroshima and Nagasaki; after the war it produced radioisotopes used in medical research. America's largest nuclear accelerator is in a 166-foot tower at the Holifield Heavy Ion Research Facility. A visitors' overlook at the laboratory provides a view of its operations and the surrounding countryside.

North of Oak Ridge and Knoxville a less carcinogenic form of energy is produced at **Norris Dam.** Impounding the Clinch River, a major tributary of the Tennessee River, it was the first dam built by the TVA, and named after its father, Senator George Norris. Providing both flood control and hydroelectrical power, Norris Dam also produced Norris Lake, a popular recreational area. South of the dam, the **TVA Interpretive Center** on US 441 contains exhibits on the history of the Tennessee Valley Authority and the recreational use of Norris Lake (open Mon-Fri 8-4:45, Sat & Sun 10-6). A state park surrounding the dam features a working grist mill and the **Will G. and Helen H. Lenoir Museum,** housing pioneer and Appalachian artifacts (open May-October, Sat-Wed 9-5, October-May weekends only, free). In **Norris,** a dispersed but verdant community constructed for the workers on the dam, the **Museum of Appalachia** is a collection of homesteads, outbuildings, gardens, barns and shops brought in from the surrounding area, featuring Appalachian made crafts and decorative arts. Live demonstrations illustrate pioneer chores (open year round, daily 9-dusk, adm.).

"For we are about to open a town here—in other words to create a new center of human life . . . in this strangely beautiful solitude," wrote the English author Thomas Hughes of **Rugby,** the utopian community he founded on the Cumberland Plateau west of Norris. Hughes's best-known novel, *Tom Brown's School Days* (1857), was largely an autobiographical account of his own experiences at Rugby, the English public school run by social reformer Thomas Arnold, father of Matthew Arnold. At Rugby, Hughes acquired Arnold's urge to reform, and after the success of his novel he turned his sights on the second and third sons of the English gentry, "our Will Wimbles" as he called them. Victorian laws of primogeniture prevented these well-educated young men from inheriting any of their father's estate, and yet as Hughes commented, their parents "would rather see their sons starve like gentlemen than thrive in a trade or profession that is beneath them." To remedy this stifling situation that wasted so many lives, Hughes decided to found a settlement in America, where England's Will Wimbles could work at a manual trade without stigma.

Hughes acquired a large tract of magnificently situated land in East Tennessee in 1879 from a group of Boston industrialists who had originally intended to resettle unemployed New Englanders there, until an economic upturn changed their plans. Hughes named the community Rugby after his alma mater, and opened it up to settlement in 1880. Rugby attracted widespread publicity and 300 settlers within six months; the principle structure, the Tabard Inn (named for the inn in Chaucer's *Canterbury Tales* and containing a bannister from that ancient hostelry) was soon a major stop for prominent travelers. An impressive library was constructed, as were homes, a church, a cafe and boarding house, as well as tennis courts, bowling greens and other amenities. Although Rugby's population of Will Wimbles was supplemented by Americans and others, the experiment gradually failed after reaching its peak in 1884 when it had 450 residents. Fires, disease, financial problems in Hughes' Board to Aid Landownership and confusion over Rugby's purpose—whether it was to make a profit, remain idealistic, or become a tourist resort—led to its decline.

In 1966 a group of Tennesseeans formed the Rugby Restoration Association to preserve the remaining physical structures of Rugby; sixteen of the pinewood "carpenter's Gothic" buildings remain, including the pretty **Christ Church,** in use since its construction in 1887 and containing the original organ, lamps and altar brought over from England. The intriguing **Thomas Hughes Public Library,** unchanged since 1882, has been dubbed "a Rip Van Winkle of books" for its over 7,000 volumes of Victorian literature and periodicals. Both of these are open to the public, as is **Kingstone Lisle,** the house built in Rugby for Thomas Hughes. Other Rugby homes are privately owned, but open during the Rugby Pilgrimage on the first weekend in August. The reconstructed **Percy Cottage** is now the Rugby Visitors Center, from where tours depart from March through November, Mon-Sat 9-5, Sun 12-5 Eastern Time (note that Rugby is on the line dividing the Eastern and Central time zones). To get there from Knoxville, take Rt. 62 to Wartburg, then Rt. 27 north to Elgin, then Rt. 52 to Rugby.

The beauty of the area surrounding Rugby inspired Congress to designate 120,000 acres on the Cumberland Plateau in Tennessee and Kentucky the **Big South Fork National River and Recreation Area.** Because of the expected influx of visitors to the area, the Tennessee General Assembly has authorized funds to rebuild the Tabard Inn, the original having burned at the turn of the century.

South of Knoxville, in **Maryville,** Sam Houston taught school in 1812 when he was 18 years old. Although Houston went on to become a Congressman from Tennessee, governor of Tennessee and Texas, and President of the Republic of Texas, he always recalled his teaching stint in the backwoods with particular fondness. The small, windowless **Sam Houston Schoolhouse** (1794), a visitor center and museum, are located on Rt. 33 south of Maryville (open mid-April-October, Tues-Sat 9-6, Sun 1-5; November-April 15, Tues-Sat 10-5, free). The adjacent town of Alcoa claims to be the world's largest aluminium center; in **Townsend,** just east of Maryville, the Cherokee Indians once lived at the entrance of **Tuckaleechee Caverns,** known for its vast "big rooms," its onyx formations and lofty waterfalls (on Rt. 73; open April-October, daily 9-6, adm.). Townsend is located on the edge of Great Smoky Mountains National Park (two roads from Townsend enter the park near lovely Cades Cove—and allow you to escape the exuberant hucksterism of Gatlinburg), and in an amphitheater next to the park, the *Smoky Mountain Passion Play* takes place from mid-June through August on Mon, Wed and Fri at 8:45 pm (tel. (615) 448-2244 for information).

Pigeon Forge received its name from the Little Pigeon River, itself named by the Indians for the great flocks of now-extinct passenger pigeons that once roosted along its banks. The pioneers built an iron forge on the river and although that no longer exists, a picturesque 1830's grist mill still grinds meal at Pigeon Forge. The rest of town is a miniature version of Gatlinburg, with such attractions as the **Elvis Presley Museum** ("no wax—just facts!") featuring Elvis' first Cadillac, his last limousine and rings and watches he designed himself; **Carbo's Police Museum,** starring "Walking Tall Sheriff Buford Pusser's Death Car"; **Hillbilly Village,** with moonshine stills, split rail fences and oodles of souvenirs; **Magic World,** "a variety of Magic, Music, Mystery, Shows and Rides"; the **Smoky Mountain Car Museum,** with Hank Williams, Jrs.'s humdinger Silver Dollar Car, James Bond's car from the movie *Goldfinger,* and Al Capone's Bullet-proof Cadillac; **Porpoise Island,** a genuine Hawaiian and porpoise show; **Tommy Bartlett's Water Circus,** where performers water ski, balance on a helicopter trapeze, jump boats and do other daredevil stunts; a 17th century-style lawn **Maze** measuring 160 by 110 feet; and **Silver Dollar City,** a replica of an 1870's mountain community featuring craft demonstrations, music shows, rides and other attractions for an all-inclusive admission. All of the above are on or very near US 441; almost all close to some extent in the winter, although a few stay open on weekends. Pigeon Forge, incidentally, is in Sevier County, near the hometown of Dolly Parton; the Dolly Parton Parkway "graced by rounded hills" runs into Newport. Tour buses in Pigeon Forge usually make a stop by her tin-roofed girlhood home.

Gatlinburg, at the main entrance to the Great Smoky Mountains National Park, is a narrow two-mile-long tourist heaven, squeezed between the Little Pigeon River and the Smoky Mountains. The sheer density of its innumerable tourist traps, motels, restaurants and souvenir shops make the main drag (US 441) a "sight" in itself, reminscent of the old Atlantic City boardwalk in the intensity of wonders and marvels peddled there "for the entire family." The contrast between this oasis of hucksterdom and the majestic beauty of the Smoky Mountains couldn't be more startling. Behind all of the pizzazz, however, Gatlinburg has been a major center for regional handicrafts since 1912, when the Phi Beta Phi School opened with the aim of cultivating the folk arts of the Smoky Mountains.

Three companies offer overviews of Gatlinburg and the Smokies: **Ober Gatlinburg** takes you up 1,000 feet to the ski lodge of Mt. Harrison via the World's Largest Aerial Tramway (2¼ miles). From the lodge you can continue on a chair lift to the top of the peak where Ober Gatlinburg has an artificial astro-turf ski slope for summer skiers. The **Sky Lift** is another chairlift, this one to the top of Crockett Mountain (2,300 feet) with equally outstanding views (April-November only). Last and least, there is the **Space Needle,** an ungainly viewing platform atop an amusement arcade.

Attractions of the wax-and-wonder school abound. For religious wax, visit **Christus Gardens** where "The Last Supper, Leonardo da Vinci's famous painting, comes to life before you. Not as a painting, but *real,"* and where the eyes of a portrait of Christ carved in a block of Carrara marble follow you everywhere; for Hollywood wax visit **Stars Over Gatlinburg;** for historical wax, where "Elvis Still Lives," take in the **American Historical Wax Museum;** for trick wax, **World of Illusions** is where "Elvis Sings Again" and you can "Make one of your friends disappear" (the one who dragged you there). For models of the world's tallest man, the largest single hot dog and yet more Elvis memorabilia, there is the **Guinness Hall of World Records** down the road from their competitors in the absurd, the **World of the Unexplained** and **Ripley's Believe It or Not Museum,** starring a circus made of sugar cubes. Then there's the **National Bible Museum,** with first editions of a Bishops and a King James Bible, a Tyndale Bible, a 32-pound bible and a bible weighing less than an ounce and hundreds of other bibles from around the world (open Mon-Sat 10-5, adm.). For folks who like their adventures vicariously, **Adventures of America** will take you for rides via a giant spherical screen; **Gatlinburg Place** features an IMAX Theater screen seven storeys tall and a special 70 mm film "To Fly" as well as an electronic animated bear musical review and a live stage show in the summer. To make sure that you get something for your money, however, take in the 8:30 nightly show at the **Sweet Fanny Adams Theater,** which promises free potato chips to any patron not satisfied with the performance.

The real attraction of the area, of course, is the country's most visited national park, **Great Smoky Mountains National Park,** half in Tennessee and half in North Carolina—see the latter for more details.

New Market, on Rt. 11E east of Knoxville, is the third home of the **Highlander School,** founded by Myles Horton in the 1930's to assist labor organizers and strikers throughout the country. During the 40's it increasingly changed its focus to the racial problems of the South, and attracted future Civil Rights leaders like Martin Luther King, Jr. The General Assembly of Tennessee, in the dark paranoia of the late 1950's, launched an investigation of Highlander School, and although it could find no evidence of Communist subversion, it countenanced a raid by local officials on Highlander and had its charter revoked. Horton moved the school to Knoxville and received a new charter—and continuous harassment. In 1972 he moved the school once more, to New Market, where it is involved in the struggle of Appalachia's poor.

Davy Crockett spent his early childhood in his father's tavern on the Abingdon-Knoxville Road (today US 11E) in **Morristown,** now reconstructed as the **David Crockett Tavern and Museum.** The museum contains items relating to the Crocketts and other early frontiersmen in Eastern Tennessee (open May-October, Mon-Sat 9-5, Sun 2-5, adm.). Another famous Tennessee resident, Reconstruction President Andrew Johnson, was a 17-year-old tailor's apprentice in 1826 when he ran away from home (Raleigh, N.C.) to **Greeneville,** the capital of the short-lived state of Franklin. Three years later Johnson won election to the Board of Alderman, the first step in a political career that led to his election as Lincoln's Vice President. The **Andrew Johnson National Historic Site** is divided into three sections in Greeneville: his Tailor Shop at Depot and College Streets, where there is also a visitors center and a museum; the Andrew Johnson Homestead on Main Street; and Andrew Johnson's tomb on Monument Hill in the National Cemetery on W. Main Street (all sites open 9-5 daily).

Hancock County, on the Virginia border, is one of the more isolated corners in Tennessee, tucked away in the Cumberland Mountains. This, if any place could make such a claim, is the capital of the Melungeons, a mysterious dark skinned people who claim Portuguese origin and who moved to Tennessee when their native Carolinas considered them legally "coloreds." Because the Melungeons (their name believed to come either from the French word "melange," mixture, or from the Greek "melas," dark) speak a dialect of old English and have English last names, some believe they are the descendants of the "lost" English colonists of Roanoke, who intermarried with the Indians; others theorize that they are of Moorish descent, their ancestors having made the crossing in the 18th century to escape persecution in Spain. But whatever long-forgotton fate brought the ancestors of the Melungeons together, the industrial age has set it into reverse, and the Melungeons are rapidly intermarrying with others and dispersing.

Harrogate, near the tri-state **Cumberland Gap National Historical Park** (visitors center in Middlesboro, Kentucky), is the home of **Lincoln Memorial University** and the Lincoln Museum, containing Civil War and Lincoln memorabilia, including a bust of Lincoln by Gutzon Borglum (open daily 9-4, June-August 10-6, adm.). A road in Harrogate leads to the top of Mount Ford, affording views of the Cumberland Gap and the Pinnacle.

Jonesboro, chartered by the North Carolina legislature on January 17, 1779, is the oldest town in Tennessee and one of the first to be established west of the Alleghenies. The state of Franklin was organized here and John Sevier chosen as its first and only governor; Andrew Jackson was "Admitted to Practiss as an Attornery" here in 1788; one of the country's first abolitionist newspapers, *The Emancipator,* was published in Jonesboro in 1820. A visitor center has been established in the **Christopher Taylor Visitor Center,** which has information on Jonesboro's historic restorations.

Neighboring **Johnson City** is surrounded by several historical attractions. **Rocky Mount,** a two-storey log cabin on US 11E, was built in 1770 by William Cob and served as a rendezvous of the "over mountain men" gathering to fight Ferguson at King's Mountain. In 1790 William Blount chose Rocky Mount as the seat of the government of the Territory of the United States South of the River Ohio, making it a "capital" for eighteen months. On the grounds today are the original house, a reconstructed kitchen and a museum (open April-mid-November, 10-5, Sun 2-6, weekends only January 15-March, adm.). The **Davy Crockett Birthplace Park** lies west of Johnson City, off US 11E and 411, featuring a replica log cabin; the **Tipton-Haynes Farm,** on US 19, was established in 1783 and has been restored with its various outbuildings to reflect four periods of Eastern Tennessee history (open April-October, Mon-Fri 10-6, Sat & Sun 2-6, adm.). On the campus of East Tennessee State University in Johnson City, the **Carroll Reece Museum** features exhibits on Tennessee crafts, music and folklore (open Mon-Fri 8-4:30, Sat & Sun 1-5, free).

In the eastern section of Cherokee National Forest, **Erwin** is the base for visiting the Nolichucky River, one of the oldest rivers on the North American continent and a principle tributary of the Tennessee River. The Nolichucky, a Cherokee name meaning "river of death," passes through Pisgah National Forest in North Carolina and enters Tennessee in the high walled Nolichucky Gorge, where it churns with rapids that challenge experienced white-water canoeists and rafters. In the forest around Erwin are a number of "balds" on top of the mountains—mysterious areas where the soil is thick and rich, but void of the surrounding dense variety of trees. The Cherokee believed a giant child-eating hornet once lived on these mountains. When it was finally killed, the Great Spirit decreed that its old haunts on the mountaintops should henceforth remain treeless, to prevent other giant hornets from hiding in the wilderness. A particularly lovely non-bald peak, crowned with a 600-acre purple rhododendron garden, **Roan Mountain** is on the North Carolina line, off US 19E (the rhododendron blooms in late June). People in the area collect ginseng and other medicinal herbs for sale in places as far off as China.

At **Elizabethton,** settlers along the Nolichucky and Watauga Rivers formed the Watauga Association in 1772, the first instance of a self government in the American colonies "for the common good of all people." Three years later these settlers and over a thousand Cherokees met at **Sycamore Shoals** in Elizabethton to witness the purchase by the Transylvania Company of almost 20 million acres in Eastern Tennessee and Kentucky from the Cherokee, in exchange for a cabin full of traders goods. Two films shown in the Sycamore Shoals visitor center (Rt. 321) depict the siege of Fort Watauga by the Cherokee in 1780, and a bronze slab in front of the Elizabethton court house marks the site of the formation of the Watauga Association, which the British governor of Virginia considered "a dagerous example to the people of America, of forming governments distinct from and independent of his majesty's authority."

Bristol to the north, is the town shared by Tennessee and Virginia (see Virginia). Here the state line is State Street, and in the 1880's a dispute arose over each state's rights in the construction of a water line. Men started toting guns as the quarrel heated up; sheriffs on either side of the line went to serve one another warrants while townsmen gathered on either side of the street, ready to erupt into civil war—when the two sheriffs slipped and fell into a ditch on the street. The Tennessee sheriff burst out laughing, and as his counterpart joined in, the tension along State Street dissipated in a gale of laughter. Relations between the two Bristols have been amicable ever since.

Tourist Information. Chattanooga Area Convention and Visitors Bureau, 1001 Market St., Chattanooga TN 37402; Knoxvisit Tourist Bureau and Welcome Center, 901 E. Vine Ave.; Forest Supervisor, Cherokee National Forest, Box 400, Cleveland TN 37311; Park Superintendent, Great Smoky Mountains National Park, Gatlinburg TN 37738.

Restaurants. *In Chattanooga*: Green Room, Read House Hotel***, Broad and 9th St; Chattanooga Choo-Choo**, Terminal Station; Eidson**,

4301 Ringgold Rd.; Loveman's Garden Room*, 8th and Market; Fehn's*, 600 River. *In Monteagle*: Smoke House*, Rt. 64; Monteagle Diner*, Rt. 41 & 64. *In Dayton*: Pierce's**. *In Sweetwater*: Dinner Bell*, Rt. 3. *In Knoxville*: The Orangery***, 5412 Kingston Pike; Regas**, 318 N. Gay St.; Union Cafe**, 501 Market St; Zeke & Dan's*, 820 N. 4th St; Louis' Inn*, 4626 Broadway. *In Oak Ridge*: Farmers Market*, 255 E. Main. *In Pigeon Forge*: Trotters**, US 441. *In Gatlinburg*: Pioneer Inn***, 373 Parkway; Smoky Mountain Trout House**, 410 Parkway; Old Heidelberg Castle**, in Ober Gatlinburg; The Burning Bush**, entrance of National Park; Traders Deli*, at the chairlift; S & M*, 762 Parkway. *In Jonesboro*: The Parson's Table**, Boone & Fox Sts.; The Widow Brown's**, Courthouse Square. *In Kingsport*: Pratt's Barn Country Kitchen*.

Middle Tennessee

Nashville

As was the case with so many American towns, what first attracted attention to the future site of Tennessee's capital was a salt lick; salt for preserving food was an indispensible resource for any band of pioneers. The early French traders knew this one well, and the first explorers to pass through the Cumberland Gap in search of new areas for settlement commented on it. When that first intrepid band of settlers led by James Robertson sailed up the Cumberland River in 1780, they decided this was the place. For Robertson's group, to come so far to establish what was then the point furthest west of the American colonies, a jump of two hundred miles beyond the other Tennessee settlements, was a strange and desperate gamble, one of the few real adventures in the opening of lands on the near side of the Mississippi.

What made them do it? The uncertainties of life in the Carolinas during the Revolutionary War, the dream of future wealth, the private deal Judge Henderson made with the Indians ceding the land, and the potential of the fertile Cumberland Valley were all good reasons, but on the other hand, the trip down the Tennessee and up the Cumberland was almost a thousand miles long and lined with hostile tribes. More Indian troubles would be waiting for them when they arrived (the actual inhabitants of the Cumberland hadn't even been party to the land deal), the first winter would inevitably find them poorly prepared, and they could expect little contact or assistance from the outside world. Just the same they took the challenge; they also took their wives and children with them. Upon arrival they set to building a fort, and not a moment too soon. By the time they had finally defeated the Indians, a year later, only seventy of the original five hundred settlers remained. They named the fort Nashborough, after a Revolutionary hero of North Carolina. Later on, during the War of 1812, they decided the "borough" was an intolerable Britishism, and made it Nashville. True grit had won out over adversity; the town and the valley prospered, surpassing the wildest hopes of the founders. In 1806 Nashville elected its first mayor, and in 1825 it became the state capital. As the center of a region that came to dominate the economic and political life of

Tennessee, Nashville in the decades before the Civil War gradually acquired fine homes and public buildings, busy riverfront wharves, gas lights, Grand Opera, slums, railroad yards, Catholics, colleges, brothels, tract-publishing houses, lyceums, and all the other things no big city should be without. By 1860, among the cities of the Southwest it was second in importance only to New Orleans. The pioneers' gamble had paid off.

Also like New Orleans, Nashville became one of the first Confederate cities to fall, in 1862. During the occupation the Yankees distinguished themselves by cutting down most of the city's trees; they had a brief scare in 1864, when that rebel Sad Sack, General Hood, made his immeasurably gallant and equally preposterous attempt to retake the city. He got as far as the southern edge of town, where the Yankees ate him up. Perhaps Nashville's early capture was its good fortune. While the rest of the South was going to pieces, Nashville boomed, and its population grew sixty percent during the 1860's. For forty years success and growth continued, and the city took on its character as an educational and religious center as a number of colleges and universities were founded (notably Vanderbilt in 1873) and denominations like the Southern Baptists made it their headquarters. Nashvillians began calling their city the "Athens of the South," and they carried this new identity to a memorable extreme in the 1897 Tennessee Centennial Exhibition, where the major attraction was the full-size model of the Parthenon that can be seen today in Centennial Park.

Today in Nashville, the "Athens idea" is still a civic commonplace, and the city is just as proud of its cultural distinctions as ever, but these have been swept into the background in most people's minds by the city's new role as the home of the country music phenomenon, and the boosters have come up with a new nickname—"Music City, U.S.A." As what started back in the 1930's with a radio show called the "Grand Ole Opry" gradually takes over the nation's airwaves and record shops, Nashville has elbowed Los Angeles aside to become the center of what is rightfully called the "music industry." Consequently, this pleasant and unsuspecting Tennessee capital has found itself in the unusual position of being the greatest repository of hype and celebrity tinsel between New York and Hollywood. In Nashville, tourists flock by the thousands to take tours of the recording studios, go to the shows, and take coach tours through the fancier suburbs for a peek at the plantation-style homes of the stars; only one of these, surprisingly, has a swimming pool in the shape of a guitar.

After the state government, perhaps, these tours seem to be the biggest business in town; Nashville's visitors come from all over, and for every eager pilgrim from Oklahoma or Ohio there's another from Great Britain or even Japan. The various tour services compete ferociously, offering stops at such sights as the Jim Reeves Museum and the Jim Reeves Plane Crash site, Dinah Shore's high school, a legendary country music bar on Broadway called Tootsie's Orchid Lounge, Johnny Cash's recording studio and the House of Cash Museum, Ernest Tubb's Record Shop, Hank Williams' car (in the Car Collectors Hall of Fame), the Country Music Wax Museum, Loretta Lynn's Western Store, Colonel Tom Parker's house and, of course, the Elvis Memorial.

It is fortunate that Nashville is enough of a city to absorb all this instead of being absorbed by it. Most Nashvillians have other things on their minds. In addition to the government the city is important as a banking and insurance center; it still has its religious bureaucracies, and its dozen or so colleges and universities make it the place where much of the South goes to school. Nashville is also a progressive city, with a strong concern for historical preservation (though it couldn't stop that beautiful old Governors' Mansion from being torn down for a fast-food stand). One of the first Southern cities to desegregate its schools peacefully, it is also one of the few cities anywhere to have instituted a form of metropolitan government, embracing Nashville and the surrounding Davidson County suburbs.

Downtown. Near the riverfront, at the foot of Broadway, is the oldest part of the city. Here, in 1930, the city built an authentic reconstruction of **Fort Nashborough** on its original site, with a museum and costumed guides (Tues-Sat 9-4, free). Currently, the city has big plans to redevelop this part of the riverfront; the old docks where the river steamers carried the city's commerce are long gone, but there's still a riverboat called the *Belle Carol,* offering excursions down the pretty Cumberland River (seasonal schedules, not running in the winter; call 356-4120, fare $5). Just behind the docks, naturally, were the warehouses and commercial blocks; dozens remain, creating an excellent 19th century streetscape that is undergoing restoration as the **Historic Second Avenue Business District.** Two groups, **Historic Nashville Inc.** and the **Metropolitan Historical Commission** oversee it all, and they share space in a building at Second and Broadway that once housed a wild establishment called the Silver Dollar Saloon. Historic Nashville operates a bookstore and the staff has plenty of information to offer on the city, past and present (Mon-Fri 9-5).

Further up Broadway can be seen a collection of Nashville's finest architecture, the pride of the blossoming city of the post-Civil War decades. The first of them, the **First Baptist Church** at 7th Avenue, has suffered an almost incredible fate. Only the graceful Gothic tower remains from the 1884 original church; a growing congregation knocked the rest down in 1970 and put up a truly ghastly modern replacement. Another Gothic building, across the street, is the 1875 **Customs House,** now converted to offices, and at 10th Avenue, the now empty **Union Station** faces an uncertain future now that the trains are gone. Fittingly, in this once-important railroad center, Union Station is by far the grandest in the South. Its Romanesque fairy-castle design is almost a copy of H. H. Richardson's famous Allegheny Courthouse in Pittsburgh.

There's only one building in downtown Nashville bigger than the State Capitol—three times as big, in fact—and that is the looming gray bulk of the **Baptist Sunday School Board Operations Building.** Tours are available, where they'll show you how they crank out hundreds of millions of Bibles and tracts each year (Mon-Fri 8-3 pm, free). The Southern Baptist Conference, which makes its home in Nashville and guides this formidable publishing empire, is by far the largest Protestant group in America, and still growing. A few blocks away, off Broadway on 5th Avenue, some less-established Protestant evangelicals built the attractive brick Gothic **Ryman Auditorium** in 1892 as a hall for revival meetings.

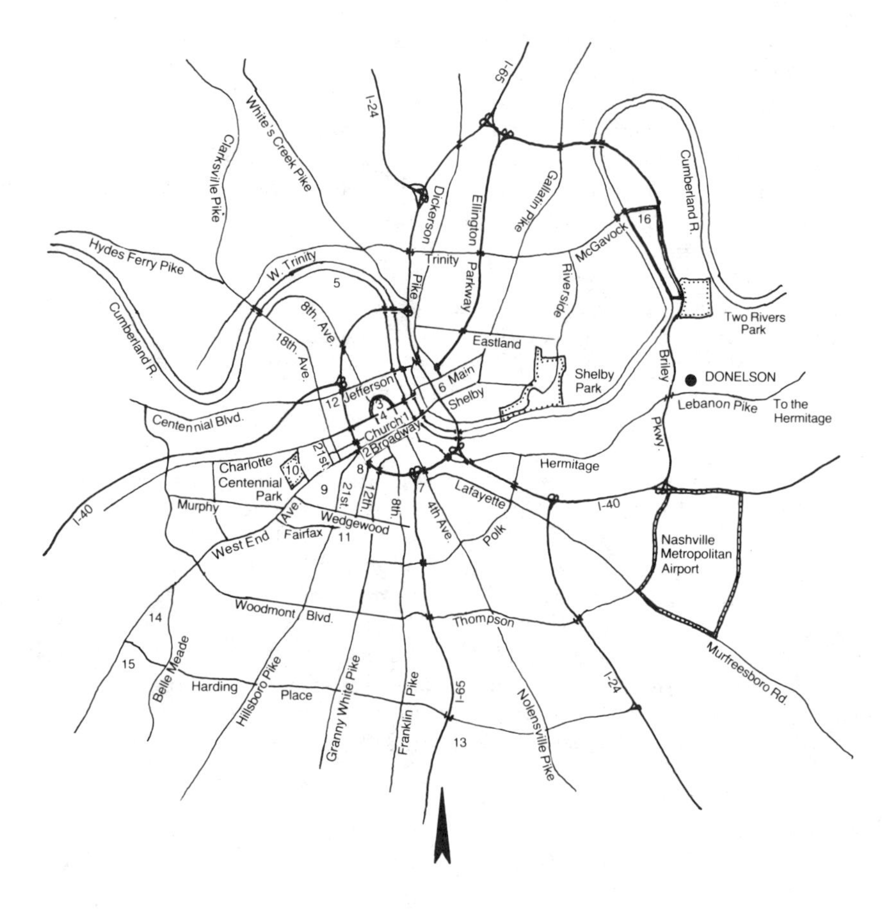

1 Fort Nashborough and Second Ave. historic district
2 Union Station
3 State Capitol
4 Tennessee State Museum
5 Metro Center
6 Edgefield
7 Cumberland Museum
8 Music Row
9 Vanderbilt University
10 Tennessee Parthenon
11 Belmont
12 Fisk University
13 Traveler's Rest
14 Belle Meade
15 Cheekwood
16 Opryland U.S.A.

Fate eventually had something very different in store for this building, however; for 34 years, beginning in 1941, it served country crooners, guitar pickers, yodelers, hillbilly comedians and harmonica and steel-guitar players as home of the Grand Ole Opry. Though the Opry has now deserted it for the wide parking lots of the suburbs, it is still maintained, with guided tours available for country music's faithful (daily 8:30-4:30, adm.).

Nashville's business and shopping districts extend north from Broadway along Church Street, 4th and 5th Avenues. Between these latter two, the city has preserved one of the few examples of a once-popular concept of commercial architecture, the **Arcade,** with two levels of shops under a glass roof. This one, built around the turn of the century, is the only one in the South. At Church and 5th, Nashville can claim another unique building, the Egyptian Revival **Downtown Presbyterian Church.** William Strickland, the architect of the State Capitol, was secure enough in his reputation by 1849 to put this over on the normally staid Presbyterians and even though it's only about as Egyptian as Elizabeth Taylor playing Cleopatra, with some gaudy windows and lotus-capitals tacked on to an otherwise sedate brick church, it is still quite the most exotic creature in town. The banks and insurance companies cluster around Church and 4th; here, the **Life and Casualty Tower** has a 31st floor observation deck (Mon-Thurs 9:30-3 pm, Fri & Sat 10-10, Sun noon-6, adm.). **Printer's Alley,** off Church, according to local legend, once had the stables where Andrew Jackson parked his horse. Later it got its name as the back door for a number of publishing houses. Prohibition filled all the old back doors with speakeasies and today many of the city's nightclubs are located here—a necessary stop for all the tour buses.

Certainly no state has a **State Capitol** like Tennessee's. Architect William Strickland, who did some of the work on the U.S. Capitol, came from Philadelphia in 1845 for this commission, and stayed long enough to do a number of fine buildings in Nashville that would set the community's standard of taste for the rest of the century. Instead of the usual dome, Strickland surmounted his austere Ionic conception with a columned cylinder modeled after the "Choragic Monument of Lysicrates" in Athens; it was a new form for the Greek Revival, and one that has been used a hundred times since (as in the Soldiers' and Sailors' Monument in New York). Tennessee provides tour guides to take you around, and they'll point out such highlights as the "chip in the balustrade," a memoir from a gunfight over ratification of the 14th Amendment during Reconstruction, a lovely spiral staircase, portraits of the governors and the "Masonic Time Capsule." State capitols can be used, if you wish, as an introduction to a state's character; they divide neatly into the plain and the fancy. Those of the latter variety give away their builders' pretensions in some unexpected ways—South Carolina, New York, Louisiana, Nebraska—and similarly the plain sisters, as you'll find them in Maine, Ohio, or Arkansas, have something to say not only about relative humility, but about the way a state sees the idea of government. Strickland's Capitol reveals Tennessee as one of the simpler states and also one of the most solid.

Outside on the grounds, along the slopes of Capitol Hill, there are some statues of interest: a defiant-looking Sam Davis, the "boy hero of the Confederacy"; Sergeant Alvin York, who singlehandedly captured a company or two of the Kaiser's troops in 1918 (and was played by Gary Cooper in the movies); the tomb of America's first great imperialist, President James K. Polk; and, of course, Andrew Jackson. Clark Mills' gallant equestrian Jackson may be the best-known statue in America, not for the casting here, but for its two copies: the one in New Orleans tips his hat to St. Louis Cathedral on Jackson Square, and the other tips it to the White House from Lafayette Square in Washington. From inside the Capitol you may pass under Charlotte Avenue through a tunnel of the very shiniest marble—Tennessee marble, of course—to the state's new **Legislative Plaza,** dominated by a futuristic building group that includes the skyscraper James K. Polk State Office Building, and the **Tennessee State Museum.**

As with any historical museum opened in the last two decades, you may take it for granted that this is no dry collection of artifacts neatly arranged in glass cases, but a kind of television-age carefully planned trip into the assumed past, an educational and thoroughly respectable theme park. In a dim spacious hall, you'll encounter log cabins, a working grist mill, tradesmen's shops, even a camp meeting. Some of the more theatrical episodes of the pioneer past—King's Mountain and the career of Andrew Jackson—are given extensive treatment, and there is a display, suitably enough in a state that has always taken politics so seriously, devoted to early campaigns; "Maury's Whigs; Defeated but never Vanquished," proclaims one parade banner from the 1850's (the decade when they were indeed vanquished). More recent Tennessee history is unfortunately neglected, but this new museum has big plans and lots of empty space, and this flaw should not go long uncorrected (Mon-Sat 10-5, Sun 1-5, free). An annex to the museum dedicated to Tennessee-at-war stands just across the plaza in the 1920's **War Memorial Building.** The **Military Branch** has the same hours as the main building.

Behind the Capitol, you're sure to notice the abundance of empty space; in the 1950's, as one of the South's first urban renewal projects, an old slum was cleared and replaced by such projects as the Municipal Auditorium, parking for state officials, motor hotels and more parking, around the broad new James Robertson Parkway.

Around Town, you'll notice that Nashville is a very diffuse city; it has always existed at an almost suburban density and there's plenty of room. The main streets radiate from downtown like wheel spokes and the way they meander gives away their origin—as Indian trails, or paths worn by deer and other animals to the salt lick. To the east, the downtown bridges lead across the Cumberland to an old neighborhood called **Edgefield,** once an independent wealthy suburb and now an active restoration area with some of the city's finest Victorian-era homes (along Russell Street or Rutledge Hill, south of Main Street). North of downtown, a potentially interesting development called **Metro Center** is beginning on a vacant 800 acre site outside a bend of the river, a "new town" project only two miles from the center of the city. Just south of downtown at 800 Ridley Avenue, the **Cumberland Museum and Science Center** has live annual shows, dioramas of the earth's natural habitats, scientific toys like the Van de Graaf generator, an excellent planetarium, and historical exhibits

(Tues-Sat 10-5, Sun 1-5, adm., free Tues).

Most of Nashville's growth and activity, however, has always gravitated towards the **West End.** At the edge of downtown, round 16th and Demonbreun, Nashville has given the name **Music Row** to the unprepossessing collection of low buildings and remodeled old homes that are the center of the country music business. The ASCAP office and all the big recording studios make their homes here, and there is also a music-oriented shopping center, differing from its millions of suburban counterparts only in that all the shops have the name of some country celebrity attached to them; inevitably, there is also a wax museum. The **Country Music Hall of Fame and Museum,** on Music Square East, has films, tapes, instruments, historical displays, a big mural by Thomas Hart Benton, and lots of sequined costumes; don't fail to miss Elvis Presley's gold Cadillac convertible. A block down the street, the museum gives tours of RCA's old **Studio B,** where many of the immortals cut their first records (both open daily 8-8 pm in the summer, 9-5 rest of the year; adm. $3.50, separate adm. for Studio B).

Vanderbilt University, the acknowledged leader of the eight educational institutions in the West End, has the most students, the most intellectual pretensions, and the best basketball team. Railroad potentate Cornelius Vanderbilt of New York made it all possible in 1873 with a million-dollar gift, and the campus, built in Nashville's post-bellum golden age, has some wonderful academic-picturesque buildings, such as Kirkland Hall (1905) and the Fine Arts Building (1888), the latter housing the prints and Oriental works of the **Vanderbilt Art Collection** (Mon-Fri 1-4, Sat & Sun 1-5, free). Fame first came to Vanderbilt in the 1920's, when writers like Robert Penn Warren and John Crowe Ransom started the "Fugitive" movement and set Southern literature on its way. Just across 21st Street are the campuses of **Scaritt College** and **Peabody College. Belmont College,** off 16th Avenue, was built around one of Tennessee's finest homes, a Corinthian-columned palace that would put almost anything in New Orleans' Garden District to shame. A German immigrant architect named Adolphus Heimann, who met his end in the war as a Confederate colonel, designed it in 1850 for Mr. Joseph Acklen; the Acklens filled it with art and furnishings from their many trips to Europe (Napoleon III was a friend). Currently undergoing restoration after many years of academic service, Belmont is especially noteworthy for the beautiful ornate iron gazebo and water tower on its grounds (Fri & Sat 10-2.30, adm.). **Fisk University,** a mile to the north of 17th Avenue, was founded during Reconstruction and remains one of the nation's most prestigious black colleges. Its **Jubilee Hall,** a spectacular Victorian Gothic creation, was built by S. D. Hatch, a black architect, in 1873, and financed by the profitable European and American tours of Fisk's Jubilee Singers, who introduced the Negro spiritual to the world and much delighted Queen Victoria with them. **Meharry Medical College,** adjacent to Fisk, was another product of Reconstruction; until recently it graduated almost all of America's black doctors.

In 1897, at the close of the three decades that saw Nashville mature into a great city, the movers and shakers did the natural thing and decided to show their city off with a fair. The Tennessee Centennial Exhibition, still the biggest fair ever held in the South, was a rousing success; the grounds, now **Centennial Park** on 23rd Avenue, became a neo-classical extravaganza in the same style as Chicago's Columbian Exposition, held only five years before. There was a Rialto Bridge, and also a Parthenon, international pavilions, lots of parades and electric lights everywhere. The plaster Rialto is long gone, but since Nashville is the Athens of the South it had to have a **Parthenon,** and when it started to crumble they rebuilt it in concrete (1930), with every detail correct down to the simulated Elgin Marbles and the complex principle of *entasis,* the trick the ancients knew of making a building's lines seem straighter by actually curving them. Don't suspect the original looked like this however; Greek specialists say the whole of it was brightly painted, but they can't even guess at the color scheme. Inside this copy there are more copies, mostly casts and reproductions of Greek sculpture, also a collection of painting, and even Indian relics (!). The city's symbol had a prominent role in Robert Altman's *Nashville* (a movie that will put all manner of dubious ideas into your head about the city) as the background for the climactic political assassination scene (the Parthenon's collections are open Tues-Sat 9-4:30, Sun 1-4:30, free).

Nashville's founders, back in 1780, were not as much interested in starting a city as a shipping center for the manorial estates they planned for themselves. Today, as a result, the city is ringed with grand homes, some of which survive from the early days. **Traveler's Rest,** south of the city on Farrell Road, was built in 1799, in the style then common to Virginia, by John Overton, a friend of Andrew Jackson and a great speculator who was one of the founders of Memphis. Perhaps the oldest substantial dwelling between the mountains and Louisiana, Traveler's Rest has been authentically restored by the Colonial Dames of America. General Hood made his headquarters here before his disastrous Battle of Nashville in 1864 (Mon-Sat 9-4, Sun 1-4, adm.). Not so old and considerably fancier is **Belle Meade,** a fine white-columned affair began in 1837 and long the social center of the area (today there's a country club and a shopping mall named after it; thus faded glamour often persists). Pretty as it is, the house is upstaged by the enormous and beautiful Victorian-era barn and stables. Belle Meade was the most renowned thoroughbred farm of its day, and it produced the first American horse to win the English Derby (Mon-Sat 9-5, Sun 1-5, tours until 4:30, adm. $2.50). Just down the road, the owner of Nashville's famous Maxwell House Hotel, famed for its coffee, built a considerably larger but less interesting palace for himself in the 1920's, somehow pillaging the country homes and royal residences of Britain of architectural details for it. **Cheekwood,** now the **Tennessee Botanical Gardens and Fine Arts Center,** functions as the city's art museum with an odd collection especially strong in contemporary American painters and antique snuff bottles. The gardens are strong in boxwoods (Tues-Sat 10-5, Sun 1-5, adm.).

Now that the money men of the music industry have turned Country Music (they don't even call it Country & Western anymore) from white lightning into stale pale ale, it is entirely fitting that the Grand Old Opry, the show on radio station WSM that has done so much since 1925 to promote the genre, should choose to be interred in the suburbs at **Opryland,** a corporate theme park with a heavy investment in sequins and torpid nostalgia, offering rides, music and fast food carefully packaged by the NLT Corporation for an experience you're bound not to forget (on Briley Parkway, east of the city; open daily in the summer, Sat & Sun in the spring and fall, closed November-March 28; open 10 am, adm. $10.75, concerts not included).

Andrew Jackson came to the Cumberland Valley in the 1790's, and he began construction of his famous home, **The Hermitage,** in 1817. Of all the presidents' homes, only Mount Vernon and Monticello perhaps receive more visitors or are as worthwhile visiting in their own right. With its monumental portico and Egyptian Revival columns, its magnificent front hall and spiral staircase and its original furnishings, this home must have seemed a strange vision in lands so recently claimed from the wilderness. Most everything Jackson owned remains here, including collections of guns and hickory sticks, a library almost entirely made up of history, law and contemporary events, and other memorabilia that show Jackson as the prosaic, practical man he was, a good soldier and clever businessman and a President who was the greatest popular leader of his day yet who left no great ideas, stirring slogans, or constructive achievements that survive to this day, only the reputation of a man who was very good at getting his own way. (Ask the Cherokee, or Nicholas Biddle, or John C. Calhoun.) Jackson exemplifies the frontier aristocrat better than anyone; as a talented young lawyer of slender means he had no sooner crossed the mountains from South Carolina when he found himself involved in writing a new state's constitution, standing for office and catching opportunities to amass fortunes in land deals. That he should be able to build so tasteful and elegant a home is a reminder of how civilization was so quickly transported over the Alleghenies by such men.

The Hermitage burned in 1834, only fifteen years after its completion and was rebuilt within the original walls. This was only one of the tragedies that attended Jackson throughout his Presidency. In 1828, on the eve of his inauguration, his beloved Rachel died, the woman whose honor he had once been moved to defend in a duel. They are both buried here, under a stone pavilion on the grounds. Several other buildings remain: the log cabin that was the Jacksons' first home on this site, another cabin, belonging to a servant named Albert who lived to 1901, a springhouse, carriage house and a museum, among others. An interesting feature is the lawn in front of the house, surrounded by trees and laid out in the shape of a guitar.

Another home, **Tulip Grove,** across the road, belonged to Jackson's nephew and was built in the 1830's. Both have been owned and operated by the Ladies Hermitage Association since 1889, and they have done as impressive a job of restoring and presenting a historic site as any private group in the nation (open daily, summer 8-6 pm, the rest of the year 9-5, separate adm. for the two homes).

Southeast of the Hermitage, the **Cedars of Lebanon State Park** contains the largest red cedar forest in the United States, and features nature trails, campsites, and square dancing every Saturday night. It lies near **Smyrna,** the home of Sam Davis, "the Boy Hero of the Confederacy" who was captured by the Union near Pulaski, Tennessee, bearing information on Federal troop movements. Convicted of spying by a military tribunal, he was offered a pardon if he would name his informant.

"Do you suppose that I would betray a friend? No, sir; I would die a thousand times first!" he replied. Davis was hanged, but in his memory the **Sam Davis Home,** on Rt. 102, has been preserved, with many of its original furnishings as well as several outbuildings and a museum of Sam Davis' life and times (open Mon-Sat 9-5, Sun 1-4, adm.).

Murfreesboro served as the state capital of Tennessee from 1819-1825 It was chosen for this honor because of its location near the geographical center of the state (an obelisk on the Old Lascasses Pike three miles from the courthouse marks the exact spot) and lost the distinction when the assembly decided by one vote to remove to Nashville, closer to Tennessee's political heartthrob, Andrew Jackson. A reconstructed village of the Old South, **Cannonsburugh** (the original name of Murfreesboro) is on S. Front Street; a blacksmith shop, a flatboat, general store and chapel are among the structures housing exhibits (open late April-October Tues-Sat 10-5, Sun 1-5, free). The 1859 Rutherford County Courthouse on East Main Street was captured in a surprise dawn cavalry attack led by General Nathan B. Forrest; on N. Maney Avenue **Oaklands Mansions,** the most elegant home in Murfreesboro, served as Forrest's headquarters. Originally built in 1815, the house was twice enlarged and embellished with a pretty arched porch, semicircular stairway, and a lovely entrance hall (open Tues-Sat 10-4, Sun 1-4, adm.).

Stones River National Battlefield, in the northwest corner of Murfreesboro, was the site of one of the bloodiest battles of the Civil War. After his invasion of Kentucky and defeat at the Battle of Perryville, General Braxton Bragg and his Confederate Army had withdrawn to Chattanooga (1862). From there he pushed north towards Nashville, and met General William S. Rosecrans at Murfreesboro. On December 31, 1862, the Confederates struck first at Stones River and pushed the Union Army back, at a tremendous cost to both sides. On January 1st, the two sides regrouped, and the next day the Confederates attacked again, with equally bloody results, but could not get past 58 massed, fire-belching Union cannons. Casualties on both sides totalled over 24,000; the next day Bragg withdrew to Tullahoma and Chattanooga. The National Battlefield, off US 70S, contains a tenth of the actual battleground and features the National Cemetery, where 6,100 Union soldiers are buried; the Hazen Brigade Monument, erected in 1863, the oldest Civil War memorial in the country; and a visitor center, the beginning of a five-mile auto tour route of the battlefield (open daily 8-5, 8-8 in the summer, free).

The beautiful, immaculate bluegrass farms and stables around **Shelbyville** help boost its reputation as "The Walking Horse Capital of the World." Many of the farms welcome visitors, especially the Shadow Valley Farm on US 231N; the **Walking Horse Hotel** in **Wartrace** features photos and memorabilia of the walking horse, famous for its smooth gait. John Gunther once asked a Tennesseean if his fondness for the walking horse extended to prejudice against other horses, and was answered: "Kill a non-Tennessee horse and one drop of its blood will poison the Atlantic Ocean."

Horse breeders weren't the only ones to be attracted to this area of Middle Tennessee. Off US 41, north of Manchester, **Old Stone Fort State Park** surrounds an ancient walled structure on the Duck River, believed to have been built as a ceremonial center by prehistoric Indians.

A museum is planned near the site to house material uncovered by archeologists from the University of Tennessee (always open, free).

Rt. 55 between Manchester and **Tullahoma** passes by the Arnold Engineering Developmental Center and its giant wind tunnels. Tullahoma, a town whose economy is based on baseball bats and whiskey, is the home of the **George Dickel Distillery** on Cascade Road (north of Tullahoma on Alt. US 41) where Tennessee sour mash whiskey had been produced for over a century. Tours are offered Monday through Friday from 9-3, free. Just to the west, **Lynchburg** (named for the man who presided over the local whipping post) is familiar to both whiskey lovers and magazine readers, who have been introduced to the homey virtues of Lynchburg by ads from the **Jack Daniel Distillery.** Jack Daniel's received whiskey license#1 in 1866, making it America's oldest whiskey distillery, and it offers tours of the limestone caves from where they draw their iron-free water to the old time charcoal processing, daily from 8 am-4 pm. Unfortunately, there are no free samples at the end of the tour because Lynchburg is in dry Moore County. Why some of Tennessee's best whiskey should be distilled in a dry county mystifies many visitors, but it keeps the local Baptists happy. The courthouse, in the middle of Lynchburg Square, is an archetype of a rural courthouse building; facing it on the square, the Soda Shop is one of Lynchburg's oldest establishments, unchanged for the past fifty years and still serving creamy sodas. The friendly folks at Jack Daniel's also like to point out the potted geraniums on the porch of the Moore County Jail, "the sign of a well-run, law-abiding community." Fed on bluegrass and the spent Tennessee sour mash from the two distilleries, the area's cattle are exceptionally fat and sleek.

Between Lynchburg and **Winchester** is the popular Tims Ford Lake and Tims Ford State Rustic Park, with campsites and boat docks. Near downtown Winchester, **Hundred Oaks Castle** was built in 1891 by Arthur Marks, the son of a Tennessee governor who had spent time in the consular service in England, where he became enamoured of the many castles he visited. After wedding a wealthy Nashville belle in Scotland, Marks decided to build his own castle, but contracted typhoid fever and died before moving in. The most remarkable feature of the castle is its exact replica of Sir Walter Scott's library at Abbotsford—there's another of these in the Tennessee State Capitol (open Tues-Sun 10-10, adm.). On 1st Ave. N.E. in Winchester, the **Franklin County Jail Museum** houses four rooms of relics from the area's history (Thurs-Sat10-4, Sun 1-4, adm.). On Rt. 64 in Belvidere, **Falls Mill,** with a still operative water wheel, is one of Tennessee's pretty-as-a-picture beauty spots. A country store has just opened in the upper floor of the mill.

To the north along the Cumberland Plateau, the **Cumberland Caverns** on Rt. 8 in **McMinnville** contain an extremely large cave room (200 by 100 feet), strange rock formations, and an old saltpeter mine. A sound and light show is presented during the cave tour (open June-August daily; weekends only in May, September and October, from 9-5, adm.). Further north, dulcimers, furniture and other items are manufactured in the Upper Cumberland Craft Center at 545 E. 20th Street in **Cookeville;** visitors are invited to watch the craftsmen Mon-Fri 7-5, and 8-4 on Saturdays from May-December.

Dale Hollow Lake, on the Kentucky line, is a favorite among divers for its large fish population and unusual fresh water jellyfish. It is near **Byrdstown** where Cordell Hull, FDR's Secretary of State, the "Father of the United Nations Organization," and winner of the 1945 Nobel Peace Prize, was born in a simple log cabin in 1871. The cabin, on Rt. 42, has been preserved and is open for tours from Memorial Day-Labor Day, 10-6, free. Another famous Tennesseean, Alvin York, was born and lived in the tiny town of **Pall Mall.** York, who grew up on a farm, accredited much of his success as a soldier in World War I to his boyhood experiences shooting squirrels. While fighting in the Battle of Argonne Forest, York became separated from his detachment in enemy territory; the next time his comrades saw him was upon his return to American lines with 132 German prisoners in tow, whom he had captured after leading seven other lost soldiers in a successful attack on a German machine gun nest. York was promoted to sergeant for his bravery, received the Congressional Medal of Honor, and was called by General John J. Pershing, "the greatest soldier of the war." **Alvin York's Farm and Grist Mill** on Rt. 28 is open daily 8-6, free. A trail from the farm leads to **Picket State Rustic Park,** one of Tennessee's most beautiful, with natural bridges, caves and other unusual rock formations. Nearby **Jamestown** was the home of John M. Clemens, the father of Mark Twain, and the model for "Obedstown" in his son's novel *The Gilded Age*.

To the west, on the north bank of the Cumberland River, **Gallatin** has two historic structures, both actually east of town. **Cragfont,** on Rt. 25, was built by General James Winchester, Indian fighter and first speaker of the Tennessee Senate, who imported stone masons and carpenters from Maryland to build this house of native stone and wood (open April-October, Tues-Sat 10-5, Sun 1-6, adm). **Wynnewood,** four miles east of Cragfont on Rt. 25, was built as a stagecoach inn and spa for takers of the mineral waters at Castalian Springs. It is believed to be the largest log building ever constructed in the state—142 feet long (open April-October, Wed-Sat 10-5, Sun 1-6, adm.).

Down the Cumberland River from Gallatin, **Clarksville** was a major 19th century river port, founded in 1784, and named by General George Rogers Clark. Although Clarksville is now an industrial town and "dark-fired" tobacco market, it has preserved pieces of its river town heritage in the **Downtown Historic District,** encompassing City Hall Square and its gazebo, Commerce, Franklin and Second Streets; in the Warehouse District along the river, in the 19th century **Port Royal State Historic Area,** on the Red River, complete with a covered bridge; and in the **Dunbar Cave State Natural Area** on Rt. 13, formerly owned by country singer Roy Acuff, and used for Grand Ole Opry square dances. Although the cave itself is presently closed, awaiting development, the old bathhouse has been restored for use as a museum and visitors center.

Just west of Clarksville, **Fort Donelson National Military Park** near Dover was the site of a Confederate fort built early in the war to protect the Cumberland River and an inter-river railroad; a twin strong point, Fort Henry, served a similar purpose on the Tennessee River. In late 1861 these two forts attracted the attention of a then obscure commander in Cairo, Illinois, named Ulysses S. Grant, who suggested a joint army-navy manoeuvre against Fort Henry. The affairs of the western Union forces at the time were in "complete chaos," according to their general, Henry W.

Halleck, but he reluctantly approved Grant's plans and appointed him commander of the expedition. Seven Union gunboats on the Tennessee supported Grant's force of 15,000 which easily captured Fort Henry after the Confederate garrison withdrew to Fort Donelson.

Grant pressed on to Fort Donelson, arriving on February 12, 1862. The Confederate army was well-entrenched, and after a brief skirmish, followed by an unsuccessful Union gunboat attack, it looked as if Grant would have to retreat. The next day, however, Grant was reinforced, swelling his forces to 27,000, against a Confederate army of 14,000. The Confederates, fearing entrapment, made a courageous sortie to reach the Nashville Road, where they beat back the Union lines. Just when it seemed that they would escape successfully, the three Confederate commanders quarreled, and the order went out to return to the trenches. Grant immediately ordered a major advance and trapped the Confederates. During the night 2,700 managed to escape, including five commanders and Colonel Nathan S. Forrest's cavalry, leaving General Simon B. Buckner, an old pal of Grant's, to ask for terms. Grant replied with his famous message: "No terms except unconditional and immediate surrender can be accepted. I propose to move immediately upon your works." Buckner accepted Grant's terms, delivering 13,000 troops as prisoners of war.

The loss of Fort Donelson was the first major victory for the Union, and for U.S. ("Unconditional Surrender") Grant, who became something of an overnight hero in the North. From here he continued a campaign to occupy the Mississippi Valley and divide the South in two. For the Confederacy, the defeat was a vital blow. Kentucky, Nashville and western Tennessee were soon abandoned to the Union and never recovered. The national park contains the preserved earthworks of Fort Donelson, 2½ miles of Confederate outer trenches, the Confederate river batteries, a reconstructed powder magazine, the Dover Tavern, where Buckner surrendered to Grant, and the national cemetery, where the graves of Union soldiers are marked with heart-shaped headstones. A visitors center has exhibits and a 15-minute slide presentation on the battle; a ten-mile auto tour of the battlefield is lined with markers from both sides.

Dover is near the TVA's **Land Between the Lakes,** a national demonstration area in the management of recreational facilities, environmental and energy education and national resources, occupying a 170,000 peninsula on either side of the Tennessee-Kentucky border, between Kentucky Lake and Lake Barkley. Land between the Lakes features a buffalo herd; bald and golden eagle winter habitats; a 19th century living history farm with 16 log cabins called The Homeplace (1850); 200 miles of trails for backpackers, horseback riders, bicyclists and canoeists; the Environmental Education Center on Lake Barkley, with its Center Station for orientation, Empire Farm, the remains of an old iron furnace and the lovely Silo Overlook; and three organized camp sites. Both fishing and hunting are extremely popular in season. The main visitors center is at what used to be the village of Golden Pond, on the Trace (the major north-south road through Land Between the Lakes) and it is open daily 9-5; tel. (502) 924-5602 for information.

Franklin, one of the prettiest towns in Tennessee, is located about twenty miles southwest of Nashville. The fifteen block downtown area of Franklin is on the National Register of Historic Places; many of the renovated 19th century shops now sell antiques. On November 30, 1864, the "Battle of the Generals" took place in Franklin, pitting the Confederates under General Hood against the Federals under General Schofield; the previous day Hood had missed his chance to trap Schofield in Springfield. He pursued and caught him in Franklin and waged a massive frontal assault against the Federals, in the spirit of Pickett's charge at Gettysburg and with equally tragic results. Hood lost six generals and seven other officers, along with 6,000 casualties. Schofield then retreated to Nashville, within the protection of Thomas' lines; Hood's Army of the Tennessee followed, to its crushing defeat at the Battle of Nashville. The story of the Battle of Franklin is told at **Battle-o-rama,** at 1143 Columbia Avenue, with a 3-D mural and slides (open Mon-Sat 11-4, adm.). The 1830 **Carter House,** a National Historical Landmark on US 31 in Franklin, was in the center of the battle; the Carter family hid in the basement while the house was battered with bullets and artillery. It has been restored and refurnished with period pieces as a memorial to the Battle of Franklin; a newly opened interpretive center by the house recreates the battle (open May-October, Mon-Sat 9-5, Sun 2-5; November-April daily 9-4, adm.).

Franklin is the seat of picturesque Williamson County, known for its rolling hills of blue grass, rich farmland and the stables of magnificent show horses. Although Kentucky's nickname is the "Bluegrass state," Tennessee has over three million acres of the stuff, three times as much as Kentucky. The "blue" derives from phosphates in the soil, which help keep it green all year and make it ideal for raising strong-boned horseflesh.

Columbia, south of Franklin, has the only surviving home of the North Carolina-born 11th president, the **James K. Polk Ancestoral Home,** an elegant Federal style home built by his father in 1816. Many of the furnishings inside belonged to the president and were used in the White House (on US 43 in central Columbia; open Mon-Sat 9-5, 10-4 in the winter, Sun 1-5, adm.). The exotic 1835 Moorish-Gothic **Athenaeum,** at 808 Athenaeum Place, is the only surviving structure of the old Columbia Athenaeum for females. To the west, on the Natchez Trace Parkway near Hohenwald, the **Meriwether Lewis Monument** marks the site of Grinder's Stand, a tavern along the Trace where explorer Meriwether Lewis (leader of the famous Lewis and Clark Expedition) was found dead in 1809. His death was extremely mysterious, and no one is sure whether he was murdered or committed suicide. His monument, a broken column, symbolizes his broken career.

On US 64, west of **Lawrenceburg,** the **David Crockett State Park** is on the banks of Shoal Creek, where Davy, who lived in Lawrenceburg during his terms in the Tennessee legislature (1817-1822) operated a powder mill, a distillery and a grist mill. The latter has been reconstructed. **Pulaski,** east of Lawrenceburg, has the ignoble distinction of being the birthplace of the Ku Klux Klan, organized in late 1865, originally as a kind of social club for bored young blades, who would ride around the countryside in hoods, playing tricks on the country people. When they observed the terror these antics created, the Klan turned their play into a serious secret organization committed to taking political control from the Republicans by frightening black voters. General Nathan B. Forrest became the first "grand Wizard of the Empire" in 1867, although he resigned in disgust within two years. Governor Brownlow hired a detective to discover the identity of the Klansmen, only to discover the detective's bullet-riddled body in the Duck River. The General Assembly passed laws against the Klan, and it went into a dormant stage when Radical rule ended in Tennessee. Pulaski was also the birthplace of John Crowe Ransom, one of the South's leading literary lights.

Restaurants. *In Nashville*: The Stockyards***, 901 Second Av. N. (the favorite of the Grand Ole Opry stars); Mario's***, 1915 West End Ave.; Vizcaya***, 1907 West End Ave.; Boots Randolph***, 209 Printers Alley; Anderson's Cajun Wharf**, 901 Cowan St.; Peking Garden**, 1923 Division; The Brass Rail**, 206½ Printers Alley; Sperry's**, 5109 Harding Rd.; The Old Spaghetti Factory*, 160 Second Ave. N.; O'Charley's*, 402 21st Ave. S.; Portside*, 7111 Charlotte Ave.; Gerst House*, 228 Woodland. *In Murfreesboro*: The Saddle**, 823 N.W. Broad St.; Briarpatch**, 1433 Memorial Blvd. *In Smyrna*: The Omni Hut** (Polynesian), New Nashville Hwy. *In Shelbyville*: Shelbyville Inn***, 317 N. Cannon Blvd.; Bridle**, Fayetteville Hwy. *In Tullahoma*: Vi's*, 507 S. Washington. *In Lynchburg*: White Rabbit Saloon**, on the square. *In Winchester*: 100 Oaks Castle**, US 64 W. *In Gallatin*: Gondola House**, 698 S. Water St.; Duncan's Diner*, 642 N. Blythe St. *In Clarksville*: Hachland Hill Dining Room**, 1601 Madison. *In Franklin*: Miss Daisy's Tea Room**, Main St.

Memphis

Tennessee's largest city, the South's fifth largest, the birthplace of the Blues and the Mecca of the Elvis cult, Memphis has forsaken its romantic past of riverboats, cotton bales stacked on the wharves and memorable dance halls for a safer, more comfortable position as a dominant Deep South commercial and transportation center—air freight is its big growth industry right now—with lots of new boxy skyscrapers and more the appearance of a midwestern city than one at the edge of the Mississippi Delta. Commerce has always been its talent; Memphis gave America both the supermarket and the Holiday Inn. One of the few cities with a metropolitan area in three states, Memphis exerts more pull over Mississippi and Arkansas than the more distant quarters of Tennessee. One of its distinctions is that, at least according to one set of statistics, it is the poorest metropolitan area, per capita, in the U.S., though the city's prosperous, solid air makes this difficult to believe.

Nashville was founded as a bold pioneer adventure, but the beginnings of Memphis were purely a matter of business. The Chickasaw Bluffs above the Mississippi, safe from most of the river's depradations, were a logical spot for a trading center in the newly-opened lands of West Tennessee, on the eve of its boom years. None other than that greatest of all speculators, Andrew Jackson, in partnership with John Overton and James Winchester, bought up the land and laid out the town in 1819. Local folklore credits Jackson himself with inventing the name—a year after Cairo was founded further up America's Nile in Illinois, along with a

Thebes and a Karnak—but the aspiring politician sold all his shares in the venture four years later. The land company was then busy rousting squatters and Jackson thought that would hurt his presidential campaign, in which he purported to be the "candidate of the common man." At first the project met with only limited success; frequent epidemics and the other health problems that would plague Memphis throughout the century kept settlers and merchants away, and for a while the now deceased town of Randolph boded fair to become the prime river port. The boom finally reached Memphis in the 1830's, establishing the city as a cotton market second only to New Orleans. By 1860 Memphis was a genuine city. Its population of 30,000 made it ten times as big as Atlanta and of that number almost one-third were Irish and German immigrants.

Like the rest of West Tennessee, Memphis badly wanted to secede. The city contributed to the cause not only the fire-eating Governor Isham Harris, who cajoled the state into rebellion, but the famous General Nathan Forrest, who had served as a Memphis alderman while making his fortune as one of the South's biggest slave traders. Hardly had the ballyhoo subsided when Memphians got the honour of being among the first Southerners to meet General Grant. On June 6, 1862, Union and Confederate gunboats slugged it out a few miles below the city while Memphians with picnic lunches watched from the bluffs above, confident of a victory. Instead, the Confederates got all except one of their boats sunk and as the spectators fled back into town Yankee troops were right behind them. For the next three years the army alternated between leniency and harshness, but neither approach really slowed down the city's new career as the Smuggling Capital of the Southland, working on the meretriciousness of Yankee traders and Union officers to keep the rebel armies supplied with munitions, medical supplies, shoes and salt. A brief thrill in an otherwise uneventful occupation came on a Sunday morning in August, 1864, when General Forrest and his men, many Memphians among them, made a surprise raid on the city and captured 600 prisoners, narrowly missing the two commanding officers.

Peace brought with it nothing but more trouble. The influx of freed blacks—by 1870 they made up half the population—resulted in increasing racial tensions and violence on the part of whites. Of the frequent disturbances, the greatest was the Riot of 1866, where 44 blacks were murdered and all the freedmen's schools burned: the incident was widely publicized in the North and proved a powerful argument for Congressional Reconstruction. Even worse, in the 1870's the city's negligence in public health matters finally caught up with it. With no healthy source of water and no real sewage system, Memphis had always been subject to epidemics, but when yellow fever appeared in 1873, panic-stricken Memphians abandoned the city, leaving only the blacks, who believed they were immune and got a nasty surprise. The disease returned in 1878, and once more Memphis became an overnight ghost town. This time, however, many never returned; trade and industry fled in all directions and most of the Germans left for St. Louis. Meanwhile the city had gone broke, as much from corruption as the disruption of the epidemics. To mollify the creditors, the state government simply took back the city charter; in 1879, Memphis legally ceased to exist, and was now known as the "Taxing District of Shelby County."

Perhaps Memphis, instead of Atlanta, should have adopted the pheonix for its symbol, for this city literally came back from the dead, building sewers, drilling artesian wells, and adopting every other progressive public health measure science could suggest, and throughout the 80's it tenaciously recaptured its business and wealth. In 1893, in the midst of a modest boom, Memphis got its charter back and entered the new century as a prosperous modern city, perhaps best known for its carryings-on around the waterfront, in the vicinity of Beale Street, that legendary black main street and entertainment district where the blues took form, brought by country boys from the Mississippi Delta and elsewhere in the rural South. As in New Orleans' Storyville, the music was only the accompaniment for a wide open district of gambling and prostitution.

Of course there were constant reform movements in the Progressive era with the purpose of "cleaning up" the town; in one of them, during the election of 1909, two young men who would be in later years Memphis' best known citizens, crossed paths. E. H. Crump was an obscure, red-headed reform candidate. As was the custom, he hired a black orchestra to ride in a wagon round town and stump for him. The bandleader, for whom Memphis elections were always rich harvests, was W. C. Handy. Musical historians today tell the story of how the song that made Handy famous, that venerable tune of innumerable reincarnations called the *Memphis Blues*, started life as the *E. H. Crump Song*. It was the first blues composition, and so immediately popular that Handy cashed in, playing it for all other candidates too. For the reformer Crump, however, he added these words:

> "Mister Crump wont 'low no easyriders here,
> Mister Crump won't 'low no easyriders here,
> I don't care what Mister Crump don't 'low,
> I'm gwine to barrel-house anyhow—
> Mister Crump can go catch hisself some air!"

It was a splendid joke; neither Crump nor the rest of the white folks had any idea what he was talking about. Crump did win the election, though, and he turned out to be an unusual kind of reformer indeed. Memphis didn't get rid of him for forty-five years.

This Dixie version of a city machine that Crump led was something entirely different from its counterparts in Chicago or Jersey City. For one thing, it was efficient and determinedly honest; Crump wasn't interested in money, only power, and he made sure nobody else had their fingers in the treasury either. There was a Crump Insurance Company, though (it lives today in a big suburban skyscraper), and anyone doing business in Memphis found it expedient to patronize it. And Crump did clean up the city, Beale Street included. After a decade or two Memphis began to look as puritanical as Knoxville, carving a nationwide reputation for censoring movies. No machine anywhere ever had such an iron grip over a city. With all the modern scientific methods of vote catching, and enormous patronage salary kickbacks, Crump was able to control the entire state in most years, and experienced no opposition whatsoever in Memphis. Democracy, in the city, ceased to exist, and not many Memphians missed it. Totalitarian wasn't quite the word for it, though any hack who stepped out of line, even accidentally, soon found himself moving to another city; against his upstate opponents, Crump was largely limited to printing his famous full-page newspaper advertisements, in which he went through dozens of fragrant paragraphs calling them apes, mangy bubonic rats, skunks, misbegotten coons, pestilential worms, and so on. On the home front he was very fond of throwing big picnics for the faithful, where he would hand out firecrackers to the children under big banners reading "Thank You, Mister Crump!" Amazingly, he never made a public speech; even so he stage-managed a string of over eighty consecutive successful local elections. When he died in 1954, his machine died with him, but today, almost thirty years later, bring up the subject with any Memphian and you'll notice, whatever their opinion of the man, it's still always *Mister* Crump they're talking about.

Whilst spending a half century under such authoritarian rule, together with the consequent sound business climate, Memphis slowly metamorphosed from a Delta cotton port to a kind of minor Chicago, dependent on transportatin, distribution and industry, built of solid brick bungalows and apartments (and much denser than the usual Southern town) and with a burgeoning nest of Art Deco skyscrapers at its center. Today, with democracy restored (Memphis is one of the few big cities with non-partisan mayoral elections) and with time obscuring the city's colorful past, Memphis is a modern, progressive city with some of the best of both North and South—not a place increasingly distant from its Deep South hinterlands, but a very useful American community whose job it is to lead the Deep South through the uncertain waters of a new age.

Downtown: Court Square has always been the center of it (even though the courthouse long ago migrated a few blocks away), and it contains everything the proper Southern town square should have: magnificent old trees, a beautiful cast-iron fountain, and the human touch, in this case the tidy little house the city maintains for the park's squirrels. The outlandish Arabian Nights structure at one corner of the square is the former **Tennessee Club,** and the big shopping street that runs past on the western edge is Main Street, now liberated from auto traffic and landscaped as the **Mid-American Mall.** Some of the city's earliest skyscrapers, each elegant in its own way, can be found on the blocks south of the square, for this was the very center of the business district at the turn of the century. Front Street, just a block away along the riverfront, was **Cotton Row** back then, famous throughout the South: it's still the center of the business, and such cotton as is still grown in the Deep South will have its destiny decided at the **Cotton Exchange,** Front at Union, which like the stock exchanges in New York welcomes visitors to see the show (Mon-Fri 8:30-4:30, free).

Further up Front, **Confederate Park,** with memorials to the Lost Cause, sits on the edge of the bluffs overlooking not the Mississippi, surprisingly, but the Wolf River, a sluggish stream that flows through the industrial areas of North Memphis; it meets the Mississippi here, at **Mud Island,** a long undeveloped spit that has finally found a purpose as a river museum. Memphis' newest and biggest attraction, scheduled to open some time in 1982, is planned as a tribute to the Mississippi and its people; the star of the show will be an enormous working model of Big Muddy himself. **City Hall,** the Municipal Auditorium, and the big new

Convention and Exhibition Center are all on this part of Front Street, where the Hernando De Soto Bridge crosses over the Mississippi. There are no bluffs on the Arkansas side, and consequently the land is entirely undeveloped; Memphis has cotton and soybean farms right at its front door. Down on the riverfront itself, at Monroe Street and Riverside Drive, you can board the *Memphis Queen*, a replica of an old-time steamboat, for a Mississippi excursion (daily, seasonal schedules; call (901) 527-5694 for information, fare $5 adults).

When the **Peabody Hotel** closed in 1975, victim of an age of cussedness, Dixie mourned. This is the legendary establishment at 2nd and Union whose most honored guests were ducks, whose lobby is traditionally the spot where the Mississippi Delta begins, and the place where Mississippi farmers pray they'll go when they die. Lately the Peabody has been reborn, as old-fashioned and classy as before, and when the ducks drop in on their migrations they still get the (literal) red-carpet treatment; you may see them on their daily grand procession to the fountain in the lobby. Just two blocks from the hotel, on the edge of downtown, is **Beale Street** and **Handy Park,** where there are still occasional outdoor blues sessions under the statue of the man who made the blues famous. Some urban renewal atrocity of the past has turned Beale Street, once one of the busiest places in town, into a gigantic neatly-mowed vacant lot, punctuated by a few lonely buildings now protected by a National Historic District designation: the Orpheum Theater, a nightclub or two, and the ancient A. Schwab department store, which has been around over a century and has a small Beale Street Museum inside. Memphis has great plans for redevelopment of the area, but for now the survivors wait patiently while sharing the street with the disconcerting ten-foot memorial in **Elvis Presley Plaza.** The King was still warm in his grave when his fans put up this heroic bronze image; Elvis, with physique and features greatly idealized, in a ghastly sort of way, strikes the pose of one of the later Roman emperors. Only the guitar and half-unbuttoned fringed shirt give him away.

Four blocks south of Beale, at Mulberry and Calhoun Streets, the otherwise unpretentious **Lorraine Motel** earned a spot in history for the assassination of Martin Luther King, as he stood on its balcony on an April night in 1968. Memphis, not a town given to violent bigotry, was profoundly embarrassed (they immediately named a new freeway after Dr. King; it runs right next to Elvis Presley Boulevard). The motel maintains King's room as a shrine, with a small museum devoted to black art.

In the last century, when Memphis was a good deal smaller, the prime residential neighborhood was Adams Avenue, on the eastern edge of downtown. On Adams at Third, **St. Peter's Cathedral** (1854) is one of the city's oldest churches and an interesting example of early Gothic Revival, unusual in Dixie. The **Magevney House,** at no. 198, was built in 1831, a simple cottage on what was then the outskirts of the city, now open as a museum (Tues-Sat 10-4, Sun 1-4, free). Further up Adams, in the preservation district Memphis has given the cutesy name of **Victorian Village,** two fine eclectic American mansions have been restored and are open for tours: the **Mallory-Neely House** (1860) at no. 652, which may be the grandest house ever built in the antebellum South without Greek columns, and the **Fontaine House** built in 1870 (both houses open daily 1-4 pm, 10-4 in the summer, adm.).

Across Manassas Street, and past Forrest Park, on Manassas at Union, is what the city calls **Memphis Medical Center,** an impressive 35-block neighborhood of hospitals and related institutions that has made the city itself the biggest medical center of the South. The growing complex includes the University of Tennessee Center for the Health Sciences, the City of Memphis Hospital, the Baptist Memorial Hospital, and a dozen others.

Around Town: Another thing Memphis has in common with Chicago (but almost no other Southern city) is the influence of the City Beautiful movement. After the turn of the century, the city built a ring of boulevards—called South, North, and East Parkways, all lined with characteristic brick bungalows that almost would not look out of place in Chicago—connecting with the new civic embellishment of **Overton Park,** home to two of the city's then-new cultural institutions. The highwaymen almost succeeded in devastating this park for one of their four-lanes in the 1960's. As with New Orleans' Vieux Carré Expressway, the result was a tremendous battle, both legal and psychological, that attracted national attention. Reason prevailed, and the meadows and groves of Overton Park survive today. Among its attractions are the **Memphis Zoological Garden and Aquarium** (daily, 9-6, adm.), the **Memphis Academy of the Arts,** and the **Brooks Memorial Art Gallery,** a marble temple modeled after that Beaux-Arts jewel, the Morgan Library in New York, with a small but well chosen collection of European paintings, contemporary art, glass and ceramics. There is also one of the largest of the Kress collections (Tues-Sat 10-5, Sun 1-5, free). If you've been wondering, whilst reading this book, what a Kress collection is, Samuel Kress was a dime store magnate—you can see his distinctively ornate shop fronts in any Southern city (as on Main Street in Memphis)—who amassed a huge collection of mostly medieval and Renaissance paintings and sculpture. Rather than leave it all in one place, he split it up among several Southern cities as an impetus to build a museum, or improve collections they already had. Memphis was his home town.

Another benefactor, Hugo Dixon, left Memphis another art museum, the **Dixon Gallery and Gardens** at 4339 Park Road, off Poplar Street on the eastern edge of town. Mr. Dixon liked English portraitists and Impressionists, and consequently his museum has lots of each, including works by Reynolds, Constable, Turner, Gauguin and Matisse. The home is decorated with English antiques, and there are seventeen acres of gardens full of azaleas and dogwoods around it (Tues-Sat 11-5, Sun 1-5, adm., free Tuesday). If you prefer roses, irises and magnolias, stop at nearby **Audubon Park** for the **Memphis Botanical Garden** (conservatory open Mon-Fri 9-5, Sat & Sun 1-5, grounds open sunrise-sunset, free).

Back towards Overton Park—this is the choice part of town, and it is full of parks—the **Fairgrounds,** the spot where Mr. Crump was wont to entertain the masses, now contains a very patriotic amusement park called **Libertyland** (March to May, weekends only; daily 10-10 June through August; adm. $6 adults; on East Parkway at Southern Avenue). Nearby, at 3050 Central Avenue, a man named Clarence Saunders built himself a million-dollar home he named Cla-Le-Clare in the crazy 1920's, but Memphians preferred to call it the **Pink Palace.** Everyone in town knew Clarence Saunders; as the most conspicuous grocer of all time, he meant it that way. If Clarence had been in politics, he would have been Huey Long (there's a slight resemblance) but instead he invented the supermarket in 1916; the word supermarket he hadn't invented yet, and so he called them Piggly Wiggly. With such a merchandizing genius, it isn't hard to see how Clarence swept across Dixie with his stores, and became a multi-millionaire. He may have been a little too clever, for he lost it all, and his chain with it, as fast as he made it. After a few sad chapters of this instructive life, there's a grand finale called Keedoozle. In 1937, Memphians who had missed Saunders' famous advertisements now read in their morning papers, "Let's do some Kissing, Let's do some loving, Let's go see Keedoozle! . . . " What they saw, downtown on Union Avenue, was the first *electronic* supermarket, run by a proto-computer of 10,000 circuits that allowed shoppers to stick funny little keys in slots and have all their groceries waiting for them at the end of the line. Grim old World War II killed off Keedoozle, or rather allowed it to collapse under its own weight, but Piggly Wiggly is still a part of the Southern scene.

The house too remains. The city owns it, and you can take a tour of it on alternate Sundays, but adjacent to it they have built the **Memphis Pink Palace Museum,** a still-growing, combination civic and natural history museum of great promise. There's a planetarium, a number of natural exhibits including an oxbow lake habitat, and lots of insects. If you haven't already met the fearsome Southern species of cockroach (like the three-inch Florida Death's Head) this is a convenient spot to watch them at play. Historical exhibits concentrate on the Civil War, the Mr. Crump Era, and of course Clarence Saunders, with a full size replica of his original Piggly Wiggly from 79 Jefferson Avenue. It's disappointingly small; the great idea was only a plain grocery store with self-service baskets and a turnstile, but Clarence made it seem fun. His newspaper ads, on display here, are as outrageous in their way as Crump's. We can wonder which one got the idea from the other. Those travelers who go only to seek out examples of that distinctly American art form, the hand-carved, mechanically operated model circus that takes someone a lifetime to make, have a real treat in store at the Pink Palace. "Clyde W. Parke's Miniature Circus" is every bit as good as its counterparts in Sarasota and Bridgeport, and it holds a prominent place in the museum (Tues-Thurs 9-5, Fri & Sat 9-10, Sun 1-6, adm.).

A grab-bag of other Memphis attractions: At 5151 E. Raines Road, the Schlitz Brewing Co. offers tours, with complimentary beer and pretzels, and also a look at the *Schlitz Belle,* another riverboat replica (Mon-Fri at 10:30, 11:30, 1:30, 2:30 and 3:30, free). The **Chucalissa Indian Museum,** nearby in the T. O. Fuller State Park on Mitchell Road, is a project of Memphis State University, a reconstruction of a late temple-mound culture town circa 1000-1500 A.D. "Chucalissa," a Choctaw word meaning "abandoned houses," is the name they've given the town, which currently includes nine very aesthetic thatch huts and a temple atop the original mound and also a museum. Excavations are still in process on the site, and on some weekends Indians who live around Memphis come here for cultural programs, or for a session of their wild and woolly Choctaw stick-ball game (Tues-Sat 9-5, Sun 1-5, adm.). Memphis trendies gather at **Overton Square,** Madison at Cooper, which isn't a square at all, but a chic shopping center near Overton Park that has restaurants, an ice-skating rink, and even a repertory theater group among its block of old-looking buildings. And finally, there is **Graceland,** on Elvis Presley Boulevard south of Mitchell Road, not far from the Mississippi line, an ordinary and discouraging suburban setting that holds much magic for the millions of weepy star-struck votaries for whom the King still lives.

Whatever sacred truths are imparted here on the Boulevard will probably always be unknown to many of us. Those initiated in the mysteries will already know how to do Graceland; for the rest, we suggest this brief itinerary: First, you'll stop at the Elvis shopping center across the street to select appropriate mementoes (a carefully sculpted Elvis bust that serves as a lamp base, perhaps) and perhaps take in "The King on Stage," a show that may be a movie, a hologram, or a wax dummy. I don't know. Then it's across the street to the manor itself. Bring a felt pen to record your thoughts with the thousands of others on the low stone Wailing Wall around Graceland. At writing, the house itself is not open to visitors; the City of Memphis is being difficult about the zoning change necessary to allow the heirs to charge admission, so while the pool, the trophy room and the piano room itself are denied you, you may of course visit the Tomb, in the Meditation Gardens.

Sad to relate, the Elvis Eternal Flame is out, thieves or fans having made off with the propane tanks, and the Elvis Memorial Park across the street has gone back to being a used-car lot, with thieves again (or creditors, according to the newspaper reports) removing the buildings and the life-size plywood statue of the King. There are plenty more of Elvis' tracks to follow in Memphis, however: Humes High School (on Jackson Avenue), where he graduated, the trucking company where he got his first job, the Sun Recording Studio, etc. Take a tour bus; there are lots of them.

Southwestern Tennessee

Is as Deep South as Mississippi, which makes it all the more surprising to find a fine 1880's Gothic Synagogue, the **Temple Adas Israel,** located in Brownsville, northeast of Memphis. It has outstanding stained-glass windows and is on the National Register of Historic Places, as is the **Zion Church** across the street. Brownsville is one of the prettiest towns in west Tennessee; note especially the homes in the College Hill Historic District. **Bolivar,** south of Brownsville, has several antebellum plantation houses and no less than three historical districts; one includes the homey **Little Courthouse** on E. Market Street, converted into a residence and later into the Hardeman County Museum (contact the Chamber of Commerce for tours).

Jackson, "the Hub of West Tennessee," located halfway between the Mississippi and Tennessee Rivers, has three colleges, the East Main Street Historic District, and the **Casey Jones Home.** Casey Jones sacrificed himself to save his passengers in a spectacular train wreck in Vaughn, Mississippi; his last home was in Jackson, and his house has been converted into a railroad museum, with memorabilia from Casey's life and times (located on I-40 and the US 45 Bypass; open Mon-Sat 9-5, Sun 1-5, adm.). He's buried in Jackson's Mt. Calvary Cemetery, on the outskirts of town.

South of Jackson, on the Forked Deer River (US 45), the **Pinson Mounds** comprise Tennessee's largest prehistoric Indian site. An unusual feature of the thirty-two mounds at Pinson is the extensive earthworks that surround major portions of the site; most of the mounds are burial mounds. Relics and other clues discovered by archaeologists are in the three-storey mound-like underground museum on the site. For opening hours call the Southwest Tennessee Tourism Organization at the Casey Jones House (901) 668-1223. Further south, **Henderson** is a pretty town, home of Freed Hardaman College, founded in 1870.

Shiloh National Military Park on the Tennessee River commemorates one of the more famous and bloodiest battles of the Civil War. It changed Federal thinking on the war. "I gave up all idea of saving the Union except by complete conquest," Grant commented afterwards.

The visitors center of the battlefield is on Rt. 22 south of Crump, and contains maps, relics, exhibits, and a movie on the battle. A ten-mile auto tour takes in the major scenes of fighting, the Union and Confederate cemeteries, and some ancient Indian mounds (daily June-August 8-6, 8-5 the rest of the year, free).

In **Savannah,** the largest town in this section of the Tennessee River, **Cherry Mansion** was Grant's headquarters prior to the Battle of Shiloh. Another river town, **Cerro Gordo,** north of Savannah, has a general store that opened in 1880 and is still doing business. On TVA-created Pickwick Lake, **Pickwick Landing State Resort Park** has become one of western Tennessee's most popular recreation areas, with cabins, campgrounds, a marina, a golf course and beach.

Interstate 40 bisects the **Natchez Trace State Park and Forest,** which is quite a distance from the Natchez Trace itself, but boasts of the world's largest pecan tree. Another park, **Nathan Bedford Forrest State Historic Area** is on Kentucky Lake east of Camden. It overlooks the site of the Battle of Johnsonville, where in late 1864, General Forrest and his cavalry surprised a Federal supply depot and left 8 million dollars worth of property in smouldering ashes. A monument to Forrest, erected in 1929, is on Pilot Knob, a landmark among river pilots and the highest point in West Tennessee, with a commanding view of Kentucky Lake and the surrounding area. A museum in the park has interpretive exhibits on the battle (open April-September 7:30 am-10 pm, 7:30 am-8 pm the rest of the year, free). On either side of Kentucky Lake, and to the north, near Land Between the Lakes, are the three sections of the Tennessee National Wildlife Refuge. The waterfowl and migratory birds that frequent the refuge make it popular among bird watchers.

In the municipal building on 309 College Street in **Trenton** is one of the world's largest collection of veilleuse-thieres (18th century food and medicine warmers) with over 500 of these ornamental gizmos on display (Mon-Fri 8-5, Sat 8-12, free). Tiny **South Fulton,** on the Kentucky border, was at one time America's largest banana distributor. Large shipments of bananas still wend their way to South Fulton in August for the International Banana Festival, when 3,000 bananas are used to create a one-ton banana pudding.

In the extreme northwest corner of Tennessee, beautiful **Reelfoot Lake** was born in the New Madrid Earthquake of 1811, one of the world's most powerful. The earth caved in and the Mississippi reversed its flow in monstrous waves, filling up what is now Reelfoot Lake. Beneath the dark waters of the lake you can see the ghostly shadows of the forest engulfed by the Mississippi; water lilies and cypress add more shelter to what has become America's best natural fish hatchery, the spawning grounds of some sixty species. In the middle of the 19th century, the fish attracted a large population of American bald eagles who lived year round by the lake, building their nests in the cypress trees. The fish also attracted thousands of sportsmen, and the eagles, valuing their privacy, took up quarters around the Great Lakes in Canada. However, over 200 of the endangered species still return every winter to their old hunting grounds around Reelfoot Lake, and their annual arrival in November causes much excitement; free eagle watches, sponsored by the Tennessee Department of Conservation, run from December 1 to March 15, departing daily at 9 am from the Lake State Airpark Inn in Tiptonville.

Reelfoot Lake is a state resort park partially located in what was one of Tennessee's most violent counties, Obion. In the early 19th century, this area of the Mississippi lived in terror of John Murrell and his band of outlaws. Murrell roamed up and down the Mississippi killing travelers, disemboweling them so that bodies wouldn't float, hacking babies to pieces, and at one point, planning to ravage the whole city of New Orleans. In the present century, Obion County was sometimes referred to as "Night Rider Country"; for when a land company planned to turn Reelfoot Lake into a private fishing resort in 1908, the Night Riders kidnapped two of the company's lawyers, demanding the preservation of their old fishing rights. When the lawyers refused to promise any such thing, one was murdered and the other barely escaped by jumping into a bayou. By 1913 Reelfoot Lake came under state control.

Fort Pillow State Historic Area, between Reelfoot Lake and Memphis, was another scene of violence. The fort, built by the Confederacy early in the war and named for General Gideon J. Pillow, was captured during the Memphis campaign and remained in Federal hands until General Nathan B. Forrest attacked it on April 12, 1864. The fort was defended by 550 troops, half of them black and half white. When they surrendered, "that devil Forrest," as the Union knew him, massacred them—although some claim that the disproportionate number of Federal deaths were casualties of the battle. In any event, few lived to tell the tale. Remains of Fort Pillow's earthworks can still be seen on the lofty Chickasaw Bluffs overlooking the muddy expanses of the Mississippi.

Restaurants. *In Memphis*: Grisanti's***, 1489 Airways Blvd.; La Tourelle***, 2146 Monroe; Vieux Chalet***, 3264 Summer Ave.; Justin's***, 919 Coward Place; Le Cafe du Louvre***, 2125 Madison; Captain Bilbo's River Restaurant**, 263 Wagner; Charlie Vergos' Rendezvous**, in the alley between 2nd and 3rd St.; Ronnie Grissanti and Sons**, Union & Marshall; Peking**, Poplar-Highland Plaza; Germantown Commissary*, 2290 Germantown Rd.; Dollie's Deli*, 810 Washington; Bullies*, 3378 Poplar; Buntyn*, 3070 Southern Ave. *In*

Jackson: Baudo's**, Wiley Parker Rd. *In Crump*: River Heights*, US 64; Pickwick Landing Resort*, off Rt. 57 in state park. *In Parsons*: Tennessee River Catfish Restaurant*, Rt. 20.

Annual Events in Tennessee

In January: Eagle Tours, *Tiptonville*, in Reelfoot Lake State Resort Park.
In February: Grand National Field Trials, *Grand Junction*, to decide the National Champion bird dog.
In March: Valleydale 500 NASCAR race, *Bristol*.
In April: Dogwood Arts Festival, *Knoxville*; Mule Day, *Columbia*; Old Time Fiddlers' Championships, *Clarksville*; Spring Wildflower Pilgrimage, *Gatlinburg*; World's Largest Fish Fry, *Paris*.
In May: Ramp Festival, in *Cosby*, honoring a pungent, onion-like vegetable that grows only in the upper Appalachians; Memphis in May, *Memphis*; Iroquois Steeplechase, *Nashville*; East Tennessee Strawberry Festival, *Dayton*; Appalachian Music Days, *Bristol*; Spring Music & Crafts Festival, *Rugby*; Museum of Appalachia Spring Festival, *Norris*.
In June: International Country Music Fan Fair, *Nashville*; Dulcimer Convention, *Cosby*; Country Music Days, *Elizabethton*; Rhododendron Festival, *Roan Mountains*; The Tennessee River Bluegrass Festival, *Savannah*.
In July: Frontier Days, *Lynchburg*; Old Time Fiddlers' Jamboree, *Smithville*; Historic Jonesboro Days, *Jonesboro*; Gatlinburg Craftsmen's Fair, *Gatlinburg*.
In August: Rugby Pilgrimage, *Rugby*: International Grand Championship Walking Horse Show, *Murfreesboro*: International Banana Festival, *South Fulton*; Tennessee Walking Horse National Celebration, *Shelbyville*.
In September: TVA & I Fair, *Knoxville*; Tennessee State Fair, *Nashville*; Mid-South Fair, *Memphis*.
In October; National Storytelling Festival, *Jonesboro*; Craftsmen's Fall Exhibition, *Gatlinburg*; Oktoberfest, *Memphis*; Museum of Appalachia Fall Festival, *Norris*; Fall Colour Cruise & Folk Festival, *Chattanooga*.
In November; American Cup International Hang Gliding Championships, *Chattanooga*; Blue Music Week, *Memphis*.
In December: The Twelve Days of Christmas, *Gatlinburg* (on four weekends preceding Christmas); The Liberty Bowl Football Classic, *Memphis*.

Accommodation in Tennessee

Eastern Tennessee (Area Code 615)
Chattanooga Choo Choo, 1400 Market St., Tel 266-5000, *Chattanooga*. Expensive accommodations in Victorian style train cars or hotel on a 24 acre complex.
The Read House, 9th and Broad, tel. 266-4121, *Chattanooga*. Moderate-expensive; Chattanooga's oldest hotel.
Drake Inn, 3515 S. Broad, tel. 266-5656, *Chattanooga*. Moderate.
Holiday Motel, 5011 Dayton Blvd., tel. 877-7112, *Chattanooga*. Inexpensive.

Lockmiller's Motel, 2531 Cummings Hwy., tel. 821-9230, *Chattanooga*. Near Lookout Mountain and Rock City, inexpensive.
Dunlap Motel, US 127 N., tel. 949-2184, *Dunlap*. Inexpensive.
Monteagle Motel, tel. 924-2011, *Sewanee-Monteagle*. Inexpensive.
Loret Resort Villa, Rt. 58 N., tel. 344-8311, *Lake Chickamauga*. Moderate, many facilities.
Watts Bar Resort, Rt. 68, tel. 365-9595, *Watts Bar Dam*. Lake front cottages, inexpensive to expensive.
The Village Inn, Keith St., tel. 478-1161, *Cleveland*. Moderate; restaurant.
Kelly's Motel, 1505 Rt. 27 S., tel. 775-1181, *Dayton*. Inexpensive.
Falls Creak Falls Resort Inn, Rt. 30, tel. 881-3241, *Pikeville*. Moderate priced accommodations in Falls Creek Falls State Park; restaurant.
Hotel Taylor, 500 N. Main St., tel. 484-5841, *Crossville*. Moderate.
Princess Motel, US 129 & 411, tel. 982-2490, *Maryville*. Moderate.
Vols Inn, 2000 Chapman Hwy., tel. 573-1921, *Knoxville*. Moderate.
Colony Motel, 5102 Kingston Pk., tel. 584-4672, *Knoxville*. Moderate.
Treemont Motel, 4405 Clinton Hwy., tel. 687-2560, *Knoxville*. Moderate.
University Travel Inn, 1700 Clinch Ave., tel. 546-5974, *Knoxville*. Moderate.
Clark Motel, 7130 Clinton Hwy., tel. 947-9961, *Knoxville*. Inexpensive.
Black Oak Motel, 6417 Maynardville Hwy., tel. 922-8425, *Knoxville*. Inexpensive.
Capri Motel, 2810 Magnolia Ave., tel. 524-2755, *Knoxville*. Moderate-inexpensive.
Sunset Motel, 6245 Chapman Hwy., tel. 573-7701, *Knoxville*. Inexpensive.
The Ridge Inn Motel, 1590 Oak Ridge Tpk., tel. 483-1385, *Oak Ridge*. Moderate.
Alexander Motor Inn, 210 E. Madison Rd., tel. 483-3555, *Oak Ridge*. Moderate.
Colonial Motor Inn, US 25 W., tel. 426-2816, *Lake City*. Moderate-expensive, on Norris Lake.
The Lamb's Inn Motel, US 25 W., tel. 426-2171, *Lake City*. Inexpensive, near lake.
River Lodge, 311 Parkway, tel. 453-0783, *Pigeon Forge*. Moderate-expensive.
Vacation Lodge Motel, US 441, tel. 453-2640, *Pigeon Forge*. Moderate.
Rivermont Motor Inn, 293 Parkway, tel. 436-5047, *Gatlinburg*. Expensive, overlooking stream.
River Edge Motor Lodge, 948 River Rd., tel. 436-9292, *Gatlinburg*. Expensive.
Brookside Resort, Rt. 73, tel. 436-5611, *Gatlinburg*. Expensive rooms and cottages.
The Cobbly Nob Resort, Rt. 73, tel. 436-9333, *Gatlinburg*. Expensive.
Rocky Waters Motor Inn, US 441, tel. 436-7861, *Gatlinburg*. Expensive, on stream.
Morgan Motel, 150 Airport Rd., tel. 436-4129, *Gatlinburg*. Expensive-moderate.
Reagan Motel, 948 River Rd., tel. 436-9292, *Gatlinburg*. Moderate.
Carr's Northside Cottages & Motel, Poplar St. & Laurel Rd., tel. 436-4836, *Gatlinburg*. Moderate, on Fork Creek.
Alto Motel, 251 Airport Rd., tel. 436-5175, *Gatlinburg*. Moderate.

L Ranch Motel, Rt. 73, tel. 487-2498, *Gatlinburg*. In rural area outside of Gatlinburg, inexpensive.
Mansard Motor Inn, Ski Mountain Rd., tel. 436-7015, *Gatlinburg*. Inexpensive-moderate.
Tally-Ho Motel, Rt. 73, Tel. 448-2465, *Townsend*. Moderate.
Valley View Lodge, Rt. 73, tel. 448-2237, *Townsend*. Inexpensive.
Parkway Motel, US 11 E., tel. 639-2156, *Greenville*. Moderate.
Camara Inn, 505 W. Elk Ave., tel. 543-3511, *Elizabethton*. Moderate.

Middle Tennessee (Area Code 615)
Maxwell House Hotel, 2025 Metro Center Blvd., tel. 259-4343, *Nashville*. Expensive edition of the hotel that gave us the coffee.
Spence Manor, 11 Music Square E., tel. 259-4400, *Nashville*. Nashville's most luxurious hotel.
Opryland Hotel, 2800 Opryland Dr., tel. 889-1000, *Nashville*. Expensive, plantation style hotel, in the theme park.
Congress Inn, 2914 Dickerson Rd., tel. 228-1371, *Nashville*. Moderate-expensive.
Nashville Central, 211 N. First St., tel. 254-1551, *Nashville*. Moderate.
Capitol Park Inn, 400 Fifth Ave. N., tel. 254-1651, *Nashville*. Moderate.
Close Quarters Hotel, 913 20th Ave. S., tel. 327-1115, *Nashville*. Small, moderate.
Madison Square Motel, 118 Emmitt Ave., tel. 865-4203, *Nashville*. Inexpensive.
York Motel, 2501 Franklin Rd., tel. 297-4648, *Nashville*. Inexpensive.
Twelve Oaks Motel, 656 W. Iris Dr., tel. 385-1323, *Nashville*. Inexpensive.
Metro Motel, 1404 Dickerson Rd., tel. 228-2531, *Nashville*. Inexpensive.
Cedars Inn, Rt. 231 S., tel. 444-5635, *Lebanon*. Inexpensive-moderate.
Jackson Motel, 831 N.W. Broad St., tel. 893-2100, *Murfreesboro*. Moderate.
Lambs Motel, Lebanon Rd., tel. 893-3576, *Murfreesboro*. Inexpensive.
The Shelbyville Inn, 317 N. Cannon Blvd., tel. 684-6050, *Murfreesboro*. Moderate.
Walking Horse Hotel, tel. 389-6407, *Wartrace*. Elegant old hotel full of Walking Horse memorabilia; moderate-expensive.
Ambassador Motel, Rt. 53, tel. 728-2200, *Manchester*. Inexpensive, with restaurant.
Park Motel, 1504 Hillsboro Rd., tel. 728-3555, *Manchester*. Very inexpensive.
Holiday Marina, tel. 455-3151, *Tullahoma*. Five chalets; moderate.
Frassrand Terrace Motel, 700 S. College St., tel. 967-3846, *Winchester*. Inexpensive.
Americana Motel, 809 Sparta St., tel. 473-2159, *McMinnville*. Inexpensive.
Riviera Plaza Inn, Rt. 42, tel. 526-9521, *Cookeville*. Moderate.
Shoney's Inn, 221 W. Main St., tel. 452-5311, *Gallatin*. Moderate.
Mid-Towner Motel, 890 Kraft, tel. 647-6536, *Clarksville*. Moderate.
A. & W. Motel, 1505 Madison St., tel. 647-3545, *Clarksville*. Inexpensive.
Celina Hill Resort, tel. 243-3201, *Celina,* on Dale Hollow Lake. Houseboats, cabins and rooms; moderate.

James K. Polk Motel, US 31, tel. 388-4913, *Columbia*. Moderate.

West Tennessee (Area Code 901)
Peabody Hotel, 149 Union St., tel. 529-4000, *Memphis*. A recently renovated classic; deluxe.
Executive Plaza Inn, 1471 E. Brooks Rd., tel. 332-3500, *Memphis*. Expensive.
River Place, 100 N. Front St., tel. 526-0583, *Memphis*. Expensive.
Elvis Presley Boulevard Inn, 2300 Elvis Presley Blvd., tel. 948-1522, *Memphis*. Moderate.
Tennessee Hotel, 80 S. Third St., tel. 525-6621, *Memphis*. Moderate-inexpensive.
Riverbluff Inn, 340 W. Illinois Ave., tel. 948-9005, *Memphis*. Moderate.
Lakeland Inn, I-40 and Canada Rd., tel. 388-7120, *Memphis*. Moderate.
Lorraine Motel, 406 Mulberry, tel. 525-6834, *Memphis*. Downtwn motel where Martin Luther King was assassinated; inexpensive.
Royal Oaks Motel East, 4941 Summer Ave., tel. 683-2411, *Memphis*. Stay in the original Holiday Inn, since retired by the enormous chain.
Leahy's Motel, 3070 Summer Ave., tel. 452-7456, *Memphis*. Inexpensive.
Shelby Motel, 6803 Summer Ave., tel. 386-3311, *Memphis*. Inexpensive.
Skylit Motel, 105 S. Grand Ave., tel. 772-3605, *Brownsville*. Inexpensive.
Arisctocrat Motor Inn. 1357 W. Market St., tel. 658-6451, *Bolivar*. Moderate.
The Hearthstone Motor Lodge, 626 W. Market St., tel. 658-4472, *Bolivar*. Moderate-inexpensive.
Gentry Inn, 1919 US 45 Bypass, tel. 668-3444, *Jackson*. Moderate.
Thunderbird Motel, US 45, tel. 422-5536, *Jackson*. Inexpensive.
River Heights Motel, US 64, tel. (615) 632-3376, *Crump*. Inexpensive.
Bellis Motel, tel. 925-4787, *Savannah*. Expensive; on Pickwick Lake.
Savannah Motel, Adams St., tel. 925-3392, *Savannah*. Inexpensive.
Pickwick Landing Resort Inn, Rt. 57, tel. 689-3135, *Pickwick Dam*. Moderate; in state park, many facilities.
The Four Seasons Motel & Cabins, Rt. 57 S., tel. 689-5251, *Pickwick Dam*. Moderate.
Parisian Motel, 501 Tyson Ave., tel. 642-1822, *Paris*. Inexpensive.
Fulton Plaza Motor Inn, US 45 Bypass & 51, tel. 479-3040, *South Fulton*. Inexpensive.
Trenton Motel, Rt. 45 W., tel. 855-0321, *Trenton*. Inexpensive.
Shaw's Lodge, tel. 253-7074, *Reelfoot Lake*. Small, moderate.

For more information on Tennessee, write the Tennessee Department of Tourist Development, P.O. Box 23170, Nashville TN 37202. The Tennessee State Parks Division, 2611 West End Ave., Nashville, TN 37203 has information on the state's recreational facilities; the Tennessee Wildlife Resources Agency, Ellington Center, Nashville 37220 can supply details on fishing and hunting regulations.

Arkansas

Traveler: ... Sir! will you tell me where this road goes to?
Squatter: It's never gone anywhere since I lived here. It's always there when I get up in the mornin'.
Traveler: Well, how far is it to where it forks?
Squatter: It don't fork at all, but it splits up like the devil . . .

Arkansas, the Land of Opportunity, is something of a puzzle for the inquiring visitor today. The state itself doesn't even know, for example, whether it's part of the South or the West. That difficulty is nothing compared to the 1840's when Colonel Sandy Faulkner composed the celebrated dialogue and fiddle tune of *The Arkansas Traveler* to honor a brand new state that had acquired the reputation of a backwater almost as soon as its settlement commenced. This now thoroughly respectable state (with occasional lapses) established its character in the wild and woolly half century before the Civil War, as the gateway to Texas and the Indian Territory of Oklahoma and character is something it has in large helpings, as well as a fierce local pride.

You wouldn't call Arkansas self-possessed and truculent, like South Carolina, just mildly ornery in an entertaining sort of way. In the last century, the Bishop of Arkansas cast the only dissenting vote in the whole world in the church council that adopted the doctrine of papal infallibility. A few years before, an Arkansan had been the only man in the U.S. Senate to vote against making duelling a federal crime. Today, after a century and more of one-party rule as rigid as that of Russia or Mexico, Arkansas politics have become crazily unpredictable—witness the election of 1968, when the state gave majorities to George Wallace for President, to the liberal anti-war Senator Fulbright, and to Republican outsider Winthrop Rockefeller for Governor. Recently the state came to the nation's attention when the legislature passed a bill mandating the teaching of Biblical creationism in the schools, fifty-seven years after the Scopes trial (the Federal courts weren't amused). But don't get the impression that Arkansas is backward; actually the state's politics are right now more enlightened than in most of the South, it's only that in Arkansas everyone, sooner or later, gets his innings.

As we said, both the South and the West have a claim on Arkansas, and if you add the purely Appalachian colony of the Ozarks, the picture becomes even more complicated. The flat eastern and southern parts of the state grow cotton, rice, soybeans, peaches, and watermelons. A look at their list of festivals gives away the affinity with Dixie. For every crop that grows there's a festival somewhere, and thanks to them Arkansas has more beauty contests, probably, than even Alabama—there's a Peach Queen, a Pink Tomato Queen, a Miss Long Grain Rice, and dozens more, including the Mallard Queen at the World Championship Duck Calling Contest held every year in Stuttgart. The Ozarks prefer to celebrate the preservation of their mountain ways with festivals that feature a good deal of country crafts and fiddle playing, while Western Arkansas, mostly around Fort Smith, is fondest of rodeos.

Arkansas' tourist propaganda touts it as "the natural state" with good reason; it's the least densely populated of all the states in this book, with an abundance of clean air, clear streams, and vast stretches of lovely mountain forest. Arkansas travelers, who drop over a billion dollars in the state each year, come not so much to see the sights as to join in with the locals in their passion for fishing, hunting, camping, and other outdoor activities. There are thirty-nine state parks, from Mississippi oxbow lakes to the tops of Ozark peaks, the big Ozark and Ouachita National Forests, as well as nineteen recreation areas created by the Corps of Engineers around their artificial lakes in the Ozarks, along the Arkansas River valley, in the Ouachitas, and aroud Texarkana. The Buffalo River, the first "National River" to be designated by Congress, is a star attraction for canoeists and fishermen, but it is only one of over twenty popular float streams in the northern and western parts of the state.

Getting There

By Train. Amtrak's **Inter-American** train from Chicago, St. Louis, and to Houston stops at Newport, Little Rock, Malvern, and Texarkana. In Little Rock, **Union Station** is at Markham and Victory Streets. The Arkansas toll-free number is 800-874-2775.

By Bus. In Little Rock, the Greyhound station is at 6th and Broadway. Trailways is at Markham and Main Streets near the Old State House. These lines have service across the state in conjunction with a number of smaller companies such as Great Southern and Arkansas Motor Coaches.

By Air. Little Rock is easily reached from most of the larger centers of the South by American, Delta, Frontier, and Texas International Airlines. Frontier, in addition, serves Fayetteville, Fort Smith, and Harrison, and there are some flights to El Dorado, Hot Springs, Pine Bluff, and Texarkana. Little Rock's Adams Field is only two miles east of downtown and served by taxis and airport limos.

Tourist Information. As in many southern states, Arkansas has large, elaborate Information Centers along all the major highways at the border; you almost can't get into the state without passing one: *from Missouri,* US 69, north of Corning, Interstate 55 at Blytheville, US 71 north of Bentonville and Rogers: *from Tennessee,* Interstate 40 at West Memphis: *from Mississippi,* US 49 at Helena, US 82 at Lake Village: *from Louisiana,* US 167, south of El Dorado: *from Texas,* Interstate 30 at Texarkana, US 71-59 at Ashdown: *from Oklahoma,* Interstate 40 at Fort Smith.

History

Thanks to the Mississippi and its tributaries, Arkansas was known to European explorers even before many areas further east. Hernando De Soto passed through in 1541, just before his personal demise on the Mississippi and his men's long ordeal crossing the southwest. Over a century after the Spanish appeared in the South the French sent their own explorers down from the Great Lakes to see what role the great, barely-intimated river system could play in the seizure of a continent. When Marquette and Joliet drifted down the Mississippi in 1673, they met the peaceable *Akansa,* or Quapaw Indians (the latter from their name for the tribal confederation), who warned them of less amenable tribes to the south, and their advice made enough of an impression on the Frenchmen to send them paddling all the way back to Canada. Five years later La Salle made it to the Gulf of Mexico, and his later attempts at encouraging the occupation and settlement of the river route resulted in the founding of Arkansas Post in 1686. That Arkansas can claim seniority in respect to settlement over all its neighbouring states, credit can be given to the friendliness of the Quapaw, who were, the explorers thought, the most virtuous and prosperous Indians they had seen. In return, the debilitating influence of contact with the white man brought them to cultural extinction in just about a century and a half.

Arkansas became a part of France's Louisiana Territory, which in 1717 passed under the control of John Law. Law was hardly the con-artist-at-large that most of the history books portray; he seems to have been rather the first serious economic theorist to be entrusted with an entire national economy on which to test his ideas. He had founded France's first national bank, and the Regent, the Duke of Orleans, had little interest in himself getting the nation out of its current depression, and so bestowed upon Law not only Louisiana, but France's national debt, with the assumption that the Scotsman would somehow make them balance. The printing presses went to work all over France, while the men of Law's Mississippi Land Company, spiritual ancestors of the Florida real estate sharks of two centuries later, began deluging Europe with tales of a new paradise on earth—gold, sunshine, leafy bowers, cute Indian girls, thousands of slaves to help you found your own personal dynasty . . . yes, Arkansas! The first thousand settlers spent an often mortal winter listening to their teeth chatter at Arkansas Post, and once again the Quapaw were called upon for a good deal of charity relief. Meanwhile the news arrived of how the "Mississippi Bubble" had burst; Law quitted France, speculators in his stock were jumping out of windows, and the predominantly German colonists left for new homes in the swamps around New Orleans. Arkansas, for its part, left the stage of world affairs forever.

With the rest of Louisiana Territory, Arkansas joined the United States in 1803. You can still see the stone commemorating the acquistion in a bog just west of Helena on Route 49. Do not suppose it is just another historical marker; Jefferson's surveyors found the meridian they were looking for here, and every piece of property as far north as the Canadian border is aligned to it. President Jefferson himself thought so little of Arkansas' prospects that he gave much of it as new homelands for the Cherokee and Choctaw. Manifest destiny, however, always abhorred a vacuum, and in the years before the Civil War the loose ends of emigration began to spread across the territory.

Settlement came from diverse sources; there were of course the typical pioneer homesteaders, many of them veterans of the War of 1812 with government land grants, also a contingent from the Appalachians, who found the rugged Ozarks much to their liking. The slave and cotton empire came shortly thereafter, establishing itself in the Mississippi bottomlands in the 1820's. But besides these, there was a large number of the more unconventional breed of westward-bound transient. In those days, when the bankrupts, speculators, gamblers, squatters, embezzlers, flatboat hi-jackers, fiancee deserters, horse thieves, lawyers, and politicians of the western states found themselves in exposed positions, it wouldn't be long before the famous sign "Gone to Texas" appeared on the doors of their abodes. Arkansas, being the great highway from Tennessee to Texas, saw them all, and many found the prospects there inviting, or got lost, or befuddled, and never left. In a sense, Arkansas is the place where the legendary Old West went to school, where the more colorful characters of later decades, including the bandits and adventurers, learned their trades. With the "Choctaw Line," and later the Indian Territory of Oklahoma on its borders, Arkansas, or at least its western reaches, took on the aspect of a permanent frontier, while serving as a staging point for some of the great movements in America's territorial expansion. Texas independence was plotted just over the border in the town of Washington, the U.S. Army readied itself for the 1848 Mexican War in the state, and a year later many of those who meant to seek their fortunes in the California gold rush gathered at Fort Smith to begin the long trip westwards. And Washington, of course, gave birth to the "Arkansas Toothpick," the Bowie knife.

The cast of characters would include Sam Houston, who on a whim deserted the governorship of Tennessee to embark on one of the nation's legendary binges with his Indian friends in the Ouachitas, where he spent four years before his apotheosis in the Texas wars; also such famous frontiersmen as Archibald Yell and Albert Pike, both of whom eventually led groups of irregulars for the Confederacy. Pike, an outlandish dresser of considerable education from Boston, was not only a soldier and explorer, but a teacher, poet, newspaper columnist, Whig politician, and the leading authority on the symbolism of Freemasonry. Among the outlaws who infested this stretch of the Mississippi, we must mention the greatest, John A. Murrell. From hidden fastnesses in the piney bottoms between Blythedale and Memphis, Murrell led his "Mystic Confederacy" of crime—a thousand or so outlaws as far south as New Orleans and also, secretly, many leading citizens of the river towns, all of whom recognized each other by special signs and grips. Murrell created his empire by being the most thoroughly vicious of them all. He murdered dozens, always taking time to disembowel them, and set a precedent for later outlaws like John Wesley Hardin by once killing a man for snoring too loud. His ambitions were Napoleonic; at the time of his capture in Tennessee, he was working on a scheme for a massive slave revolt, after which he hoped to gain control of the entire Mississippi valley.

Despite the likes of Murrell, Arkansas was beginning to fill up. By 1819, settlers were spreading far enough across the territory to cause the capital to be moved to a more central location at Little Rock; Arkansas Post, already a century and half old, began to wither and eventually disappeared. Statehood came in 1836, somewhat prematurely—the leading men weren't quite ready to give up the territorial subsidy, but the South needed another slave state to balance the admission of Michigan. Already the new class of planters, self-made men for the most part with little of the aristocratic pretension of their counterparts in the Old South or Louisiana, were beginning to assert their dominance over Arkansas politics. In the 1840's their business boomed, along with the rest of the state; in the next twenty years the population doubled, and the number of slaves increased tenfold. As the Civil War began, and the first fighting came to Arkansas (Arkansas claim the first shot fired, at the seizure of a Federal arsenal in Little Rock) the slaveowners manoeuvred the state into secession with no real opposition save in the Ozarks.

Although the state contributed its share of men to the cause (as well as 10,000 to the Union forces), little fighting of any consequence actually occurred there. Grant passed through in his 1863 campaign for control of the Mississippi, and throughout the war small forces on both sides tried to increase their slice of the hinterlands with little success; 1864 found the state with two governments, the Confederates installed in Washington and a newly elected Unionist administration protected by Federal troops in Little Rock. Reconstruction proceeded more smoothly than in most states, with the brief comical interlude of the "Brooks-Baxter" War in 1874, when the armed forces of two rival Republican claimants to the governorship milled about the streets of Little Rock for several weeks, dearly trying to avoid any incidents beyond the usual saloon fights. Both sides were commanded by Confederate colonels, and composed largely of blacks. The historians are sure that Baxter won, and one of his cannons can still be seen outside the Old State House.

Beyond that, it is to Arkansas' credit that the state passed through Reconstruction more gracefully than the rest of the South. Blacks maintained their political rights into the 1890's, and until the Jim Crow fever swept in from across the Mississippi in that decade, there was little of the racial hatred and everyday discrimination they faced elsewhere. Jim Crow's career in Arkansas makes a tragic story. In the previous decade, Arkansas had been one of the hotbeds of agrarian radicalism, first through the Grange, and then with a home-grown farmers movement that spread from Arkansas throughout the south and west, the Agricultural Wheel, founded in Prairie County. The Wheelers' foes were clearly marked—the bankers and railroads, who held the farmers in thrall while maintaining a firm grip over the state Democratic Party—and in the election of 1888 only widespread voting fraud kept their Union Labor party from throwing the Democrats out of the statehouse. The frightened party leaders, faced with the political nightmare of the radical farmers joining forces with what was left of the Republicans in the state—namely the blacks—to make Arkansas for the first time ever a two-party state, found Jim Crow the only solution, and soon, without any real popular agitation for it, the Democratic legislature passed the "Separate Coach Act". Next came the disenfranchisement of blacks, ironically through the adoption of the secret ballot, discouraging both white and black illiterates from voting, and later the poll tax and white primary. Meanwhile the radicals were co-opted by a shadow-populist, the colorful Jeff Davis, who served three terms as governor after 1900.

In this century progress came to Arkansas, after a fashion. Electrification arrived, and resulted in the state coming under the control of the Arkansas Power & Light Co. Still, the movers and shakers pondered the question of how to bring Arkansas, with its vast mineral resources, into the developed and industrialized world. For a while they tried a new state nickname, "The Wonder State" before finally settling on "Land of Opportunity," but it remained for the Second World War, with its mobilization of rural areas to the new plants, to work the changes in Arkansas that lack of capital and absentee ownership had precluded in the past. That, building on the rural programs of the New Deal, began the slow, gradual political and economic upheaval that continues today. Some Arkansas counties had a postwar "veteran's revolt" against corrupt local governments, as in Tennessee, and the result was the election of a reform governor in 1948, the well-remembered Sid McMath.

One of McMath's major contributions to Atkansas was the undertaking of the state's extensive highway program. In later years, he joked that the worst mistake he ever made was "building the first paved road in Madison County and letting out Orval Faubus". Faubus, the man who in the 1950's brought Arkansas to the center of national affairs in the worst possible way, ironically started out as a McMath protege, a nominal progressive whose father had been a follower of Eugene V. Debs. Although he did nothing to repudiate this background in his first term as governor, beginning in 1954, in his second term the "hillbilly from Greasy Creek," as he called himself in campaign oratory reminiscent of Jeff Davis, had the bad luck to come against the burning issue of school desegregation. In 1957, a plan for intergration of Little Rock's Central High School had quietly been arranged under threat of federal court action. Facing the first challenge to Southern racial practices, Faubus found himself politically squeezed by the new and rapidly growing Citizens Councils and segregationist politicians, and found the path of least resistance in the kind of outraged defiance that set the pattern for George Wallace and Lester Madox. He ignored a court order to admit nine black students to Central, and had his National Guard occupy the school to keep them out. When segregationist agitators (many from outside Arkansas) started a riot, Little Rock blazed across the nation's headlines, as if everything that was bad about the South and festering for a century had somehow chosen that particular spot to explode.

Little Rock, actually, had acted responsibly throughout; both the citizenry and its elected officials had done their best to avoid a crisis, but once again in Arkansas history the state had fallen victim to the ambition of its politicians. Faubus' intervention caused President Eisenhower to send in the Army, and the 101st Airborne Division spent the year dug in at Central High, to show that Uncle Sam meant business. The State's political lines were redrawn by the desegregation hysteria, however, and Faubus' outrage only earned him twelve more years in the governor's chair.

When Orval finally stepped down in 1968, the damnedest thing happened; Arkansas elected as its new governor not only the first Republican since Reconstruction, but a man named Rockefeller. Perhaps it isn't so strange after all. At that time, the third generation of that famous family was collecting states the way the first one had collected oil companies: Nelson Rockefeller was firmly installed in New York, and a few years later Jay Rockefeller would be governor of West Virginia.

Brother Winthrop, "a Republican mountaineer who owned his own mountain" as Arkansas writer Harry Ashmore put it, was a gentleman rancher in his adopted state. As governor, he turned Arkansas politics upside-down, making the old political obsessions of the Faubus era obsolete and replacing them with a drive for modernization, industry and progress, to get Arksansas out of the Old South and into the New South.

Largely thanks to Rockefeller, Arkansas is enjoying a small industrial boom. Even so, timber, agriculture and mining still put the goods on the table for most Arkansans; the state exports cotton, soybeans, rice, turkeys, and famous Hope watermelons, while its miners claw up the nation's largest deposits of aluminium around the Ouachitas, as well as more esoteric minerals like vanadium and manganese. In the Ozarks, a new economy is being created from tourism and from out-of-staters seeking country homes for retirement or for pleasure where they can spend their days enjoying some of the nation's best fishing. Although still the third poorest state of the union, Arkansas marches on, or rather ambles at its own pace, keeping a respectful distance from the rest of the South in style and temperament and experimenting in a new kind of politics in a changing economy.

Little Rock

To the earliest French traders on the Arkansas River, the "little rock," a mossy boulder on the southern bank, was an important landmark where the plains toward the Mississippi rose into the Ouachita Mountains (the Big Rock was another landmark upstream). By 1819, with the Arkansas Territory newly established, the central location of the site and its promise as a potential river port attracted two rival cabals of speculators to start buying up land with the intention of founding a town. Arkansas' territorial commissioners were just then in the market for a new capital, and when they selected the site of Little Rock in the following year, the two parties—after some legal skirmishes and desultory burning of cabins—reached a gentleman's agreement and set the surveyors to work plotting out streets and lots.

The steamboats came, and later the railroads, Davy Crockett paid a memorable visit on his way to Texas, and cotton bales stacked up on the docks in ever-increasing piles, but this backwoods capital of 3,000 souls generated nothing to catch the nation's attention until the Civil War. In 1862, when the west was still an important theater of the war, Little Rock became the second Confederate state capital to fall to the Northerners. The railroads and the government made Little Rock grow; today it is the only city of any size in Arkansas, and surprisingly one of the pleasanter cities of the South. The oldest part, including downtown and the residential neighborhoods to the south along Main St. and Broadway, is called the **Quapaw Quarter.**

Perhaps alone among the states, Arkansas has three capitol buildings, offering in themselves a quick course in the state's history. The earliest is a cabin among the thirteen buildings of the **Arkansas Territorial Restoration,** 3rd Street at Cumberland (Mon.-Sat. 9-5, Sun. 1-5, adm.). It was in 1939 that the citizens of Little Rock realized that some of their city's original settlement from the 1820's and 30's was still standing, decayed and forgotten, just two blocks from Main St. All have been returned to their original condition; besides the capitol, homes and shops there's an example of an old "dog trot" cabin and the original office of the Arkansas Gazette, distinguished "old lady" of the state's journalism and the oldest newspaper west of the Mississippi.

Main Street, the shopping district, has been redone as an exceptionally attractive pedestrian mall—though the unimpressed citizens of the metropolitan area continue to shift their trade to the suburbs. A block away, at Center and Markham, the **Old State House** (Mon.-Sat. 9-5, Sun. 1-5, free), after many years of service as the Civil War Memorial, has been restored like its older counterpart, and serves as a museum of Arkansas history, natural and otherwise. Here, in 1833, three years before statehood, the frontier territory cast all its pretensions and hopes for the future into one stately Greek Revival vision of urbanity. To build it, the first thing they had to do was start a brickyard; next, they enticed architect Gideon Shyrock from Kentucky, where he had just completed the state capitol at Frankfort. Many of the rooms have been decorated and furnished to replicate their appearance when this was the only substantial public building in Arkansas, and it isn't too hard to imagine a scene from a busy legislative session in the early days, with dandied lawyers and one-gallus farmers in attendance, accents of plain, bottomlands and hills in the air, and spittoons overflowing.

By the 1890's, although the government had outgrown the building, Arkansas' frontier boosterism was long gone. The **State Capitol,** begun in 1899, is an austere, even humble creation; it's certainly large enough, well proportioned in the usual American style with a democratic dome and rows of marble columns, but it is as quiet and unassuming a capitol as any of those in the New England states. Populist Governor Jeff Davis, who hated to spend a dime of the taxpayers' money for any purpose, let the project languish for a decade, but he was eventually replaced by a real estate man named Donaghey (who also gave Little Rock its first skyscraper). The new governor hired architect Cass Gilbert to finish the job, and the capitol was finally completed in 1915. Inside, the **Visitors Information center** on the ground floor under the rotunda is prepared with information about the building and the state government, as well as Little Rock and other Arkansas destinations. Behind the capitol, the miniscule state bureaucracy fits neatly into a group of office buildings around a mall. The capitol's slight elevation reminds us of the importance of Little Rock's location: it is the spot where the eastern plains end, and behind the government buildings the first foothills of the Ouachitas rise into the city's choice residential area, **Pulaski Heights.** Here War Memorial Park, Markham at Monroe Sts., contains the **Arkansas Zoo** (daily 9:30-5, free).

Little Rock has good reason to be proud of its efforts to retain some urban character in the face of its atomizing Sunbelt prosperity—not only downtown, in such projects as the rehabilitation of the picturesque old **Pulaski County Courthouse** on West Markham, but particularly in the restoration of the Victorian residential districts of the Quapaw Quarter, a shady, quiet neighborhood that has more of the Midwest than the South in it. Many lovely homes can be seen on Spring, Gaines, Scott, and 19th Streets, and around **MacArthur Park,** 9th at Commerce. General Douglas MacArthur, Little Rock's most famous citizen, was actually born here, in the Old Arsenal where his father was commanding officer. Today, that 1836 building is the **Museum of Science and History,** with exhibits of Arkansiana (Mon.-Sat. 9-5, Sun. 1-5, free). It faces the city's newest museum, the 1963 **Arkansas Arts Center,** with a small permanent collection concentrating on prints and drawings of the last two centuries (Mon.-Sat. 10-5, Sun. 12-5, free).

Restaurants. Jacques & Suzanne***, First National Bldg. (30th floor); Bruno's Little Italy**, 1309 Old Forge Rd.; Cajun's Wharf*, 2400 Cantrell Rd., seafood.

Eastern and Southern Arkansas

From the capital, the road to Memphis passes through the rich agricultural regions of Prairie and Lonoke Counties. The latter is a good example of the facetiousness of so many American place names; railroad men building the first line to Little Rock in the 1830's, finding the site distinguished by a "lone oak," tacked up a signboard, and local geography was born. Off Route 15, just south of Scott, are Arkansas' most impressive examples of the work of the Mound Builders, the **Toltec Mounds State Park,** with a small museum. Further east, there's **Stuttgart,** where the Arkansas prairie begins to decline into the Delta bottomlands. Stuttgart proclaims itself the "rice and duck capital of the world." The abundance of rice fields, lakes and streams in the area make it a major stopover for migrating ducks and geese, and the Stuttgartians celebrate their guests each year at Thanksgiving with the World Championship Duck Calling Contest. The **Arkansas County Agricultural Museum,** E. 4th at Park, plays on nostalgia for the area's past, with relics of everyday life as well as farming, and a replication of an Arkansas prairie village of the last century (Tues.-Sat. 10-12 & 1-4, Sun. 1:30-4, free). If that's not enough, two of the town's big cooperative processing plants, Riceland Foods and Producers' Rice Mill, offer guided tours.

There's more rice, and soybeans, in the northeastern corner of the state. That's a profitable combination for Arkansas farmers; rice drains the soil, and soybeans planted in alternate years replenish it. The flat expanses of fields are boken here by one of the South's geological oddities, **Crowley's Ridge,** a long, narrow elevation covered with wind-blown loess that stretches one hundred miles from north to south paralleling the St. Francis River. The geologists puzzle over it, speculating either that it may be the space between two former beds of the constantly shifting Mississippi River, or that it is a fold in the earth's crust, and still rising. Early settlers from Missouri used it as a path southwards to avoid the soggy bottomlands; today, the ridge supports peach orchards (near Wynne) as well as species of trees and wildflowers not normally seen in Arkansas. There's also a huge ancient deposit of oyster shells—most of Arkansas was a prehistoric sea—and petrified trees that are so common that the town of **Piggott** (where Hemingway wrote *A Farewell to Arms*) was given to using them for tombstones.

Two prosperous agricultural towns flank the ridge, and both are the seats of colleges: **Blytheville's** local community college is an experimental building entirely powered by solar energy, with solar cells covering acres of ground, and **Jonesboro,** to the west, has Arkansas State University and the **Arkansas State University Museum,** with an art gallery and more about Arkansas, historical and prehistorical (Caraway Road, on campus; Mon., Wed., Fri. 1-4, Tues., Thurs. 9-12 & 1-4, free). Southwest of Jonesboro, the town of Newport survives because, in the 1870's, the railraod came here instead of to the once thriving, now quite disappeared town of Jacksonport; here, only the fine old courthouse remains, in the **Jacksonport State Park.** It serves as a museum, and shares the park with a lovely restored riverboat, the **Mary Woods No. 2,** moored on the White River. **Harrisburg,** a tiny county seat, nonetheless has one of the most elegant courthouses in the state. There are more Indian mounds east of **Parkin,** on Route 64, and the **Cross County Museum,** at the courthouse in **Wynne,** to elucidate them and some other Indian cultures found in the area that are among the oldest yet discovered in the South. More of the same, actually one of the most noteworthy collections of mound builders' artifacts anywhere, is the **Hampson State Museum** (Tues.-Sat. 9-5, adm.) in **Wilson,** an agricultural "company town" started by Robert E. Lee Wilson in the 1890's on the banks of the Mississippi. Further downriver, **West Memphis** is a growing suburb of the Tennessee metropolis across the bridge; it is probably best known in these parts for **Southland Greyhound Park,** one of the few dog racing tracks outside of Florida.

Arkansas' frontage along the Mississippi, referred to as the "Delta," is subject to the same ills that the river carries everywhere along its southern half: erosion, washed out roads on swampy ground, continual shifting of the landscape, and Old Man River just rollin' on through your kitchen when he has a mind to, all the modern wizardry of flood control notwithstanding. One spectacular flood in the 1930's, on both the Mississippi and the Arkansas, left one-fifth of the state under water. There are miles of Arkansas farmland that currently find themselves on the Mississippi side of the river, and at least six chunks of that state's territory on the Arkansas side. Just the same, the bottomlands were fine for cotton, and consequently it is this corner of Arkansas where the Deep South culture took root, with its slaves, manorial economics and Corinthian columns, and it is here where the spirit of Dixie still exerts its strongest pull. Cotton isn't so important anymore, though; rice and soybeans are more profitable, and the omnipresent sharecropper of just a few decades ago is giving way to modern mechanized farming techniques.

The most Southern place in Arkansas is the pretty town of **Helena.** De Soto may have stopped here, at the Indian settlement that occupied these bluffs—above most years' floodwaters. By the 1830's with the plantation culture firmly established in the Delta, Helena was the chief river port and a kind of frontier Charleston, a place where the elite could build themselves grand houses and throw lots of parties. Firmly committed to the Confederate cause, Helena gave the rebel army no less than seven generals, and itself became an early casualty (1862) to the Union drive for control of the Mississippi. In 1863, after Grant took Vicksburg, the

Confederates tried unsuccessfully to recapture Helena to replace it. Today the town is a minor Natchez, with a small collection of restored homes of the 1840's and 50's, and an annual "pilgrimage" in April. The rest of the year, you'll have to be content with the small historical museum in the town library on Pecan St. (daily 9-5, free). The **National River Academy,** where today's Mississippi captains and pilots learn their trade, is in Helena. Route 44 from here to Marianna passes through the small but beautiful **St. Francis National Forest:** here and elsewhere around Helena you'll note that determined oriental vine, kudzu, turning parts of the bottomland into thick jungles. The hamlet of **Elaine,** south of helena, was the site of one of the darker incidents in Arkansas history. In 1919, the local black sharecroppers were attempting to form a tenant's union; hysteria among the white population led to several incidents, and finally to a massacre of about 100 blacks. The state tried to send twelve more to the electric chair, but the U.S. Supreme Court freed them.

The confluence of the Arkansas and the Mississippi, like that of the Missouri and Mississippi, is a wilderness of swamps and doomed islands, where the shifts of the rivers make settlement tenuous at best. When Mark Twain was traveling the rivers writing his *Life on the Mississippi* in the 1870's, he was determined to revisit the bustling port of Napoleon, once legendary as the wide-openest town on the river where general brawls occurred daily by the docks, and where the writer, as a young man, "had used to know the prettiest girl in town." His request to disembark at Napoleon occasioned some mirth in the wheelhouse: "There *isn't* any Napoleon any more . . . the Arkansas River burst through it, tore it all to rags, and emptied it into the Mississippi!" It was in fact no sudden disaster, only the steady process of erosion. Only one shanty and a part of a chimney remained—and today those are gone too. **Arkansas City,** downriver, was founded to replace it, but the river is retreating from there and this once prosperous town would probably be entirely abandoned by now if it weren't the county seat. Little has changed here since the 1880's. Near the southern corner of the state, across from Greenville, Miss., there's a state park around Arkansas' biggest natural lake, **Lake Chicot**—really fifteen miles of the river cut off long ago to form a crescent-shaped "oxbow lake."

McGehee and **Dumas** are the largest towns in the lower Delta; near the latter, on the Arkansas River, is the **Arkansas Post National Memorial.** John Law's suckers, mostly Rhineland Germans and black slaves, founded the first settlement in Arkansas here in 1718, where the French had already maintained their outpost for thirty years. When the Mississippi Bubble burst, the settlers deserted Arkansas for New Orleans, where Governor Bienville granted them lands in what is today known as the "German Coast." Arkansas Post revived under the Spanish, who built a fort in the 1760's, and served as the territorial capital under American rule until 1820. Only ruins remain today, but the National Park Service maintains a **Visitor's Center** on the site (daily, 8-5, free), and the **Arkansas Post County Museum** is a mile away on Route 1 (Tues.-Sat. 9-4, Sun. 1-4:30, adm.). Upstream, towards Little Rock, past the Cummins Prison at Varner where they hold the annual Prison Rodeo, is the state's largest city, **Pine Bluff.**

Pine Bluff suffers from the usual dreariness inherent in the cities of the cottonbelt, but it has made a game attempt at reviving its declining center by commissioning native Arkansan Edward Durrell Stone to build their new **Civic Center,** on main Street. There are some ante-bellum homes on West Barraque Street and West Fifth, and also the restored home of Martha Mitchell, wife of Nixon's Attorney General famous for her midnight telephone calls to journalists, eventually becoming a strange martyr of the Watergate era.

Beyond the Mississippi and Arkansas valleys there isn't much, only the cotton fields gradually giving way to the dense pine forests that cover much of the southern portion of the state. Logging has long been important here—much of what you see is second-growth forest—and an insight into the more progressive side of that industry today comes courtesy of the Georgia-Pacific Company at their **Levi Wilcoxon Demonstration Forest,** on US 82 near Crossett, where you can learn anything and everything about the South's family of trees and modern timber management; loggers, it seems, are really farmers now. Further west, across the Ouachita River, a neat triangle is formed by the cities of **Camden, Magnolia,** and **El Dorado.** The first was a French trading post in the 18th century; De Soto and his men preceded them, probably spending the winter of 1541 camped on the bluff. Camden has several ante-bellum homes, and a branch of the **University of Southern Arkansas,** the main campus of which is in Magnolia.

Although El Dorado has been around since 1843, it was only for a few years in the 1920's that its name was singularly appropriate. When oil was discovered in the great "Smackover field," the sleepy cotton center became an instant boomtown. Within a few weeks 20,000 souls were added to the population, and the main streets of downtown became an oil workers' camp. Surprisingly, El Dorado landed on its feet after the boom was over to become a pleasant small city with some cultural pretensions (it has a symphony) and a good number of splendidly Babbitish offices and public buildings left over from the 20's.

The village of **Reader,** Route 24 west of Camden, may be exceedingly tiny, but it has its very own railroad, and if you're around on a weekend (April through October) you may take a ride on the ancient, steam powered **Reader Railroad** through the Ouachita County countryside. Further west, in the valley of the Red River, agriculture reasserts itself against the pines. Other localities, other states, may make their trifling brags about big watermelons, but don't dare mention them in **Hope,** the land of true champions. Hundred-pounders are commonplace here; any so unlucky as to be smaller are served as hors d'oeuvres. Hope currently has the official, certified world champion, a 200 pound brute as big as your bathtub, and each year the assembled populace meets at the Watermelon Festival, in August, in anticipation of the next inevitable record-breaker. Six miles north on Route 4, the old historic town of Washington has dwindled to less than 300, but the state has stepped in and turned the town into **Old Washington State Park.** Washington is best known as the place where Jim Bowie, Sam Houston, Davy Crockett and their companions spent time planning their Texas adventure from just over what was in the 1830's the U.S.-Mexico border. With a population of over 2,000, it was as big and important as Little Rock or Arkansas Post, and between 1863 and 1865, when Union forces were occupying Little Rock, it served as the capital. Much of the town survives, including the courthouse where the rebel government installed itself, the old tavern where the Texans stayed, several other churches and buildings from the 1840's, and a Gun Museum (Mon., Wed.-Sat. 9-4, Sun. 1-5, adm.). The story of the Bowie knife is one of the classic Western legends. Equally handy for chopping underbrush, skinning game or fighting, the original, made for Jim Bowie, was supposedly a survival of the ancient secret of Damascus steel: it rang like a bell when struck, and it never grew dull. Following Bowie's tracks across the continent, various stories have grown up around purported inventors, in locations from Philadelphia to New Orleans. In Washington, they claim that a Philadelphia craftsman named James Black turned out the original here, and today at the state park there is a reconstruction of James Black's forge, where smiths produce Bowie knives—without the Damascus secret—for visitors.

At Arkansas' southwestern corner, **Texarkana** can fairly be called a border town—in fact, you can stand on the "photographer's island" downtown on State Line Avenue and have your picture taken standing in two states at the same time. Texarkana is two legally separate municipalities, in Arkansas and in Texas, but really a single city, a growing industrial town of 50,000 (about 22,000 on the Arkansas side). The **Federal Building** interrupts State Line Avenue to sit squarely on the border—and the address of the post office inside is Texarkana, U.S.A.

Restaurants. *In Pine Bluff*:El Cocina** (Mexican), Route 365 North. *In Paragould*: Linwood Steak House**, US 49 South. *In Jonesboro*: Conch's Bar-B-Q*, 5323 E. Nettleton. *In Marianna*: Armstrong's Bar-B-Q*, Route 1 South. *In Camden*: Duck Inn*, 952 Adams. *In Stuttgart*: Mallard Restaurant*, W. Michigan St. *In Texarkana*: C.J's Red Barn*, US 67 North. *In El Dorado*: Eagle's Nest**, downtown airport.

The Ozarks

"The hills ain't so high; it's the hollers is deep . . ."

This old saying is truer than the Ozarkers know; the patch of mountains they call home, stretching across northern Arkansas and southern Missouri, and even including some parts of Oklahoma and Kansas, really isn't "mountains" at all. In the geological sense, the Ozarks are an uplifted plateau, carved into mountains by innumerable rivers and streams—like the Catskills in New York—over millions of years of constant erosion. Geologically, Arkansas' Ozarks are the oldest part of the state, and culturally they are the solidest, home to a unique mountain people who have been here a long time and survived in spite of a total lack of economic opportunity. Until very recently, they were the most backward and isolated parts of the state, and gained a reputation nationwide as the preserve of the archtypical hillbilly—bare feet, moonshine still, and everything else that endeared them to cartoonists and comedians since the pattern was cast with the Ozark squatter of Sandy Faulkner's "Arkansas Traveller" in the 1840's. The real hillbilly succumbed to modernity decades ago, but the mountain culture endures, and in this somewhat more enlightened time the rest of the nation has begun to appreciate the Ozarks on its own terms, as one of the more pleasant mountain regions anywhere, and one of the last great strongholds of folklore and folk life in the United States.

Perhaps "appreciate" would be an understatement, for the Ozarks happen to be, just now, the fastest growing rural area in all America; for the last thirty years big-city people from all over have been beating the Ozarks' doors down in a rush to settle, or merely vacation, in this rugged wilderness of unspectacularly beautiful scenery, low living costs, and a determinedly unhurried style. There seems to have been a kind of conspiracy to develop for tourism; while the state was building a network of roads in the late 40's and 50's to many previously inaccessible areas, the Army Corps of Engineers was beginning a plan to dam up the Ozarks free-flowing rivers. The half-dozen or so lakes they created have become the prime recreational areas of the region, with hundreds of resorts, both plain and fancy, growing up around them. Fishing, even more than in the rest of this trout and lunker-bass-crazed state, is the big deal. In addition, the Ozarks, in their new role as one of the prime vacation areas of the South, can now boast of dozens of "attractions," from folklore festivals, old mills, and some lovely caves, to the more dubious sort—a theme park called "Dogpatch U.S.A.," wax museums, and "country stores."

Ozark folklore has been more than adequately chronicled by the life work of one man, Vance Randolph, who has written over a score of books of Ozark stories and songs, folkways, and superstitions. Perhaps the most interesting is the most recent, an earthy collection of tales called *Pissin' in the Snow,* including everthing Randolph culled in a half century that he figured would have offended his editors at the university publishing houses. Randolph's works are also the best access to Ozark magic and superstitions, subjects now somewhat in disfavor with modernized Ozarkians of today. Crafts and music, on the other hand, are enjoying a renaissance, nowhere more prominently than at the state-run Ozark Folk Center at Mountain View.

The Ozarks begin at the Black River. **Batesville,** on the White River, is the major town of the foothills and one of the oldest in Arkansas, also the site of **Arkansas College,** a private school founded in 1836. Eight miles north on Rt. 69, the 1867 water-powered **Spring Mill** is still in operation—one of the few left in the South—and maintained as a museum. Further north, as part of the general rehabilitation of the Ozarkian image, Barren Flat is now **Mount Pleasant,** and Hookrum, its very name an old butt of jokes, now **Evening Shade,** with a historic district of Victorian homes. **Salem,** near the Missouri border, is famous for its programs of mountain music every Saturday night (at the Civic Center and the Music Barn east of town on Rt. 62, both free). One of the world's largest springs, at **Mammoth Springs,** pumps 220,000,000 gallons a day that provide the source of the Spring River. Although dammed, it is still impressive, and it now supplies electric power to a few neighboring counties. Twelve miles downstream, the old resort town of **Hardy** has a "public beach" of sorts, on the river and another musical show, the **Arkansaw Traveller Folk Theatre.** Like so many other Ozark attractions, it's only open in season, Memorial Day to Labor Day.

Further west, on the White River (which is crossed by more ferries than bridges—free 24-hour ferries built by the state that aren't really boats, but floating roadways) there's the pretty town of **Calico Rock,** draped on three levels over a steep hillside. The **Blanchard Springs Caverns,** near Fifty Six in the northernmost section of the Ozark National Forest, were discovered only recently, and have only been open since 1973, but they have some wonderful stalactite formations, grottoes, and a giant "flowstone" (daily 9:30-4:30, adm.; for tour reservations call 757-2211). With the aim of encouraging the old mountain ways—and also attracting more tourists—the state created the **Ozark Folk Center** in 1973, on a hill outside **Mountain View.** Here, in a dozen or so cabins devoted to the old "cabin crafts," you may observe not only such specialities as woodworking and the production of musical instruments, but also the homely necessities of the Ozarks' past—spinning and weaving, blacksmithing, candle-making and more. There's also an "herb doctor" and his garden, and rightfully so, for the culinary and medicinal use of wild plants is probably as complicated a science among the Ozarkers as anywhere else in the world. Musicians are everywhere, and there are nightly performances of mountain music from all over Arkansas, anything from fiddle and dulcimer to ballads to gospel, in the large circular theatre that dominates the Center (open daily 10-6, from June 1 to Labor Day; Wed.-Sun. 10-6 in May and Sept.; Tues.-Sun. 10-6 in Nov., adm.). More music can be found in Mountain View, in such institutions as the Jimmy Driftwood Music Barn, as well as informal concerts on the courthouse steps Saturday evenings, and more crafts at nearby Sylamore Creek, at the **Ozark Foothills Guild Sale Shop.** To the south, a big vacation area is building around **Greer's Ferry Lake,** near the town of Heber Springs. Another, **Bull Shoals Lake,** is on the Missouri border, and its center is **Mountain Home.**

By the 1960's, all the Ozark's rivers save one had been dammed, and it took a major effort by conservationists to save that one; the **Buffalo National River,** the first designated national river, was set aside by Congress in 1972. Its 148 meandering miles, between two sections of the Ozark National Forest, run through narrow valleys and limestone bluffs, in an area that a hundred years ago enjoyed a brief zinc-mining boom (it has at least one ghost town) but now are as empty and unspoiled as any scenic corner of the U.S., and now a major destination for the nation's canoeists and hikers.

US 65, the main road north from Little Rock, heads for the heart of the Ozarks, passing **Conway,** a small college town, and **Clinton.** Just south of Clinton, at the village of Choctaw, the **Watergate Museum** is a recently established attraction, a completely furnished replica of an 1890's town, populated by wax dummies (open March through November, daily 9-5, adm. $2.50). Where the route crosses over the Buffalo River, near St. Joe, a side road trails off for the unaffectedly old-fashioned general store at **Gilbert,** only purveyor of necessities to the National River's woodsy clientele. For the traveler with time to spare, a more interesting way into the Ozarks is Route 7, from Russellville; the local boosters claim it "the most scenic highway in Arkansas" with some justification, and as you follow it through the Ozark National Forest, you'll pass any number of scenic overlooks. Pay attention to the signs on the back roads, almost all of which promise a waterfall, a national bridge or some other wonder. **Diamond Cave,** near Jasper, is one of the largest in the country, and has some beautiful calcite formations.

Route 7 meets US 65 at **Harrison,** an old railroad town most famous today for that inescapable consequence of the Ozarks popularity: **Dogpatch U.S.A.** Al Capp may be gone, but his comic strip characters L'il Abner, Daisy Mae, and the rest survive among the undead in this theme park for other people's children, with rides, games, country music, fishing and a cave (Memorial Day to Labor Day, daily 9-6, adm. $6.50). Yet another cave (and Ozark grottoes are almost always more interesting than their fellows east of the Mississippi) awaits near US 65 between Harrison and St. Joe. **Hurricane River Cave** was an Indian habitation, and its caverns, subterranean rivers, and fossils make it one of Arkansas' most popular (Memorial Day to Labor Day, daily 8-7 pm; from then until November 9-5 pm; the remainder of the year weekdays only, 9-5; adm.).

Eureka Springs. The eventual destination of most Ozark tourists, this town grew up on its most improbable site by virtue of the curative properties of its sixty odd natural springs. Tales of its singular geography have become a mainstay of Arkansas folklore—that you can walk from your backyard onto your neighbor's roof, or that no two streets in town intersect at right angles. It may not be true that there's a church whose parishioners enter through the steeple, but there is in fact a seven-storey hotel where every floor is the ground floor; the **Basin Park Hotel** on Spring Street is now a museum, but at least two other distinguished hostelries of the 1880's and 90's still cater to the tourist trade. In season, gaily painted jitney buses carry visitors along Main Street, a National Historic District of 19th century commercial buildings, many of which house artist's studios and craft shops. Some of this lovely town's attractions are: the **Historical Museum,** on Spring Street (Apr.-Nov., daily 9-5, adm.): **Hatchet Hall,** the last home of that foul old Prohibitionist and saloon wrecker Carry Nation, on Steele (Apr.-Nov., daily 9-5, adm.): the **Miles Musical Museum,** with guided tours through its collection of calliopes, music boxes, nickelodeons and other interesting old trinkets, on US 62 just west of downtown (May-Nov., daily 9-5, adm. $3.00): also the **Hammond Bell Museum** on Spring, and the **Bank of Eureka Springs,** on Main Street, recently restored to its 1880's appearance, at once working bank and museum.

There's more outside of town, in this rugged landscape hard by the Missouri border: **Beaver Lake** is another creation of the Corps of Engineers, and a nascent resort community with another restored grist mill, **War Eagle Mill** near its southern shore on Route 12: **Inspiration Point,** a beautiful overlook, west of town on US 62, with a mountaintop "castle" predictably converted into a museum of nostalgia; **Onyx Cave,** also on 62, and **Cosmic Cavern,** on Route 21, with a huge underground lake. The **Eureka Springs & North Arkansas Railway** is an 1890's engine that once ran along the Panama Canal; now its colorful modern coaches carry visitors on excursions through the countryside from the old depot in Eureka Springs. And finally, fundamentalist Christians from all over flock to Mount Oberrammergau, off US 62, to see what must be the most stirring panorma of religious depravity in the entire U.S., the many projects of the **Elna N. Smith Foundation.** All this isn't the work of Elna, but of her husband Gerald L. K. Smith, a man who started his career as Huey Long's chief rabble rouser in the Louisiana backwaters. When Long passed from the scene and populism became unfashionable, Smith set out on his own, publishing a venomous newsletter called "The Cross and the Flag" and earning a reputation as America's leading Red-baiter, Jew-baiter, and Negro-baiter. His gift to the Ozarks begins with a seven-storey high concrete Jesus of grotesquely distorted features, the "Christ of the Ozarks." Then there's the **Bible Museum,** the world's largest collection of old and rare bibles: the **Christ Only Art Gallery,** Mr. Smith's own collection of art portraying Jesus: **The Great Passion Play,** five days a week from May to October: and the last and most ambitious project, **Holy Land U.S.A.,** a life-size replica of all the famous sites in both Old and New Testaments—the Sea of Galilee is already complete, and the River Jordan, the Temple and the rest are planned as the funds become available (museums open May-Labor Day, Tues., Wed., Fri., Sat., Sun. 8-8, Mon.-Fri. 8-5:30; the rest of the year daily 8-7, separate admission for both). Eureka Springs has attracted religious groups perhaps ever since Carry Nation, but their manifestations aren't always of the Smith variety; it's certainly worth the three-mile trip west on US 62 to see **Thorncrown Chapel,** the dream of a local minister realized by the nationally respected Fayetteville architect E. Fay Jones, a disciple of Frank Lloyd Wright. The lofty, open, wood and glass chapel seems to have grown up naturally with the forest that surrounds it, a rare case of religious impulse and contemporary design speaking the same language.

Across Beaver Lake from Eureka Springs, northwest Arkansas' pocket conurbation stretches along US 62 through the cities of Bentonville, Rogers, Springdale, and the largest, **Fayetteville,** the home of the University of Arkansas. Fayetteville is built on seven hills, and has a small botanical garden filling the spaces of Fayetteville Square around the old Post Office. The University's sports teams are the chief repository of Arkansas state pride, holding their own with Texas and the other southern football powerhouses. On campus, there's the **University Museum** in Hotz Hall, with exhibits of historical and anthropological interest (Mon.-Sat. 9-5, Sun. 1-5, free). The next city along the string, **Springdale,** has a large collection of frontier artifacts at the **Shiloh Museum,** in the old town library, and **Rogers,** like Springdale presently a booming little city, is famous as the BB gun capital of the world. The Daisy Company makes 65 million BB's every day at their plant on US 71, and every grown American boy who spent his formative years in the 50's and 60's terrorizing the neighborhood with these toys will want to visit their International Air Gun Museum (weekdays 9-5, free) and take the plant tour (at 1:30). Surprisingly, this corner of the state on the Ozarks' western slopes is an important agricultural area, for apples, chickens, and grapes; **Tontitown,** which still has an annual grape festival, was founded in 1897 by Italian refugees, not immediately from Italy but from the Mississippi valley in Arkansas, where malaria and poor land were causing their newly established colony to founder. Also surprisingly, Arkansas' ony two significant Civil War battles were fought in this distant, sparsely-settled corner of the state, commemorated at the **Pea Ridge National Military Park** just north of Rogers (daily 8-5, free), and the **Prairie Grove Battlefield State Park** in Prairie Grove (daily 8-4:30 from Memorial Day to Labor Day, otherwise Tues.-Sun., free). At the former in 1861, Union troops under Gen. Franz Sigel (who has a park named for him in New York City) slugged it out inconclusively with Confederate forces that included a band of Cherokees led by Albert Pike, both sides retiring to other parts of the state. Prairie Grove, in November 1862, was equally inconclusive; much blood was spilled and both sides erroneously claimed victory.

Southwest of Fayetteville, the Ozarks show their most impressive face, the steep, rugged **Boston Mountains** in the western portion of the Ozark National Forest. Route 23 is a difficult mountain road, traversing the chain from Ozark to Huntsville in this wild and unpeopled stretch, but it rivals the more travelled Route 7 for scenic beauty.

Arkansas River Valley. The very highest peaks of the Ozarks are not where you would expect them, in the heart of the range or even in the Boston Mountains; they stand alone on the southern side of the Arkansas River, where the Ozarks end and the Ouachitas begin. The river, between Little Rock and the Oklahoma border—and indeed, halfway across Oklahoma—is under the tender care of the Corps of Engineers, and planted with locks and dams throughout. When completed in the 70's, the job was the Corps' greatest boondoggle ever, costing well over a billion dollars.

Russellville and Morrilton are the two big towns of the valley, on the northern bank of the river; between them, off Route 154 on the southern bank rises **Petit Jean Mountain,** with a state park at its summit. The name comes from early French traders, and there are two conflicting legends for it, equally romantic and equally improbable—the locals prefer the one about the Parisian girl who disguised herself as a boy to follow her lover into the wilderness and met a melodramatic end here. Governor Rockefeller's Winrock Farm, where he raised prize Santa Gertrudis cattle, is here, and his collection of antique cars has become the **Museum of Automobiles** (daily 10-5, adm.). **Mount Nebo** is another peak within a state park, and **Mount Magazine** a third, the highest point in the state, a steep 2,300 feet straight up from the valley. Beginning in the 1870's, this part of the valley attracted a good number of German and Swiss immigrants, who found the soil and climate excellent for vineyards. The industry they began survived Prohibition and prospers today. Of the wineries around the town of **Altus** at least four welcome visitors, notably the largest of them, **Wiederkehr Wine Cellars,** just north of Altus (Mon.-Sat. 9-4:30, free) and the **Post Winery** (Mon.-Sat. 8-8, free)—both are on Route 186.

Fort Smith, on the Oklahoma border, has little to do with the South; it celebrates its entirely western character every year at the Old Fort Days in May with such activities as a rodeo, an "Indian Pow-wow," and a chili-cooking contest. Only a century ago the town, now heavily industrial and the second largest city in Arkansas, was the Army's frontier post on the edge of the Indian Territory. The first log fort went up in 1817, and the town began to grow around it with the boom that accompanied the California Gold Rush. The Cherokee across the border, who had followed the "trail of tears" across Arkansas to their new home, were as civilized as the white settlers, but after the Civil War, the border area became a frontier as wild and lawless as any Hollywood western fantasy. In those days (when the neighboring Ozarks were overrun by gangs of armed freebooters), Indian courts had no jurisdiction over whites, and the parts of the Indian Territory near Arkansas became a sanctuary for every outlaw spawned by opportunity and the social disruption of the war. In response, President Grant appointed as federal judge for the district the legendary Isaac C. Parker, a man who by his appearance "always reminded the children of Santa Claus," but who saw over ninety desperados hanged in his twenty-one years on the bench—western folklore's original "hanging judge." Parker only lost sixty-five deputy sheriffs, shot while tracking down miscreants, and so retired with the score thirty men in his favor; when he died, the penitentiary rocked with celebrations.

Today, in the **Old Town** restoration area along the riverfront, Parker's courtroom survives in the 1836 barracks building at the **Fort Smith National Historic Site,** Rogers at Third St. (daily 8:30-5, free). You'll also see the last surviving gallows in the U.S., where Parker kept the hangman so busy he often did three at a shot. The **Old Fort Museum** occupies the only other original structure from the fort, the Commissary, but there are plans to reconstruct the whole of it as a tourist attraction (museum open daily 10-5, adm.). Judge Parker, and soldiers from both sides of the Civil War, are buried in the **National Cemetery** three blocks away.

North of downtown, between the river and 10th St., many of the fine homes of Fort Smith's 19th century elite are being restored in the **Belle Grove Historic District.** Continuing in that direction, US 64-71 (Midland Blvd.) will carry you across the river to **Van Buren,** Fort Smith's sister city and long-ago commercial rival, an important steamboat stop in the 1850's. Van Buren is restoring its historic downtown district along **Main Street,** featuring the attractive County Courthouse from the 1870's and the old **Frisco Depot,** which houses the Chamber of Commerce and a railroad museum. Van Buren's effort at restoring the elegance of the past is a little more serious than most preservation efforts; they plan to tear up the asphalt and repave Main Street in brick, replace ornate old street lighting they once threw away in the name of progress, restore the shop fronts to their 1890's appearance, and even build a trolley line. To see the twentieth century being repealed, even in a small corner of Arkansas, is certainly an encouraging sign, and they should have quite a town when they're finished.

Hot Springs and the Ouachitas. The mountains of west-central Arkansas are pronounced wa-SHEE-ta. The difficulty, as in so many Indian names, is their phoneticization by the first explorers—in French. In the foothills, an area of geological wonders that it is said to contain more different minerals than any other on earth, the city of Hot Springs has been Arkansas' biggest tourist attraction ever since there's been an

Arkansas. Even earlier, in fact; the 47 hot natural springs within the city limits were a sacred ground for the Indians, who also recognized their curative properties. The U.S. Government did too; they bought the land as a national preserve in 1832, four years before Arkansas statehood, and today the **Hot Springs National Park,** including much of the city, is the oldest of the national park system. Hot Springs fits snugly into its beautiful location in the Ouachitas, its skyline dominated by palatial old hotels such as the Arlington (they're just like the ones Atlantic City is busy demolishing). Central Avenue splits the town from north to south, and the magnolia-shaded stretch of it downtown is **Bath House Row,** with eight quite fancy, pastel-colored turn of the century bathhouses on landscaped grounds. Four are still in operation, and another is the Park Service's **Visitor Center and Museum** at Central and Reserve Avenue (daily 8-5, free). Three of the springs are open for display on the Row, behind which runs a pleasant promenade. You may try the cure yourself, here or at the thirteen other establishments in Hot Springs, many of which are in downtown hotels; a session in the 144 degree waters costs $5-7. As you might expect, Hot Springs is full of doctors, hospitals, and institutes for patients suffering from arthritis or back problems, or recuperating from injuries, but the waters are understandably promoted also as a tonic for everybody. Hot Springs, incidentally, is the source of America's only widely popular *eau minerale,* Mountain Valley brand.

A number of peculiar attractions have sprung up to amuse Hot Springs visitors, none more peculiar than the **I.Q. Zoo** on Whittington Avenue, where "psychologically trained" animals perform—many of them have careers as character actors on TV or in movies. Chickens play baseball, raccoons shoot baskets, and other small critters play in a band, tell fortunes, dance, or otherwise show off (Apr.1 to Oct., daily 10-4 pm; Oct., weekends only; closed in winter, adm.). There's also **Tiny Town,** a miniature village, **Magic Springs,** a 1890's theme park, an alligator farm, and more. The city and the region are full of lapidaries and rock shops, offering such local specialties as "Hot Springs diamonds"—perfect, polished quartz crystals. **The Mid-America Museum,** run by the state, is a participatory lesson for children in the sciences and natural history (west of town on Route 227, open Tues.-Sun. 10-5, adm. $3.50).

A chain of artificial lakes almost surrounds Hot Springs—Lakes Ouachita, Hamilton, Catherine, and De Gray—dammed either by the Corps of Engineers or Arkansas Power & Light; like their counterparts in the Ozarks, they too are ringed with resorts and state parks, with plenty of fishing and water sports. The pine-clad Ouachitas are of a lower range than the Ozarks, not heavily populated and almost entirely within the **Ouachita National Forest.** From **Mena,** in Polk County, the famous **Talimena Scenic Drive** (Route 88) traverses the highest parts of the range into Oklahoma; *Rich Mountain* here would be Arkansas' tallest, but its summit is just over the state line. **Queen Wilhelmina State Park,** on the mountain, gets its name from the resort lodge whose developer, in the 1900's, dubbed it thus in hopes he might get the Dutch queen to pay a visit. She didn't.

South of Hot Springs, on the fringes of the Ouachitas, are the state's most important mineral producing regions. **Arkadelphia,** at the center, collects the vast quantities of gypsum and bauxite (aluminum ore), among others. A more romantic sort of mining is indulged in by visitors at the **Crater of Diamonds State Park,** on Route 301 near *Murfreesboro.* Although this is the biggest deposit of diamonds in the U.S., there aren't enough to make commercial exploitation pay off (it was tried, from 1908 to 1924). The state bought the land, and has maintained it ever since as their strangest—and probably best attended—tourist sight. They'll rent you mining tools, and if you are lucky, it's strictly finders keepers; an expert is on hand to appraise and weigh all gems found. Over sixty thousand diamonds have turned up since 1908, some as big as 40 carats, but of course most prospectors-for-a-day go home empty-handed. Nevertheless, they'll tell you about the man from Texas who dug up a stone worth $100,000 a few years ago, and named it the "Star of Amarillo" (open daily 8-5, adm. $3).

Also near Murfreesboro a significant prehistoric Indian site has recently been excavated and opened to the public. The **Ka-Do-Ha Discovery** was one of the largest villages of the Mound Builders in Arkansas, and the well-fashioned artworks and artifacts retrieved by the archeologists are on display in a museum at the site (open Apr. through Oct., daily 9-6, adm.).

Restaurants. *In Fort Smith*: Emmy's German Restaurant**, N. 16th St.; The Red Barn**, 3716 Newton Rd. *In Hot Springs*: Sawmill Depot**, North Valley Street, in the old railroad station; Bohemia Restaurant**, North Route 7; Millers Restaurant**, Route 7. *In Lakeview*: Gaston's***, at Gaston's White River Resort; Col. Jack's Country Kitchen*. *In Springdale*: Heinie's**, 2407 S. Thompson. *In Rogers*: Tale of the Trout***, New Hope Road. *In Mountain Home*: Little Pines Restaurant**, US 62 East. *In Hardy*: Pioneer Restaurant**, US 62 East. *In Fayetteville*: Restaurant on the Corner*, 324 W. Dickson. *In Heber Springs*: Stockholm, Inc.*, 600 W. Main (Swedish cuisine). *In Tontitown*: Mary Maestri's Casa Bianca*, Route 68 (Italian). *In Altus*: Wiederkehr Weinkeller**, Route 186.

Annual Events in Arkansas

In March: Jonquil Festival, the second week in March, *Old Washington State Park*; Pioneer Crafts Festival, in *Rison.*
In April: Spring Pilgrimage, tours of antebellum homes, in *Helena*; Arkansas Folk Festival, at the Ozark Folk Center, in *Mountain View.*
In May: Old Fort River Festival, on the riverfront in *Fort Smith,* early May; later in the month, the Old Fort Days and Arkansas-Oklahoma Rodeo.
In June: Arkansas Fun Festival, in *Hot Springs,* early June; Pink Tomato Festival, in *Warren*; Ozark Mountain Music Makers String Band and Fiddle Contest, in *Salem.*
In July: Ding Dong Days, in *Dumas.*
In August: Confederate Air Force Air Show, with antique warplanes, in *Pine Bluff*; Johnson County Peach Festival, in *Clarksville*; White River Water Carnival, in *Batesville;* Watermelon Festival, in *Hope*; Tontitown

Grape Festival, at *Tontitown*; Arkansas Prison Rodeo: "See over 500 of Arkansas' most closely guarded rodeo stars participating along with Free World contestants," at the Cummins Prison, in *Varner*.
In September: Fiddlers' State Championship, in *Lincoln*.
In October: Stat Fair, first week of the month, in *Little Rock*; Rice Festival in *Weiner*; National Wild Turkey Calling Contest and Turkey Trot Festival, in *Yellville*; Ozarks Arts and Crafts Festival, at *War Eagle Mill*.
In November: Frontier Days, at *Old Washington State Park*; World Championship Duck Calling Contest, in *Stuttgart*.
In December: Ozark Christmas, at the *Ozark Folk Center* and *Mountain View*.

Accommodation in Arkansas (Area code 501)

In Little Rock

Americana Inn, 707 1-30, tel. 372-4392. Moderately expensive.
Camelot Inn, Broadway & Markham Sts., tel. 372-4371. Expensive downtown hotel.
Vagabond Inn, 8001 New Benton Hwy., tel. 565-0111. Moderate.
Magnolia Inn, 3601 Roosevelt Rd., tel. 666-5481. Inexpensive.
YMCA, 6th and Broadway, tel. 372-5421. Men only, inexpensive.
Passport Inn, 400 W. 29th St., tel. 758-5100, *North Little Rock*. Moderate.

Eastern and Southern Arkansas

Town House Motėl, US 79 West, tel. 673-2611, *Stuttgart*. Moderate.
Delta Lodge, US 62 South, tel. 382-5115, *Dumas*. Moderate.
Delta K Motel, US 61 at I-55, tel. 763-1410, *Blytheville*. Inexpensive.
D & M Motel, US 70 West, tel. 633-3214, *Forrest City*. Inexpensive.
American Motor Inn, St. Louis., tel. 793-5751, *Batesville*. Moderate.
Starlight Motel, US 64 at Rt. 1, tel. 238-2722, *Wynne*. Moderate.
Harbor Inn, Rt. 49B, tel. 572-2597, *West Helena*. Moderate.
Townhouse Motel, US 79 at 65, tel. 532-2875, *Pine Bluff*. Moderate.
River Port Inn, 4125 Rhinehart Rd., tel. 535-1200, *Pine Bluff*. Inexpensive.
Town House Motel, 10th & Caddo, tel. 246-6792, *Arkadelphia*. Inexpensive.

Ozarks and Quachitas

Crescent Hotel, Prospect St., tel. 253-9766, *Eureka Springs*. Built in 1886. Expensive.
New Orleans Hotel, 63 Spring St., tel. 253-8630, *Eureka Springs*. Equally old and decorative, also expensive.
Joy Motel, US 62, tel. 253-9568, *Eureka Springs*. Inexpensive.
Arlington Hotel, Central Av. & Fountain St., tel. 623-7771, *Hot Springs*.Moderate, expensive in season.
Grand Central Motor Lodge, 1127 Central, tel. 624-7131, *Hot Springs*. Moderate.
Majestic Hotel, Park & Central Ave., tel. 623-5511, *Hot Springs*. Moderate.
Avanelle Motor Lodge, Grand & Central, tel. 321-1332, *Hot Springs*. Central location, moderate.

Ina Motel, 741 Park Ave., tel. 624-9164, *Hot Springs*. Moderate.
Capri Motel, 1606 Central, tel. 623-1668, *Hot Springs*. Inexpensive.
Margarett Motel, 216 Fountain, tel. 624-9745, *Hot Springs*. Inexpensive.
Traveller Motor Lodge, 1045 E. Grand Ave., tel. 624-4681, *Hot Springs*. Inexpensive.
Country Lodge & Trout Dock, te. 453-2422, *Flippin*. Modest White River resort.
Stetson's, tel. 453-2523, *Flippin*. Another fishing resort.
Red Apple Inn, Rt. 110, tel. 362-3111, *Heber Springs*. Expensive resort.
Lakeshore Resort/Motel, Rt. 4, tel. 362-2315, *Heber Springs*. Moderate.
Pines Motel, tel. 362-3176, *Heber Springs*. Inexpensive.
Silver Leaf Lodge, Rt. 4, tel. 492-5187, *Mountain Home*. Moderate resort.
Mockingbird Resort, Rt. 3, tel. 491-5151, *Mountain Home*. Moderate.
Royal Motel Resort, Rt. 62, tel. 492-5288, *Mountain Home*. Inexpensive.
Ozark Folk Center Lodge, Rt. 382, tel. 269-3871, *Mountain View*. Inexpensive.
Dogwood Motel, Rt. 14 East, tel. 269-3847, *Mountain View*. Moderate.
Harvey House Inn, US 71 North, tel. 394-3710, *Mena*. Moderate.
Riverview Motel, US 63 South, tel. 625-3218, *Mammoth Springs*. Moderate.
Town House and Sands Motel, 215 N. College, tel. 442-2313, *Fayetteville*. Inexpensive.
Townhouse Motel, Rt. 64 & 65B, tel. 329-3846, *Conway*. Inexpensive.
Continental Motel, 1421 N. 11th St., tel. 785-1471, *Fort Smith*. Inexpensive.
Gaston's White River Resort, Rt. 178 South, tel. 431-5202, *Lakeview*. Moderate resort cottages.
Hiway Host Inn, 915 S. 8th St., tel. 636-9600, *Roberts*. Inexpensive.
Jan-Lin Motor Inn, 1601 S. 8th St., tel. 636-1733, *Rogers*. Inexpensive.
Park Motel, 2615 W. Main St., tel. 968-4862, *Russellville*. Inexpensive.

Further information is available from the Arkansas Department of Parks and Tourism, Capitol Building, Room 149, Little Rock, Arkansas 72201 (toll free 1-800-643-8383). Fishing and hunting regulations are available from the Game and Fish Commission, 2 National Resource Drive, Little Rock, AR 72201.